Advance praise for *Crossing Oceans*

"Gina Holmes explores the beauty, tenderness, and tenacity of mother love in *Crossing Oceans* with marvelous skill and insight. An outstanding debut from a gifted storyteller. Bravo!"

SUSAN MEISSNER, AUTHOR OF *THE SHAPE OF MERCY*

"Moving, heartrending, and poignant—a stunning debut. Holmes returns us to what matters in a too-short life— what it really means to come home."

TOSCA LEE, AUTHOR OF *HAVAH: THE STORY OF EVE*

"What a touching story! Beautifully written, it is a lyrical testament to the hope we have when we believe."

DEBORAH RANEY, AUTHOR OF *ALMOST FOREVER*

"*Crossing Oceans* is a confident debut, understated yet powerful."

ERIC WILSON, *NEW YORK TIMES* BEST-SELLING AUTHOR OF *FIREPROOF*

"This story will wring you out and hang you up to dry. It's beautifully written and deep as a river."

LAURAINE SNELLING, AUTHOR OF *A MEASURE OF MERCY*

"A stunning debut novel about love, loss, and the circle of life. Gina Holmes knows how to find laughter in tragedy. . . . Her characters will grab you by the heart and have you laughing, crying, and holding your breath."

MARSHALL KARP, AUTHOR OF *THE RABBIT FACTORY*

crossing *Oceans*

---❀---

GINA HOLMES

TYNDALE HOUSE PUBLISHERS, INC.
CAROL STREAM, ILLINOIS

Visit Tyndale's exciting Web site at www.tyndale.com.

To learn more about Gina Holmes, visit www.ginaholmes.com or her blog, www.noveljourney.blogspot.com.

TYNDALE and Tyndale's quill logo are registered trademarks of Tyndale House Publishers, Inc.

Crossing Oceans

Copyright © 2010 by Gina Holmes. All rights reserved.

Cover photo of woman copyright © by Image 100 Limited/photolibrary. All rights reserved.

Cover photo of girl copyright © by Masterfile. All rights reserved.

Cover photo of hands copyright © by Brand X Pictures/Jupiterimages. All rights reserved.

Designed by Jennifer Ghionzoli

Edited by Kathryn S. Olson

The author is represented by Chip MacGregor of MacGregor Literary, 2373 NW 185th Avenue, Suite 165, Hillsboro, OR 97124.

Scripture quotations are taken from the *Holy Bible*, New Living Translation, copyright © 1996, 2004, 2007 by Tyndale House Foundation. Used by permission of Tyndale House Publishers, Inc., Carol Stream, Illinois 60188. All rights reserved.

This novel is a work of fiction. Names, characters, places, and incidents either are the product of the author's imagination or are used fictitiously. Any resemblance to actual events, locales, organizations, or persons living or dead is entirely coincidental and beyond the intent of either the author or the publisher.

Library of Congress Cataloging-in-Publication Data

Holmes, Gina.
  Crossing oceans / Gina Holmes.
    p. cm.
    ISBN 978-1-4143-3305-2 (pbk.)
    1. Self-realization in women—Fiction. 2. Life change events—Fiction. 3. Family secrets—Fiction. 4. North Carolina—Fiction. 5. Domestic fiction. I. Title.
    PS3608.O494354C76 2010
    813'.6—dc22   2009046949

Printed in the United States of America

16 15 14 13 12 11 10
7   6   5   4   3

For my sister, Jodi, who has already crossed.

Yet what we suffer now is nothing compared
to the glory he will reveal to us later.

ROMANS 8:18

Acknowledgments

I've been on this journey toward publication for something like a decade. Along this path were many who have encouraged and taught me. So many, in fact, it would take an entire book just to name them. My dear friends, you know who you are, so if I fail to mention you, it's not for lack of appreciation, but for lack of brain power and white space. Forgive me.

Before anyone else, I must thank my Redeemer, Jesus Christ. May my meager words always point to Your divine ones. You've picked me up, dusted me off, and kissed away my tears again and again. I hope this novel gives a glimpse of the grace You give and the future awaiting those who believe. What sting has death?

Thank you to my dear friend and biggest cheerleader, Cindy Sproles, and to the two very special ladies in my "strand of three threads": Jessica Dotta and Ane Mulligan. We began this path together, admonishing, uplifting, and teaching one another without ceasing. You have almost as much time and effort invested in my writing as I do. Thank you for reading, rereading, and reading again. You are not only amazing writers but as close as sisters. I love you!

No one suffers the obsession of a writer more than her family. My parents—Nancy and Alberto, and John and Mary—don't get nearly as many visits or calls as we'd all like because of my obligations. Thanks for understanding and all your years of love, sacrifice, and believing in me. Thank you to Gordon for keeping the children so I could attend writers' conferences. My sons, Jacob and Levi, know the top of their mother's head as much as her face. I couldn't ask for two sweeter, more wonderful and understanding boys. You've never complained once over the years. Thank you, babies. I love you so much. And to my three beautiful and ridiculously lovable daughters by marriage—Catherine, Jessie, and Becky—your grace inspires me. I cannot, of course, forget my biggest supporter, best friend, and the love of my life: my amazing husband, Adam. He brings me coffee with kisses, gives me time and space to write, then gushes over me and my writing. Words are inadequate to describe the depth of my love and appreciation.

Thank you to my agent, Chip MacGregor. I hit the lottery when you took me on. Your friendship and confidence in me has made all the difference. Also, Karen Watson and the fiction team at Tyndale. You've taken a chance, believed in my writing with an enthusiasm that has humbled me. Kathy Olson, my editor, made this novel so much stronger, thinking of things I hadn't even considered. I cringe to think of what would have slipped by without your eagle eye and insight. Of course, I can't forget our fantastic publicity and marketing team or the bookstore owners, sales reps, and book distributors, who are all the unsung heroes of publishing. Thank you so very much.

A special thank-you to Sue Brower for her suggestions and encouragement in the early stages of this novel.

Thank you to the critique groups I've been part of over the years: Silver Arrows (Elizabeth "Lisa" Ludwig, Michelle Griep, Ane, and Jess), the amazing Penwrights, and the group that gave me my first taste of criticism, Kingdom Writers.

Also to the Novel Journey team, my friends: Ane Mulligan, Jessica Dotta, Kelly Klepfer, Mike Duran, Lisa Ludwig, Noel DeVries, Marcia Laycock, Yvonne Anderson, Ronie Kendig, and S. Dionne Moore. You work so hard for nothing more than a love of words. I appreciate you more than you know. Thank you for all you do.

It also wouldn't be right not to thank the teachers I've had over the years who've cultivated in me a love of words. I can't remember all of your names, but I haven't forgotten the lessons. You're getting through more than you know.

I promise I'm almost finished, but I can't forget the many published and not-yet-published authors who've encouraged me and answered my never-ending barrage of questions: Alton Gansky, Sara Mills, Michael Palmer, Dineen Miller, C. J. Darlington, Deb Raney, Don Brown, Colleen Coble, Kathy Mackel, Eric Wilson, Claudia Mair Burney, Robert Liparulo, Gail Martin, Charles Martin, Heather Tipton, Bonnie Calhoun, Nora and Fred St. Laurent, T. L. Hines, Brandilyn Collins, Kristy Dykes, and countless others. Thank you for your open hand. Special mention to a few who helped me with certain scenes: David Rodgers, Mike Bowie, and Dr. Anuj Sinha. Last but not least, thanks to my volunteer copy editor, Randy Hurrt, who found many a boo-boo.

CHAPTER ONE

NOTHING DEEPENS A stream like a good rain . . . or makes it harder to cross.

Just a few hundred feet away from the home I'd sworn never to return to, I sat on the smooth surface of a boulder. With my jeans cuffed and toes wiggling in the cold water, I reflected on how recent rains had caused these banks to widen and swell.

Perhaps a decent relationship with my father might also rise as a result of the storm we'd endured. Much could happen in six years. Maybe my absence had, as the adage promised, made his heart grow fonder. Maybe my homecoming would be like that of the Prodigal and he'd greet me with eager arms. Together we'd cry for all that had passed between us—and all that should have but didn't.

Maybe. Maybe. Maybe.

It's going to go just fine, I told myself as I traced the slippery surface of a moss-covered branch with my foot.

"What's funny, Mommy?"

Isabella's voice startled me. I didn't dare admit that what my five-year-old interpreted as mirth was really a grimace, because then of course she'd want to know what was the matter. "Nothing, sweetness."

She threw a pebble at the water, but it dropped inches from its goal, clinking against slate instead. "You were smiling like this—" She bared her teeth in a forced grin.

Gently, I pinched her cheek.

"You're beautiful, Mommy."

"Thank you, baby. So are you."

"Yes, I am."

I smiled at that. I smiled at just about everything she said and did.

"Mommy, why'd we drive here 'stead of Cowpa's house?"

Cowpa was her name for grandparents of either gender. I probably should have corrected her long ago, but I found the odd term endearing. Besides, I reasoned, she'd grow out of baby talk all too soon without any help from me. I found myself wondering what other lessons she would learn in my absence.

The thought overwhelmed me, but I refused to cry in front of my daughter. Unloading my heavy burden onto her delicate shoulders was not an option. I might not be able to control much in my life lately, but I could still protect her. Nothing mattered more.

"This was my thinking place when I was a little girl. I wanted to show it to you in case you wanted to think sometimes." I breathed in the area's familiar fragrance—a combination of damp leaves, pine, and earth—and eyed my surroundings. Same trees. Same sounds. Nothing much ever changed in this spot. That, more than any other reason, was why I loved it so much. Especially now.

I'd spent half of my life here, sitting on this unyielding rock, trying to make sense of the world. The loss of my mother. My father's neglect. The sometimes-sweet, often-bitter, words of my ex-boyfriend, David. It was here I'd first gotten real with God, begging Him not to take my mother. Railing at Him when He did.

Isabella bounced on one foot. "What did you think about here?"

I poked my toes through water, watching droplets glide down my pink toenails. "Well, when I was little, I thought of catching frogs and grasshoppers and wondered whether I would ever have a best friend to share my secrets with."

"Did you find your best friend?" A dangling pine needle twirled from one of her curls.

Love overwhelmed me. "Yes, sweetness. I got you."

She gave me one of her endearing smiles, pulled the debris from her hair, examined it, then dropped it in the stream. I scooped a handful of the cool water and let it slip through my fingers like the life I'd just left behind—my studio apartment that never really felt like home, the corporate ladder I'd just begun to climb, my coworkers who never became the close friends I had longed for. All of it now gone, as though it had never existed at all.

My daughter looked at me askance. "I wanna go."

The hum of nature faded. The only thing I heard now was the sharp tick of my wristwatch reminding me just how short time was. Standing, I assured myself that I could do what I had come to do. For Isabella, I could do it. I slipped my damp feet into my Birkenstocks and brushed off my rear before collecting my daughter's chubby hand in my fingers.

I forced one leg in front of the other and made my way past my car, along the winding dirt road.

A familiar picket fence dressed in tangled braids of morning glories came into view. I clutched my daughter's fingers tighter, feeling more like child than mother.

Placing a hand over my heart, I stopped and took it in. I'd forgotten how beautiful my childhood home was and how much I'd missed it. As I remembered running barefoot through this yard and cannonball jumping into the pond out back, joy pricked at me . . . until my gaze settled on the bare dirt beneath the stairs. How many times had I hidden under that porch, wounded by my father's words? Too many. My smile died.

Isabella looked up at me eagerly, giving the motivation, if not the courage, I needed to continue. Ghosts of summers past faded as the fragrant scent of roses washed over me, and with it another wave of doubt so tall and wide, I felt as though I might drown in it.

What if my father wouldn't receive me? Or worse, what if he didn't accept my daughter? I felt sure Mama Peg would embrace her, but could he? Accepting me had proven impossible for him, but perhaps a child as charming as Isabella could thaw his arctic heart.

Now on the second stair, I paused to look behind me at the road, feeling a sudden urge to retreat. Isabella bounced on the balls of her feet, anxious to continue.

When we reached the porch, I squatted to her level. "Are you ready to meet your grandpa and great-grandma?"

The longing in her maple syrup eyes needed no words, but she added them anyway. "Jane has a cowpa, Natalie has a cowpa, Carter has two cowpas, and . . ." She gave me a look that said, *Must I continue?*

"Okay, I get it." I stood and lifted a fist to the door. Before I could knock, Isabella lurched forward and did it for me. She tapped her sandaled foot twice, then reached to knock again.

I grabbed her hand. "Give them a chance."

The oversize wildflower wreath swayed as the door creaked open. An elderly woman with thick gray hair fashioned into a bun stood before us, oxygen tubes protruding from her nostrils. Deep wrinkles fractured her leathery skin. Her eyebrows were bushes, her lips were shriveled like raisins, and a heavy, floral perfume emanated from her.

Isabella gasped, but I beamed. "Mama Peg."

My grandmother winked at me before turning her milky gaze to her great-granddaughter. "You must be Bella."

Isabella's mouth opened and a strange squeal escaped. I don't know who was more horrified at that moment—Isabella at the sight of Mama Peg, Mama Peg at Isabella's revulsion, or me at their initial reactions to each other.

Mama Peg broke out in a deep belly laugh, intermingled with emphysemic hacks. Isabella leaped back as though she expected my grandmother and her tank to explode.

I laughed so hard tears streamed down my cheeks. That seemed to calm Isabella, and soon she was grinning too.

"I'm a wretched sight now, little girl, but not so long ago, I used to be as pretty as you," my grandmother managed through her own amusement.

Isabella looked at me to dispel this ridiculous claim. I could only nod. I should have prepared her for this.

Mama Peg raised an unruly eyebrow at me. "I don't think she believes me."

Catching my breath, I wiped my eyes. "I'm not sure I do either." I added a wink to soften the jab. I knew she had been lovely, of course. I'd seen the proof in photographs. She still was in my eyes—one of the most beautiful women I had ever known, despite the cruel effects of tobacco and time.

An exaggerated scowl deepened her wrinkles. "Genevieve Paige Lucas, you're still a brat."

Leaning in, I hugged her with all I had. "I missed you, Grandma."

"You too, Jenny. You stayed away far too long." She hugged

me tight, then slowly pulled away from me. Her eyes glistened, but her tears, every bit as stubborn as she, refused to fall. She scanned the porch. "Where are your bags?"

"In the car. I'll get them later."

She squinted past me at the empty brick driveway. "You parked in front of the stream, I gather?"

I nodded.

A glint of understanding crinkled her eyes as she stepped back, motioning us into the house. My grandmother, more than anyone, understood my need to commune with nature.

When I entered my father's home, my heart once again found my throat. I ushered Isabella across the threshold and hastily scanned the living room, searching for him. I watched Isabella take in the cozy surroundings. Braided rugs protected the hardwood floor. Vases of garden flowers rested on lace-covered tabletops. Everything was just as I remembered . . . including the chill creeping through me, which had nothing to do with air-conditioning.

"It's beautiful, Cowpa!"

Mama Peg shut the door and turned to me. "What did that child call me?"

"That's her word for Grandma—" I cleared my throat— "and Grandpa."

My grandmother shook her head, eyeing my daughter. "Call me Mama Peg. Understand?"

Without responding, Isabella made her way toward the stone fireplace, enthralled with the portrait hanging above it. A woman with long chestnut curls flowing about her narrow waist sat sidesaddle on a white horse. My mother's painted gaze followed me. Her sad little smile made me long to comfort her.

Isabella moved as close to it as she could without stepping onto the hearth. "It's you, Mommy."

Mama Peg grabbed the black handle of her oxygen canister and rolled it to where my daughter stood. "That's your mama's mama. They look a lot alike, don't you think?"

Isabella nodded.

"She died before you were born."

A familiar ache settled within me as memories of my mother's last days forced their way into my mind, elbowing away more pleasant memories.

Isabella picked at the glitter on her T-shirt. "Where do you go when you die?"

I flashed my grandmother a warning look. "Never mind." I had no desire to explain death to her at that moment. "Where's Dad?" I asked.

Mama Peg's shoulders sank. "Upstairs being him."

"What did he say when you told him I was coming?" I held my breath and fingered my thick braid.

"You know him. He . . ." Without finishing the thought, she made her way to the kitchen and we followed. The hard rubber heels of her shoes scraped against the tile floor as she shuffled to the back door. She pulled the lace curtain to the side and looked out the window at the pond out back.

Isabella lifted the top from a white candle in the table's center, releasing a waft of vanilla.

I wrinkled my nose at the sickeningly sweet smell, took the lid from her, and replaced it. "You didn't tell him everything, did you?"

"I told him he had a granddaughter."

"That's all?"

Her voice began to break up. "Of course. A mother should never have to tell her son—"

"Bella?" I interrupted before Mama Peg could say more in front of my child than I was prepared to answer for.

Isabella's gaze ping-ponged between us.

"See if you can find Sweet Pea." The thought occurred to me that there I was, trying to avoid the subject of death, and the cat might be long gone. I lowered my voice, though Isabella stood no farther away than Mama Peg. "He is still—?"

"Alive?" With a chortle, she let the curtain drop back into place and turned to face me. "His Royal Stubbornness refuses to cash in his ninth life. You really must want to change the subject badly to send your sweet girl searching for that homicidal monster."

Isabella's expression filled with alarm.

"Not a monster." I tousled her soft curls. "Just a kitty."

Mama Peg hacked, her skin taking on a grayish hue. I rubbed her back, hating the plastic feel of her polyester top. When her cough subsided, she plucked a napkin from a pile on the table and wiped her mouth. "That furry devil will scratch her bloody."

"She'll never catch him."

"You forget, six years have passed. He's old and slow now."

Considering what the tabby might do to Isabella if she tried to pet him gave me pause. I took her hands in mine and squatted to eye level. "Look for him, Bella, but don't get too close. He's got a bad temper and sharp claws that will give you boo-boos."

She promised obedience, then raced off for the hunt.

Mama Peg turned to me. "She's braver than you were at her age."

"Who isn't?" I had never been the fearless child Isabella was. She saw everything as a ray of sunshine living just to warm her. No matter how many times I counseled her that not everyone had her best interests at heart, she refused to believe it. After all, she loved everything and everyone, so why wouldn't they love her back?

Mama Peg adjusted the tubing threaded over her ears. "When are you going to tell your father?"

I walked to the stove and picked up the teakettle. Finding it heavy, I set it back down and turned on the burner. A snap preceded a flame.

"I want to see how he treats her first."

"Of course he'll love her. She's part of you. Part of your mother."

An old, familiar dagger lunged into my chest and I hated that even now it could penetrate me. "He hasn't loved anything since Mom passed."

"That's not true," she whispered, as if saying it softly

could somehow breathe truth into the falsehood. She pulled two ceramic mugs from the cupboard. "He's a good man, Jenny."

I felt a sudden heaviness about me as I pulled a chair away from the table to sit. "A good man with a hardened heart."

She dropped a square of tea into each mug. "Having someone you love taken from you has a way of changing a person."

I crossed my arms.

She averted her gaze. "Stupid thing to say to you, I guess."

"I guess."

"So what if you don't like the way he is with her? Then what will you do?"

It was the question that had kept me awake for the past two weeks. The most important question in my world.

"I'm not her only parent."

"I guess now would be the time to tell me who her father is." She raised my chin, forcing me to look at her. After several seconds of reading me, she withdrew her hand. "As if I don't already know."

My face burned and I opened my mouth to say his name, but it stuck in my throat—a dam holding back half a decade's worth of tears. "I never told him."

Mama Peg's face drained of what little color it held. I could almost feel her heart splinter. "Oh, Jenny."

I deserved her scorn. But she wrapped her sagging arms around my shoulders, smothering me in her generous bosom, flowery perfume, and acceptance. Relief overwhelmed me.

"I found him! I found him!" The pattering of feet accompanied my daughter's shriek.

Mama Peg released me, and we turned to the doorway in anticipation of Isabella's excited return. She appeared, dragging my father by the hand.

His short, wavy hair was more gray now than brown. He wore his polo shirt tucked neatly into creased pants and a leather belt fastened around his trim belly. I'd have better luck trying to read Chinese than gauge his emotions by his stoic expression.

My fingernails dug into my palms and I felt the need to sit before registering that I was already seated. When his gaze met mine, he gave me a quick once-over. I studied the lines around his eyes. Was he fighting a smile? If so, was it due to smugness that I'd come crawling home or joy at seeing me after so long? Or was I imagining it all?

Without a word, he walked to the kitchen window, held his hand over his eyes, and panned the side yard.

Mama Peg threw me an annoyed glance. "What the dickens is he doing?"

He turned around, this time donning a sly grin. "I'm looking for the airborne swine."

The dumb look on his face told me he expected laughter, but I just sat there slack-jawed.

"As I recall, you said you'd come home when pigs fly."

Though I promised myself I would curb my usual retorts, my mouth opened before I could will it not to. "Yeah, I get it. I'm smarter than I look."

He surprised me by waving his hand in dismissal. "So after six years of nothing, you've finally decided to let me meet my granddaughter. How very humane of you. I assume you're here because you're broke?"

My thoughts flashed back to the phone call home I'd made after leaving. I'd tearfully told my father I was pregnant. Five minutes into a lecture on the sins and consequences of fornication, I hung up without a word and never called again.

Every day for two weeks after that, his number showed on my caller ID. Not wanting further berating, I never answered or called him back. After several months of silence, the number flashed again. This time I picked up, but it was my grandmother on the other line, not my father. Never again my father.

"Assumptions have always been your specialty." As soon as the words left my mouth, I wanted them back. Why was I waving a red cape before this bull instead of the white flag I'd intended?

The teakettle's high-pitched scream pierced the uncomfortable silence. Mama Peg hurried to the stove and jerked the vessel to a cool burner.

My father squatted before Isabella. "Do you know who I am, young lady?"

Considering the question, she looked to the left. "My daddy?"

I cringed at her unexpected response and my gaze flew to meet my father's eyes. The icy glare he sent my way could have frozen an ocean.

"That's your grandpa," I managed.

She looked up at him with adoring eyes, then flung her pudgy arms around his shoulders.

I exhaled in relief when he reciprocated. After the hug, he stood. His expression once again bore the emotional void I'd come to expect since Mom died.

Clearing his throat, he straightened an already-even belt buckle. "I think I saw Sweet Pea run by."

Isabella jerked her head left, then right. My father pointed to the living room and off she went, oblivious to the manipulation.

"She doesn't know who her father is?" He glared at me as I fought back tears of frustration. I didn't trust myself to speak, and he probably felt the same. After a few long seconds, he snatched a set of keys from the wall hook, glowered at me one last time, and slammed the door shut behind him.

CHAPTER TWO

THOUGH I LAY in bed for nearly two hours, sleep never came. I counted the wobbly rotations of the ceiling fan, wondering how I could tell David he had a five-year-old daughter. As impossible as it had seemed at the time to say the words *I'm pregnant*, how much worse it was now that he'd missed Isabella's first smile, first step, first word. Would he hate me? I certainly deserved it.

I flipped onto my stomach, leaned on my elbows, and gazed up at the framed artwork that had long ago replaced my rock posters. Along sun-painted sand, a young couple strolled pinkie in pinkie. I cursed their bliss and rolled back over.

Twisting the corner of the pillow, I mentally rehearsed excuses. . . .

Remember that night in the car, David? I started to tell you, but you broke up with me first. You said things could never work for us. You told me our fathers would never get along. You told me you didn't share my desire for having a family. How could I tell you you were going to be a father right after you said you never wanted children?

When she was born, I called you from the hospital as I held her in my arms. I couldn't wait to show you what we'd created, but your answering machine picked up and I heard, "David and Lindsey Preston aren't here to take your call. . . ." I didn't know you'd gotten married. It had been less than a year since we broke up. You wouldn't believe the shock I felt, the betrayal, the pain. . . . I didn't want to cause trouble for you. . . . I couldn't . . .

Giving up on both a nap and an acceptable defense, I forced myself out of bed.

Despite the magnitude of my worries, I found myself relaxing as the scent of fried chicken and baking rolls made promises to my stomach that I knew my grandmother's cooking would make good on.

Moving around the dining room table, I laid a plate in front of each chair. A hand touched my shoulder and I nearly jumped out of my skin, dropping the last two dishes. They clanked together, making my ears ring. My gaze jetted to the plates—both intact—then to the blond frowning at me.

"Sorry, Jenny. I didn't mean to scare you."

He looked familiar and had the kind of good looks a girl wouldn't normally forget, but I couldn't quite place him.

"You startled me," I said as I picked up the dishes.

"Wow, you look exactly the same."

The same as what? I frantically searched my mind for memories of him. Tall, narrow, about my age . . .

"You don't remember me, do you?"

"Sorry," I said, feeling sorry indeed.

He took the plates from my hand and moved around the table, laying them down. "We went to Hargrove together. Same graduating class."

I searched my mind for any recollection.

"I can't believe you don't remember me." He said it with a glint of humor I didn't comprehend. "How about now?" He puffed his cheeks out like he had a mouthful of water, then expelled the air.

Feeling suddenly uncomfortable in his presence, I stepped back. He might have just walked in off the street for all I knew. Maybe I wasn't the one who was confused.

His eyebrows knit together, and he reached his hand out as though to keep me from running. "It's me, Craig Allen."

My gaze flew over him. It was clear, even through his blue Tar Heels T-shirt, that he was well-defined. The only Craig Allen I knew was a doughy sort of boy, shy and pimply. This couldn't be him. Searching his eyes, I found they were the same stormy hazel they had been back when they were peeking out from under layers of fat.

"You've lost weight," I managed.

He snickered. "Ya think?"

My cheeks blazed. "What are you doing here?"

"I live here."

"You do?"

"I rent the loft."

"Loft?"

"The apartment above the saddle barn."

"There's an apartment above the saddle barn?"

"You really need to keep in touch with your family."

I supposed by his grin that he meant his words as a joke, but the painful truth they conveyed struck me as more rude than amusing.

"Thanks for the advice, Craig. Good to see you again."

"Thank *you* for setting the table. That's usually my job."

Though I knew it was irrational, I felt the prick of jealousy. Here was this man my age, living at my father's home, eating with my family, setting *my* table. It was as if he'd taken my place. I knew, of course, that I didn't need to be present for life to go on, but the truth of it was too much at that moment. I clamped my mouth against a sudden and overwhelming desire to scream. To hit Craig. To break something.

We sat across from each other, Craig and I, with Mama Peg on one end of the rectangular table and my father on the other. Isabella inched her chair so close to his that he'd been forced to eat in the awkward position of keeping his right elbow pinned to his side.

Ice cubes clinked together as I took a sip of sweet tea. "Bella, give your grandpa some room."

She responded by sending me the evil eye. I pushed myself up from the table, but Mama Peg grabbed my arm. "She's not bothering him. Is she, Jack?"

My father stared at her, lips pressed tight. "No, she's fine."

Isabella smirked a *so there*. The dim light from the pewter chandelier cast an odd shadow over her features, making her look like a different child.

With my fork, I arranged the peas on my plate into a frown.

The clatter of silverware and an occasional cough from Mama Peg were the only sounds as we ate. Craig snuck curious glances at Isabella while I snuck glances at him. A shroud of gloomy silence continued to hang over the room until I couldn't stand it a second longer. I pushed my uneaten dinner to the side.

"So, Craig, what have you been up to?"

With a heap of mashed potatoes halfway to his mouth, he paused, meeting my gaze. He set the spoon down on his plate. "Been great. I've got my own business now. Landscaping."

"Like mowing lawns and that sort of thing?"

He furrowed his brow. "Um, no, I have guys who do that. I'm more of an artist."

"Like sculpting bushes into shapes of animals? I love . . ."

Mama Peg and my father exchanged glances. Craig looked at me as though trying to gauge whether I was joking or just plain stupid. His tone and the fresh splotches of red on his neck told me I'd missed the mark. "Not quite. I'm a landscape designer."

The fact that I had offended him offended me, but for the sake of peace, I apologized.

The room fell silent again until Isabella asked to be excused. She'd eaten most of her dinner, leaving only an untouched roll and some scattered peas.

Her child-size suitcase leaned against the maple hutch. She grabbed it by the handle and dragged it across the rug, upside down, its small black wheels pointing uselessly toward the ceiling. I opened my mouth to correct her but changed my mind.

The sound of her unloading toys took the edge off the silence. Mama Peg reached for the glass pitcher of tea and Craig cleared his throat in disapproval. They locked eyes. She huffed and set the pitcher back down. Tea splashed around in it, a trickle escaping down the side.

I grabbed the pitcher and poured her another glass, glaring at Craig as I set it in front of her. If my grandmother wanted another drink, what was it to him?

Mama Peg reached for the glass and brought it slowly to her lips. Her hand quivered as she tilted the glass to drink.

Craig crossed his arms and stared hard at her. "Enjoy your last glass of the real stuff, Peggy. From now on it's decaf."

When did he become my grandmother's keeper? I slapped

down my linen napkin. "She's a grown woman. If she wants to drink the whole pitcher, what's it—"

"Jenny," Mama Peg began.

"Jenny, nothing. Who does he think he is?"

She set the glass down, looking guilty. "He's just doing what I asked him to."

Anger melted into confusion. "What?"

"My doctor said one glass a day because of my palpita tions."

I turned to Craig. "Palpitations?"

"Your grandmother's medications make her jittery, and when she has too much caffeine, it makes her heart race. The doctor said, unless she wants to end up with a pacemaker, one glass a day. She asked me to keep her accountable."

My stomach got that queasy elevator feeling as I realized I was being the biggest jerk in the world.

My throat constricted and everything I'd been through in the past six years suddenly weighed on me until I could barely breathe. Traitorous tears blurred my vision. When I opened my mouth, intending to blame my volatile emotions on exhaustion, pathetic sobs busted out instead of words.

Mortified, I rushed from the room.

Unsure whether to retreat or return, I leaned my back against the kitchen wall. Crying at my circumstances. Laughing at myself. Wondering if the mind really was the first thing to go.

After a few minutes, Craig came to my side. "Hey, I'm sorry," he said.

Feeling self-conscious about the raccoon eyes I undoubtedly had, I rubbed away the wet mascara. Trails of black now marred my fingers. "What are you sorry for?"

"Honestly? I have no idea. I'm always saying stuff to upset women." He tucked his hands into his jeans.

"It wasn't you. I'm just going through a lot. I'm the one who should be sorry for acting like a freak."

He exhaled. "Want to talk about it?"

And then I remembered a time years ago when he'd asked me the same thing. Ninth grade. I'd just learned I hadn't made the cheerleading squad. I stood against the chain-link fence that bordered the soccer field. As my classmates chattered and laughed, I wept silently into the bend of my arm. I had thought no one was watching.

A younger Craig asked if I wanted to talk about it, just like now. I shook my head, wanting to talk about it, just not to him.

Just like now.

"Thanks, Craig." I softened toward him then, reminding myself the true nature of people didn't change. The considerate boy he had been was still a part of the man standing before me. "But it's personal."

"Stuff with your dad?"

"Actually, Isabella's dad."

"David Preston."

My heart froze. "How do you know?"

"It's not rocket science. You two were dating."

Shame filled me and I looked down. "You must think I'm . . ."

A gentle hand guided my chin up, forcing me to meet his gaze. "I think you must be very strong."

I snorted. "Yeah, real strong."

"You're raising a child on your own. I mean, I sure couldn't do that."

"You'd be surprised what you could do if you had to."

"It can't have been easy," he said.

"Easy? No, it definitely wasn't that." I felt the weight of that burden anew. "I sold my blood more than once to buy diapers, and if I ever see another ramen noodle, it'll be too soon."

"See, that's what I mean, Jenny. You're an amazing woman. Not everyone is that strong."

"If I was so amazing, I wouldn't have needed to be."

CHAPTER THREE

I LAY WITH Isabella until she drifted off to sleep, then made my way down the stairs. Mama Peg reclined in her easy chair. Veins protruded atop her feet like earthworms, which told me her legs were swollen and probably hurting. Of course if I asked, she'd only deny it.

Not taking her eyes off the TV, she reached to the end table, blindly felt around, and lifted a coffee mug resting on its *Reader's Digest* coaster. Meanwhile, Lucy Ricardo whined at Ricky, mesmerizing my grandmother as though she hadn't seen the episode a hundred times before.

The last step I touched down on creaked under my weight. Mama Peg aimed the remote at the set, muting it, then turned to me.

"Hey," I said.

"Hey, kid. Your dad's on the porch having his evening pipe."

I plopped down on the love seat. She cleared her throat and stared at me expectantly.

"What?"

"I said your father's on the porch."

"Uh-huh."

"Alone."

Oh. "What kind of mood's he in?"

"He's been giddy ever since he found out you were coming home."

I thought she needed to clean her rose-colored glasses but didn't say so. Facing forward, she hit the remote again. Ricky exclaimed, "Oh, Lucy!" and I took it as my cue to go.

When I opened the front door, the groan it made echoed my sentiments.

My father glanced over as he slipped the pipe from his lips. "You want to hit that off?" He motioned to the porch light smothered by fluttering moths of various sizes. I ducked back in, flipped the switch, then joined him again.

He sat in the same rocker he had occupied most summer nights ever since I could remember. The moon cast a soft glow over him, hiding his gray and wrinkles and making him look like the man I once called Daddy.

I took the porch swing, curling my fingers around the cool metal chain suspending it. The sweet scent of pipe tobacco flooded me with nostalgia. I never told him how much I loved that smell. "Keep smoking that—" I nodded to his pipe—"and soon you'll be dragging around a tank like your old lady."

He snorted in good humor. "There's a big difference between this and two packs of Pall Malls a day."

Sweet Pea climbed the porch steps and rubbed against my father's leg.

I motioned to the purring cat. "I think he wants you to pet him."

"No thanks. I value my fingers." He shooed Sweet Pea away with his foot.

The cat's fur stood straight up along the length of his spine as he hissed his disapproval. Sweet Pea must have heard something in the distance because he jerked his head toward the yard and slunk off into the night.

We said nothing for a few moments as a cricket choir serenaded us. "Man, I'd forgotten how loud those things could be."

Back and forth he rocked as though he didn't have a care. As though the tension between us wasn't thick enough to dull a chain saw. "What things?"

"Crickets."

"I guess I tune them out." He tapped the side of his pipe against his armrest, then slid it back into his mouth.

"You're good at that."

"Are we going to start fighting again, Genevieve?"

"It's not your fault. It's common to your gender." I winked to let him know I was playing. Or at least to pretend I was.

"That's true enough. I wonder why God made us that way."

"Coping mechanism, I guess." I walked my feet back, then picked them up, sending the swing gliding. Warm air stroked my cheeks and pushed wisps of rogue hair off my face. "I bet Eve was a talker."

An owl hooted. I searched the night for the reflection of its eyes, but the only forms visible were the silhouettes of treetops swaying against a velvet blue canvas.

"She'd have to be." He stared at the half-moon as though conversing with it instead of me. "She and her husband only had a few million things to name."

"I bet she named 90 percent of 'em too."

When his rocking stopped, so did my heart. "You want to tell me what happened five years and nine months ago?"

I really did.

And I really didn't.

I planted my feet on the porch, making the swing halt abruptly and my stomach lurch. "I guess."

And so I did.

I told him I'd had every intention of doing the right thing, of keeping myself until marriage, but when Mom died, I was hurting, and David was there. Of course I left out the gritty details. I didn't tell him I was furious with God and didn't care if I broke His laws. In fact wanted to break as many as I could. I didn't tell him David's touch served as an effective, albeit temporary, anesthetic. And if only for the short time we made love, I didn't think about my mother's suffering.

Didn't think about the fact that the person who knew and loved me best in the world was forever gone.

Moving as slowly as if he were wading through petroleum jelly, my father laid his pipe upright by his bare feet. "Mosquitoes getting you?" He stared ahead into the night.

"Not yet." I studied his face and body language for any sign of repressed anger.

"I keep meaning to get some tiki torches out here." His tone was flat. His expression stoic.

"They'll look good with the fifteen-foot totem I'm buying you for Christmas."

"Can't wait for that."

Were we really not going to mention the elephant in the room? I had no choice but to. It was crushing me. "We going to keep making small talk, Dad?"

He leaned his head against the back of the chair and turned toward me with a look that wasn't softened even by the moonlight. "What do you want me to say, Genevieve? that I'm disappointed in you? Okay, I'm disappointed in you. The last time I voiced my opinion, you hung up and I didn't hear from you again for almost six years."

"Maybe you could skip the lecture this time and—"

"I share a grandchild with the man who murdered your mother. Do you want me to be happy about that?" The tendons in his hands protruded as he clutched the wicker arms of his chair.

I kept waiting for him to continue. After the longest five minutes of my life, he started rocking again.

"Well?"

"Well what?" he snapped. "His father killed your mother."

I winced. His flaming anger hadn't cooled an iota over the past six years. "That's a little over the top. He wasn't even her doctor."

His nostrils flared, his lips disappeared, and his breath became short, angry bursts. "She trusted him. He should have sent her to a specialist. He knew he screwed up. Knew it. All he had to do was admit it. Say he was sorry." His words were clipped and an octave higher than he normally spoke.

"Daddy—"

"Did you do it just to spite me?"

I'd mistakenly thought he was on the verge of tears, but fury, not sadness, was the ledge he teetered on. "What?"

"Did you do it—"

I bolted up, lava coursing through my arteries. "I heard you. Did I get pregnant, make my life a hundred times harder than it had to be, and bring a child into the world to raise alone just to spite you? Is *that* your question?"

He expelled a loud breath, pushed himself out of the chair, and marched off down the dirt road. I watched him walk into the night until a cloud of billowy gray blanketed the moon. I could no longer see him. That was just fine, because I no longer wanted to.

CHAPTER FOUR

THE SMELL OF frying bacon woke me. My head felt like a block of cement as I tried to lift it from the pillow. The bright morning sun speared through the wooden blinds straight into my eyes. I squinted, making everything around me appear cast in golden halos and veils of gauze.

For the briefest moment, I was a child again. Eight years old, pigtailed and slight, with every dream for my life still a possibility. I rolled over and sat up, feeling pushed to hurry. If I missed the bus again, Mom was going to kill me.

No, that wasn't right. I rubbed the slumber from my eyes. The Polly Pocket backpack lying on my dresser belonged not to me, but to my own daughter.

I sighed and trudged to the bathroom.

Having showered and dressed, I made my way down the stairs, and my heart fluttered at what I saw. Still wearing her footed pajamas, Isabella sat at the kitchen table, a stub of tongue jutting from the corner of her mouth as she meticulously traced a picture with a fat blue crayon.

When I entered the kitchen, she glanced up, then went back to work. Mama Peg finished pouring a cup of coffee before giving me her attention.

"Aren't you supposed to be giving up caffeine?" I asked.

"It's *decaf*." She said it as though it were less appealing than a mug of sewer water. "Sorry to make the whole family suffer with me, but Hurricane Craig came through this morning."

The melodrama in her voice made me laugh. "You really shouldn't talk that way about your father."

"Hardy-har-har." She wrinkled her nose and took a sip of unleaded.

I pulled a mug from the cabinet and poured myself a cup, adding a splash of half-and-half from the carton resting on the counter. Behind me, a chair leg scraped the floor.

"Sit. Let me fix you a plate."

An empty cast-iron pan still lined with grease sat on the stove, along with a mound of bacon piled on a plate lined with paper towels. My stomach grumbled, and for the first time in weeks, I felt hunger instead of nausea.

Taking a seat next to my daughter, I eyed the picture she was coloring—Cinderella dancing with her prince at the ball. Isabella outlined her gown in royal purple and his suit in navy. Her strokes were almost perfect; only rarely did a small mark venture outside the lines.

"Bells, you sure are good at that."

Fighting a smile, she colored the glass slippers lemon yellow.

I looked past her, through the window, at a small tree. Its branches dripped with dark green leaves and small, pale apples. I turned and smiled at Mama Peg. "Mom's tree has fruit!"

She followed my gaze. "Ain't that something? This is the first year it's done that. I told her that thing would never produce if she didn't cross-pollinate by planting another variety. I guess she was right. I should have had a little faith."

Memories of my mother's gaunt face smeared with dirt as her bony fingers pressed the hand spade into earth replayed in my mind. I wished she could be here now to see it. "I always thought it was strange she took the time to plant that when she knew she was dying."

Mama Peg set her sponge down and looked thoughtfully at the ceiling. "The true meaning of life is to plant trees whose shade you never expect to sit under. Or something like that."

I considered it a moment. "Wow, did you just make that up?"

She shook her head. "I'm not that profound. Just heard it once or twice and it stuck with me."

I ran my hand over Isabella's soft cheek. "Did you eat breakfast?"

After a minute of silence, Mama Peg answered for her. "She had two hotcakes, four pieces of bacon, and a glass and a half of orange juice."

I snorted like a hog into the bend of Isabella's neck, sending her into a laughing fit.

Moments later, my grandmother laid three steaming pancakes, several strips of bacon, and a glass of orange juice before me. I grinned my thanks and got busy spreading butter.

Coffee in hand, she took a seat across from me. "How'd you sleep, kid?"

I drowned my plate in maple syrup. "Perfect. Where's Dad?"

I had to wait for her coughing fit to subside to get my answer. "Probably still in bed. He came in late."

Maple and butter played a delicious melody in my mouth. I swallowed my bite and took a sip of juice. Its bitter taste ended the symphony and killed my appetite. "How late?"

"Two."

A piece of bacon tried to enter my lungs instead of stomach, making me cough so hard I thought my eyes would pop out.

"Put your hands above your head," Mama Peg said.

Ignoring her advice, I took another drink instead.

"You okay, Mommy?"

I caught my breath before answering. "I'm fine. I laid your clothes out on our floor. Go get dressed for me, okay?"

She closed the coloring book without an argument, and I felt a surge of thankfulness. When I heard her feet on the stairs, I asked my grandmother, "Why did he come in so late?"

"What happened between you two last night?" Her milky gaze bored holes through me.

"I told him."

"About Isabella or about—"

"Just Bella."

She nodded as though agreeing with my decision. "So you're throwing one grenade at a time instead of taking the mushroom cloud approach. That's probably wise."

"If I wanted to tell him everything, I would have had to run after him screaming."

"He walked away?"

"Doesn't he always?"

A wry smile met me. "You might want to move out of that glass house of yours before you hurl stones at his."

The truth of her words stung. Maybe I was more like him than I'd considered. Not liking the thought, I swept it away. "I wonder where he went for four hours?"

"Finish your breakfast."

Though I no longer had any desire to eat, to please her I pushed my fork into another square of pancake.

She plucked a half-eaten piece of bacon from my plate and popped it into her mouth, speaking between crunches. "With him, who knows? He might have walked, or fallen asleep in the canoe, or—"

My father's footsteps bit off her words. He walked through the doorway with a bottom lip twice the size of the top and a left nostril crusted with red. Mama Peg and I exchanged questioning glances.

I'd forgotten I was no longer speaking to him. "What happened to you?"

He made his way to the cupboard and pulled out a coffee mug. "What happened to me when?"

Mama Peg coughed, then pointed to his mouth. "Your face."

He busied himself pouring coffee into his mug.

"Jack, what did you do?" She shook her head as though she already knew the answer.

My insides burned. "Please tell me it doesn't involve the Prestons." His silence knocked the wind out of me. "Daddy, no."

When he turned to face us, I noticed a long scratch on his right cheek.

Alarm filled me. "What did you do?"

Mama Peg stood, her face grayer than usual. "Jack?"

His gaze lingered on the linoleum as he spoke. "I confronted him."

"David's father?" This couldn't be happening. "Again?"

"I demanded he acknowledge . . ." He paused when his bloodshot eyes met mine. "He still denies it. Even now that we share a grandchild, he refuses to do the right thing."

Blood pounded against my temples. "Say you didn't tell him about Bella. Tell me. Tell me!" I was screaming now. My body seemed to be acting of its own accord while my mind floated high above the scene, watching with deaf horror.

"David doesn't know. You know I haven't told him yet. How could you!"

My father hung his head and covered his face with both hands.

"Jesus, help us," Mama Peg prayed aloud as I snatched my keys and bag from the counter and tore out the back door.

CHAPTER FIVE

I SPED OUT of the saddle barn's gravel driveway, down the bumpy road, and across the single-lane bridge leading to town. Scanning through radio stations, I flipped past the talk shows, past the easy listening, past the country, to rap. Angry and loud, it suited my mood.

As I drove, I tried to reassure myself that I was still early enough to stand a good chance of beating Dr. Preston to his son. It was Saturday, and if memory served right, my father's nemesis would not be making morning rounds as he did during the week but would have one of his residents performing this duty so he could sleep in. How many times had I heard him say in his pompous way, *"After this many years of doctoring, I think I've earned the right to my weekend."*

Though I seldom saw eye to eye with my father, in this case I was inclined to agree that the only thing Dr. Preston deserved was a kick in the pants. I didn't hate him like my father did or make him the scapegoat for my mother's death, but I did disdain his haughty nature.

When Mom passed, my father considered retribution by seeking damages. But he had been a trial attorney and had developed such a loathing for the system that he swore when he retired, he would never willingly set foot in a courtroom again. I'd heard him say more than once that he would just as soon kill a man as sue him. I had no doubt he'd like to kill Dr. Preston, but fortunately for them both, the Bible forbade it.

Of course God also said we should love our enemies, but reminding Dad of that only brought cold shoulders and colder stares. My father, the hypocrite. Obedient only when it suited him. Selfish with God. Selfish with me.

When my mother died, he retreated into a world all his own, casting a shadow over our house and over my life. Did he care that he left me to suffer alone? If he did, you wouldn't know it. If he wasn't yelling, he was giving me the silent treatment. At my mother's funeral, I buried not one parent, but two.

And now this. How dare he reveal Isabella's existence in that manner! I could just picture him standing on Dr. Preston's porch, screaming for him to come down. The way he probably spat the words, red-faced, eyes bulging from their sockets. Did he growl Isabella's name? I gritted my teeth at the thought. My daughter was precious, not something to be spewed out like a curse word.

My mouth felt suddenly dry. I patted around the passenger seat, under my purse and a pile of CDs, for the bottle of water I'd left in the car. Securing it between my thighs, I kept one hand on the wheel vibrating from the roughness of the country road and, with the other, twisted the cap off and took a swig. It was warm, but at least it was wet.

Nearing the paved main road, I began to wonder how exactly I planned to talk with David when I had no clue where he lived. From Mama Peg, I had learned he'd become a type of accountant called an actuary. So I figured he would more than likely be home on a Saturday.

I had no idea where home was, of course, but with the small fortune his grandparents had left him, I felt sure it would be a lovely place in an affluent neighborhood I could never afford to live in. Nor would I want to. His tastes had always seemed extravagant to me, and mine too simple for him.

He used to say, *"If you're going to dream, dream big. You want a cottage; I'll build you a castle."* I didn't want a castle. Like Goldilocks sitting in Papa Bear's chair, I found his dreams too big. I preferred my smaller ones, which felt just right.

Never in my dreams had I imagined I would be the big bad wolf in David's fairy tale. I had meant to be his princess. But he had chosen another. Even after all this time, that fact brought back the stabbing pain of rejection. I knew I wasn't being rational, but emotion seldom cares.

I made a sharp right onto Elm. Gravel crunched and sprayed

as my tires kicked off the last remnants of the back road onto pristine asphalt. The stuffiness of the car, all closed up and stale, suited me somehow, but as I neared a large, dusty home with an older man rocking on its porch, I felt a sudden desire to disturb the peace. I opened the front windows and cranked the music louder, relishing the dirty look he sent my way.

The warm wind whipped at my face, pulling strands from my once-tidy braid. I tilted the rearview mirror down and glanced at my reflection. Long, untamed hair hung partly in its braid, partly slapping at my oval face. I yanked out the ponytail holder and ran my fingers through to loosen the tangles. The wind finished the job. Long, crimped tresses flew about me like kite tails.

My lips, neither full nor thin, were as red as if I'd applied a lipstick too bright and then wiped it off. I smiled at my wild reflection. She didn't smile in return. While I had my mother's shape, face, and mannerisms, I had inherited one thing unmistakably belonging to my father. His eyes. Gray and disapproving, they glared at me under my own long lashes.

I pushed the mirror back into place and turned the radio down to a less obnoxious level.

A sickening feeling came over me as I glanced through the windshield at the sun, fully risen. What if I got to David too late? The clock on my dashboard read 9 a.m. The dreaded conversation between father and son might have already taken place or could be taking place at that very moment. I could almost hear it.

"David, I have news, Son. Remember that girl you were

seeing that I couldn't stand? You know, the one whose mother died and her crazy father keeps accusing me of murdering her? He always said he'd get even. Well, he finally has."

Sick of my rampant thoughts and being whipped by my own hair, I put the windows up and concentrated on a plan of action. Surely half the town would know where David lived. I sped past Theodore's Café, which looked more like Ted's truck stop—a long, characterless building, once white, now yellowed from sun and age.

Theodore was David's uncle. David's uncle would have David's address. I threw a glance in the rearview mirror, saw only an empty road lined with overgrown grass behind me, slammed my brakes, and burned rubber as I sped in reverse. The crowded parking lot offered only one unoccupied spot, wedged between two pickups, which I squeezed into.

The owner, Theodore Preston, better known to everyone as Uncle Ted, was Dr. Preston's stepbrother. Though Theodore's Café was a classless little establishment, Ted made a killing. He lived two houses down from his doctor brother and matched all the luxuries Dr. Preston enjoyed—Mercedes for Mercedes, summer home for summer home—everything, that is, except his superiority complex.

The so-called café was a strange little place, complete with vinyl tablecloths, schoolhouse chairs, and plastic flowers in chipped vases. A stuffed gopher stood guard over the rickety cash register, and the place reeked of grease and cigarette smoke. But what the atmosphere lacked, Ted's cooking made up for.

While breakfast patrons shoved biscuits and gravy into their mouths between words, I stood nervously near the counter full of men on stools drinking coffee and reading the want ads.

I asked the waitress if I could please see Ted. She jabbed a pen into her bun and disappeared into the kitchen.

Uncle Ted emerged. He took off his paper hat, revealing a bald head shimmering under a layer of perspiration. Shoving a hand out for me to shake, he spoke around the toothpick jutting from the corner of his mouth. "Jenny Lucas, I'm pleased to see you back in town."

I could tell by his expression that *horrified* was more like it.

"I'm trying to find David."

He sucked on his toothpick and stared at me unblinking. Dishes clinked in the background, and behind the kitchen doors someone yelled for someone else to move it or lose it.

He slurped on wood. "You know he's married now?"

"I know."

"Happily married."

"Listen, Ted, I'm not trying to cause trouble. I just have something of David's I thought he might want."

The way Ted eyed me gave me the impression that he thought he knew what that something was and didn't care for it one bit.

The elderly couple occupying the booth behind me threw down two dollars, picked up their bill, and shuffled to the register to pay. Ted grabbed a soppy washcloth from under the counter and hurried over, clearing away two mugs and several empty creamer containers they left behind. He wiped the table, then gestured to it. "There you go."

"I really can't—"

"You can't very well visit David on an empty stomach."

I gave him a pleading look, which he ignored. Good grief. No wonder the man was rich.

When I sat, he puffed his chest out triumphantly. "Because you're basically family, I'll take your order myself."

Oh, joy. "I'll have an English muffin and glass of water."

He crossed his arms and stared me down. "You want his address or not?"

I glanced at my watch. "What do you recommend?"

"Now, that's better. I'll fix you a stack of pancakes with bacon and sausage."

My stomach lurched at the thought. "Fine."

"How do you want your eggs?"

"Eggs?"

He raised his black eyebrows peppered with silver.

"Surprise me."

"You like surprises, eh? David's wife, Lindsey, sure don't."

"Don't tell them I'm coming, okay?"

"Don't tell them I gave you the address." With that he scribbled something on the back of my bill and laid it on the table.

Without waiting for my food, I read the address Ted had written—43 Sweet Mountain Court—paid the eight-dollar-

and-forty-two-cent bill, and made the bell above the glass door jingle as I exited.

Outside a grand, stone-faced home, smack-dab in the middle of a cul-de-sac, surrounded by manicured boxwoods and other grand, stone-faced homes, I stood. My heart threatened to slam through my chest. For what seemed like the hundredth time, I wiped damp palms down the front of my jeans.

Every minute I hesitated meant another opportunity for his phone to ring. For David to find out about Isabella from someone other than me. The thought was unbearable.

My car keys clanked against my cell as I dropped them into my purse, then slid the bag over my shoulder. I sucked in a deep breath of humid summer air and tried to exhale away the worst of my nerves. Refusing their eviction, they clung to my insides like thirsty little leeches.

I talked myself forward . . . left foot . . . right foot . . . left foot . . . right. I could do this. I had to. Gathering my last remnant of courage, I pushed the doorbell, adding a knock for good measure.

As I waited, my hands wrung together nervously, my pinkie sliding over the smooth opal of my delicate ring and the gold prongs holding it in place. Another knock and more waiting. I glanced at the garage. One of its doors was open, and inside I spied a gleaming Infiniti Coupe.

Unaffected by the storm brewing within me, the morning sun rained down a warmth I could not feel. Maybe David and Lindsey were out back, working on the yard, basking on the deck . . . sitting in matching rockers on the patio, holding hands and sharing secrets. I cringed at the thought.

As I walked over the cushion of manicured lawn to the back of the house, I pictured an older David reading the morning paper while his beautiful wife encircled her adoring arms around his waist—long, wavy tresses spilling over him like a shawl of spun gold. The intensity of the hatred I felt for a woman I had never even met alarmed me.

The privacy fence's wooden gate stood ajar, and I poked my head through. To my surprise, an English garden bloomed on the other side. Stepping inside for a better look, I marveled at its beauty. Stone paths led to scrolled iron benches. Ornate trellises dripped with flowered vines . . . and then I caught a strange sight that stole my breath.

Large, paper-white cherry blossoms burst from otherwise-bare branches. Shocking. Lovely. . . . Wrong. This tree was an early spring bloomer, not summer. I stared at it, wondering if I were really here or if I could be dreaming.

Maybe I was really fast asleep in my city apartment. The alarm clock would soon sound and I would throw off the covers, plant my feet on the soft chenille carpet, slip into my business suit, and call for Isabella to rise and shine.

Maybe I had not gone home to my father's. Maybe I hadn't had a reason to. Maybe it was still just Isabella and me, the two of us, not needing anyone but each other. I wasn't standing in David's yard about to tell him he had a daughter. I wasn't dying.

Hope budded as I smiled dreamily.

As I gazed at the blossoms clinging to bark, a feeling of déjà vu came over me, and I tilted my head, digging through the recesses of my mind, trying to recapture the memory on the tip of my consciousness. A sweet smell drifted by me on a whisper of wind. Vaguely familiar. Very comforting. Popcorn tree. That's what I'd called it as a child. Popcorn tree.

A mosquito landed on me. I swatted it and felt the pain. I touched the smear of red left on my arm and brought my fingertips to my nose. They smelled of blood, rusty and real. Not a dream. Not a chance.

Dejected, I scanned the yard for signs of human life, past the morning glories opening their mouths to drink in the sunshine, the lavender swaying to a melody only it could hear, and the crow glaring down at me from the weather vane atop a small shed.

And there, at the edge of the yard, on a hammock sandwiched between two maple trees, lay a man. An overturned coffee cup rested on the grass beneath him and an opened *Wall Street Journal* fluttered in the wind, held by his listless hand.

The back of his head faced me, covered in curls the same shade as Isabella's. My hand flew to my chest and time seemed to slow.

David.

He lay so still I began to wonder if he was alive. A grumble came from his direction as the newspaper dropped from his fingers. When he turned toward me, even my blood seemed to freeze in response. Closed. His eyes were still closed. I exhaled in relief.

I hadn't seen him since the night he'd broken up with me. My heart ached as I studied the familiar angles of his face, the lips I used to love to kiss. That I would have liked to kiss even now. Especially now.

A sudden breeze launched the cherry blossoms from their branches. They floated through the air like fairy snow. Soft, fragrant . . . magical, twirling and fluttering left and right. I reached my hand out, but not one landed on my palm, open and ready.

Not a single one.

Carried by the changing wind, they fell instead over David. His eyes twitched. I tried to move, to back away, but my feet remained anchored. When he opened his eyes, panic stopped my heart. He smiled as though seeing me after all this time was the most natural thing in the world. A warm smile. Familiar and kind. And then his eyes grew large and he sat up suddenly, the smile replaced by alarm.

We were still for a moment, taking each other in—David on his hammock in his beautiful garden, surrounded by flowers, birds, and sweet fragrances, and me, an intruder, sneaking into his yard, hiding an ax, sharpened and ready. His life would come crashing to the ground with one swing of my blade.

David's gaze moved from me to the back of his house. In the window, a dark-haired woman watched us. David stared at her.

She stared at me.

CHAPTER SIX

THE WOMAN IN the window disappeared. David turned to me, panicked and pale. "Jenny, what are you doing here?"

"We need to talk."

"You couldn't have called?"

"This isn't the kind of thing you say over the phone."

"You know I'm married?" He held his left hand up. The gold band on his finger glistened in the sunlight. "Five years now."

Jealousy bit hard as I regurgitated a smile. "Wow, that's great." A gust of wind scattered the carpet of white blooms and whipped my hair into my eyes. Hurriedly, I pushed it away, wishing I could've taken a moment to pull my hair back and myself together.

"David?" a woman called meekly from the back door. This was not the Lindsey I'd imagined with wavy blonde locks and an hourglass figure. This Lindsey wore her shiny black hair in a blunt cut that would have looked more at home in Manhattan. Her fawn eyes jetted between David and me as she approached.

Her long khaki shorts ended where knobby knees began. In an evening dress, her pasty skin might have appeared luminous, but in naked daylight it just looked like she needed a tan.

By anyone's standards, I was more attractive, but that thought brought no satisfaction. What it did bring was painful curiosity. What virtue did she possess that made her lovable when I was not?

David seemed to quickly compose himself as he stood, leaving the chains on the hammock jingling. "Lindsey, this is Genevieve Lucas. Jenny, this is my wife."

She turned in my direction, studying me. After a moment, recognition washed over her, punctuated by an exclamation. "Your prom date!"

When my eyes met David's, he looked back to his wife. "That's right, sweetie."

Sweetie was a name he'd often called me, but for her it dripped with honey. She held out her hand.

I gave it a weak shake. "It's nice to meet you."

"You should see the scrapbook I made David with his high school memories. I gave it to him for his birthday. Your prom picture's in it." Her gaze traveled over my body so quickly, if I'd blinked, I'd have missed it. "You looked so pretty in that

green dress. So pretty, I almost—" she made air quotes—
"*accidentally* lost the photo."

David shifted from one leg to another. Red mottled his
cheeks and neck. "What brings you here, Genevieve?"

Taking in a deep breath, I motioned to the glass-and-iron
table on the brick patio. "Can we all sit?"

"Is this about your mother again?" He crossed his arms.
"Your dad really needs to move on."

The cockiness that made his father so loathed in my
household shone from David's eyes like candles I wanted to
blow out in the worst way. I felt my nostrils flare. "Would
you be able to move on if you thought someone's negligence
caused *your* wife's death?"

Lindsey fingered a button on her blouse, rubbing it
absently as a child might do to the satin edge of a blanket.
"What's she talking about, David?"

He glared at me as he spoke to her. "My father supposedly—"

"Not *supposedly*," I interjected.

"According to Genevieve's dad, my father misdiagnosed
her mother. He wasn't even her doctor." He said it as though
the accusation were as insignificant as a fly he could just
wave away.

That infuriated me as I stood among green grass and
hummingbirds feeding from beautiful flowers. What did he
know of losing the person he loved most in the world? What
did he know of misery? He whose heart had never been broken. He whose parents both still breathed. He who would

most likely live to a ripe old age. "He should have insisted she get checked out."

David opened his mouth to protest, but I cut him off. I turned to Lindsey, trying my best to keep my hands unclenched and my volume down. But like every other time in my life when I felt slighted, a switch had been flipped and I was powerless to control what came out of my mouth. "Your father-in-law told my mother her fatigue and headaches were due to anemia. Without running a single test, he gave her prescriptions for ibuprofen and iron pills, which she took faithfully. Six weeks after that, she was diagnosed with a brain tumor. Three months after that, she died."

Lindsey looked pleadingly to David.

He was more focused on debating me than offering her the refuge or explanation she sought. "Jenny, what do you want? Like I've said a hundred times, what's done is done."

"All my father ever wanted was an apology."

"Right. What he wants is for us to raise her from the dead."

I slapped his face and felt the sting on my hand. Shocked at my behavior, I clutched my hand to my chest to keep it from lashing out again against my will.

Lindsey stepped back, looking lost and unsure. David grabbed my other wrist. "You come to my house, accuse my father, then attack me?"

I pulled from him and rubbed the spot he'd held. Hot streams of shame trickled down my cheeks. "David, I'm sorry."

His expression didn't soften. "I'm tired of all the grief your family's caused mine. I thought when we broke up, we could spend the rest of our lives avoiding each other. It's a big world. You'd think you'd be able to stay on your side."

I wiped the tears from my face. "I'd love nothing more than—"

"So do it," he hissed. "Go. I didn't ask you to come here. I'm married, Jenny. Married. It's time for both you and your father to move on."

I laughed bitterly. "Do you really think I'm not over you? I was over you the second I slammed the car door that night. You Prestons really think you're something."

"I want you to leave. You're upsetting my wife."

Lindsey looked embarrassed at her mention.

A tiny butterfly landed on the hammock David had been lying on, and finally I remembered Isabella.

This wasn't about me or David or Lindsey or my mother or our fathers. It was about her. This idiot was her daddy. I needed to do damage control. For her sake.

"Listen, David, Lindsey, I'm sorry. I didn't come here to hit you or to accuse your family. I came here to—"

"Save it." David rubbed the red mark I'd left on his cheek.

"Fine," I spat back. "You're not good enough for her anyway."

He whipped around and snatched the coffee cup and paper off the ground, then marched toward the house.

Lindsey stared at me, uncertain. "For who?"

"Never mind," I said. Let his father tell him. Let no one tell him. I couldn't care less. The last thing in the world I wanted after finding that David had turned into his dad was for him to be part of the upbringing of my precious daughter. Better for her to be raised by my father, half-present, than this pompous jerk.

CHAPTER SEVEN

NAKED BARBIE DOLLS lay strewn across the coffee table beside a heap of miniature clothing. Isabella was nowhere in sight. I listened for her but heard only the distant hum of the ancient refrigerator. No laughter or pattering of feet. Curiously, the house was silent.

My father's Buick sat in the driveway and Mama Peg almost never left the house these days because of shortness of breath, which made me wonder if they'd taken to napping in the mornings.

If my mother were still alive, I would be seeking her sympathetic ear to lament that David's words had ripped open the wound that had never quite healed. That I again felt his rejection every bit as raw as the night he told me he didn't love me. But I'd long since learned to live without the comfort of my parents. I used to talk to God, but He'd never seemed as far away as He had in the weeks following my diagnosis.

Isabella was the only one who could give me what I needed at that moment—love, acceptance, and as many sweet hugs as it took to smother my pain. Nothing in the world brought me more comfort than to feel her warm breath against me, her soft cheek against mine, and to hear the only words in the world I could trust without question: "I love you, Mommy."

My sandals clacked against the hardwood floor as I walked farther inside and called for her. Mama Peg's bodiless voice shushed me from the kitchen. Following the raspy sound, I found her sitting at the table, a Bible and notebook set open before her. The breakfast plates had been washed and put away. The scent of lemon dish soap still hung in the air.

Looking up at me, she laid her pen on the table. "She's taking a nap."

"She stopped taking naps two years ago."

"I think this morning upset her."

I grimaced. As I considered how the morning's altercation between my father and me must have sounded to my little girl, I felt shame for the second time in an hour. I wanted to ignore the voice in my head chiding me, but regret is not an emotion that whispers. "You think I should check on her?"

She shook her head, making the oxygen tubing jiggle from her ears. "Just did. Snoring away."

"She sounds just like Dad when she sleeps."

"He used to drive me crazy when he slept between his father and me."

I slid a chair from the table, making a scraping sound against the floor. Mama Peg frowned at the scuff mark I'd left behind.

With my foot, I rubbed it away and sat across from her. "You let him sleep with you? You gave me such a hard time about that."

"Jack refused to sleep on his own until he was six. Why do you think I tried to warn you?"

I grinned. "Is that why he's an only child?"

She tugged on the hem of her blouse to straighten it. "You laugh, but it's true. And see? So is she."

"That's not why she is. I thought if I ever did it again, I'd do it right."

Her thin lips curled downward at the mention of what would never be.

I pulled a ragged edge of paper off the notebook and rolled it between my fingers. "I hate that she'll never have any sisters or brothers."

"Builds self-sufficiency," she said. "Besides, you don't know she'll be an only child. David might give her a sibling."

I worked the paper between my fingers, bunching it into a tiny ball, not daring to meet my grandmother's gaze.

"Did you find him?" she finally asked.

I nodded slowly.

"And?"

I laid the paper ball I'd made on the table and ripped off another corner of paper. I worked this scrap, too, into a ball and placed it beside the first one.

She took a long, deep breath. "By the look on your face, I'm guessing it went over about as well as a turd in a punch bowl."

I wanted to cry but figured I'd let my pity party go on long enough. It was time to put my daughter first. Her future depended on the decisions I would make. The actions I would take.

"You guessed right. He's a total jerk," I whispered.

"Runs in the family," she said matter-of-factly. "Hard to believe that sweet angel has Preston blood running through her veins."

I ripped off another corner, not answering. I balled it up and added it to the pile I'd begun.

I was reaching to tear off another piece when a warm, shaky hand grabbed mine. "So did you tell him about Bella before his father did?"

I looked up into my grandmother's foggy eyes. "He still doesn't know."

She scrunched her face, giving her the appearance of a fleshy prune. "What? Why the dickens not?"

"He was so abusive. I couldn't tell him."

"Abusive? or angry?"

I shrugged. "How do I know he won't be that way with her?"

"How do you know he will? It's not your job to control

the results, only to relay the message. He has a right to know he's a father."

"He hates me."

She squeezed my hand. "It doesn't matter if he hates you, hates Jack, or hates me. He's her father. *Her father*, Jenny. If he loves *her*, then that's all that matters."

"His father will tell him," I mumbled. "I'm sure he probably has already."

"He should have heard it from you."

I slid my hand from under hers and wrapped my arms around myself, feeling suddenly cold. "He should've let me speak. Besides, I don't want my daughter being raised in that family."

"That's not your decision."

Not my decision? Having metastatic melanoma was not my decision. The headaches, fatigue, palpitations, and mood swings I'd been suffering from were not my decision. David's breaking up with me was not my decision. My mother's dying was not my decision. Mama Peg's emphysema was not my decision. My father's coldness toward me was not my decision. But this? This was one of the few things that *was* my decision. "She's my daughter. While I still have breath in my body, I have a say."

I looked down at the pile of tiny paper balls I had made, then closed my eyes. *It's time,* I told myself. After months of worrying about what would be best for my daughter, all choices but one had vanished. I now knew what Isabella's future would be and it was time to meet fate halfway.

I stood and swept the mess I'd made into my palm.

"Where are you going?" Mama Peg asked.

"To tell Dad."

"Tell him what?"

I walked to the sink and emptied the scraps into the garbage disposal, then turned around. "What do you think?"

She went into a coughing fit. I grabbed a glass from the dish rack, filled it with tap water, set it before her, then set out to find my father. As I neared the stairwell, I started to call his name but remembered Isabella sleeping.

Standing before my father's closed bedroom door, I clenched my fist and gave a light tap. Not surprisingly, no reply followed. Of course he wouldn't be in his room. All he did in there was dress and sleep. Most of his time was spent in his office teaching himself the banjo or in the basement studio painting, or rather, trying to. The truth was, he was even less talented in the visual arts than he was at music.

I made my way back down the stairs and found Mama Peg waiting for me. Her skin appeared ashen and her breathing resonated louder than usual. "You can't tell him today," she managed around coughs. Cyan outlined her lips.

"You don't look well," I said.

"You're perceptive."

"I mean more not well than usual."

The slamming of a car door in the driveway turned both of our heads toward the window. I walked over and drew back the curtain, revealing a blue pickup in the driveway with *Allen Landscaping* stenciled in white letters on the door.

"Who is it?" Mama Peg asked.

"Craig."

She frowned. "What's he doing home already?"

He leaned against the truck with a cell phone to his ear.

I shrugged, let the curtain drop, and turned around. "You think Dad's in the basement?"

"Didn't you hear me?"

"I can't tell him. Why not?"

She grabbed the stairway post to steady herself. "To everything, there is a season."

I let out an exasperated breath. "First you get on my case for not telling him; now you're telling me *not* to tell him?"

She opened her mouth to answer but hacked instead. She continued to cough until her face turned an alarming shade of purple. I took the handle of her tank in one hand and with the other I led her to a chair to sit. Pink returned to her skin as she sucked in several breaths.

I sat on the armrest and rubbed her back. "In case you forget that my time is short, I'm reminding you. I have no other options. I need Dad's promise to raise Isabella. I know he's not the world's greatest father, but at least he won't abuse her and will provide for her physical needs. I need to get my ducks in a row now. I have to tell him."

When she started coughing again, I walked back through the kitchen and descended the stairs. Unlike the ones leading to the second floor, more than just the last step of these creaked. Every other one squalled under my weight. The sound was familiar and comforting. I had long ago memorized which ones would shriek and which would merely groan as my weight passed over them.

A wave of soft music met me at the bottom. It was a song that stopped my heart. "Sea of Love." It was her song, or rather, theirs. The song my parents danced to at their prom, then wedding. The song my father softly hummed over my mother's casket as he leaned in to kiss her one last time.

My insides knotted as I remembered today's date. July 10—the sixth anniversary of my mother's death.

I crept toward the studio door, which stood open just a crack, and peeked in. A portable CD player sat upon a rustic wooden shelf, serenading my father with the mournful tune.

He had his back turned to me, and I could clearly see the canvas he was painting on. The portrait was amateurish at best. If he hadn't made the woman's dress lavender, I might not have known it was her. Lavender had been my mother's favorite and the color of the dress we buried her in. Seeing my father mourn her anew flooded me with crude emotion. Grief tore at my heart like barbed wire. Why did she have to leave us? It made everything that was right in our family wrong.

The steps creaked behind me, but I couldn't take my eyes off my father long enough to turn around and look. Craig whispered my name, but I didn't answer. His hands turned me around. I hadn't realized I'd been crying until he wiped the tears from my face. My shoulders trembled as he pulled me to him. There was solace in feeling his chest rise and fall against my cheek and his strong arm wrap around my shoulders. He smelled of pine and hard work, and that too comforted me somehow.

When I pulled away, I caught a glimpse of disappointment in his eyes.

"I'm sorry," I said.

"I'm sorry you're sorry." He drew me against him once again and held me.

I patted his back twice to replace any notion of romance with one of friendship, then stepped backward. "Why aren't you at work?" I glanced at my father through the cracked door. He continued on, either oblivious to our presence or ignoring us.

Craig ran a hand through his hair, making it spike. "I know today's a hard one for your dad. I just popped in to check on him."

Craig's remembering the anniversary only served to make me feel worse for forgetting it. He rubbed his neck and peeked in at my father. "At least this year he got out of bed."

It seemed strange to me that this man who had been a mere acquaintance of mine would now be so intimately connected to my family, so intimately connected to me. It struck me as more than a little odd that while most people our age had left home or were anxious to, Craig would take up residence with my family. Curiosity got the best of me. I had to know what his deal was. Besides, I told myself, he might stick around awhile. I needed to learn more about him for my daughter's sake. "Have you got time for a cup of coffee?" I asked.

He seemed taken aback by my question and threw a glance

at his watch. "I've got at least three hours' more work to do on this job. I promised I'd have it wrapped up today. How about if I take you and Bella to dinner when I finish?"

"Make it pizza at Chuck E. Cheese's and you've got a deal," I said.

He slapped a hand over his heart as though he'd been shot. "Only for you would I agree to that torture. I'll warn the old lady she doesn't need to cook for us."

Normally someone referring to my sweet grandmother as *old lady* would get my dander up, but Craig said it with affection.

He told me good-bye, then bolted up the stairs, taking them two at a time, and disappeared out of sight.

It of course dawned on me that Craig might have felt more than brotherly toward me. I had entertained that same assumption a few times back in high school when I'd turned around in class and found him staring.

He was handsome, intelligent, hardworking, and all the other things I would want in a man, but romance was the last thing a dying woman needed. And the last thing a young man in his prime needed was to develop a crush on a dying woman. I decided, for his sake, I would tell him everything over dinner.

For my father, the truth would have to wait. I leaned into the doorjamb, resting my shoulder against it as I watched him. "Sea of Love" faded to silence. He set his paintbrush on the easel, walked over to the CD player, and hit a button.

The song began again.

CHAPTER EIGHT

I STOOD NEXT to Craig as he studied the lit Chuck E. Cheese's menu hanging above the glass counter.

Taking Isabella's face in my hands, I guided her to look at me. "Do you want plain or pepperoni?"

"Pepperoni!" The way she bounced around, I'd have thought she needed to use the bathroom if I hadn't just taken her.

The teen behind the counter pulled a loose thread from her red polo shirt as she waited.

I stepped forward and ordered the family value meal. Turning to Craig, I asked, "Do you want anything besides pizza?"

He tilted his head as though considering his choices, then said no. The teen set four paper cups on the counter, a small sandwich board with a number twenty-three on it, and a cup full of gold coins. Isabella snatched them up, bent her neck over the cup, and shook it. She jangled behind us as Craig and I made our way toward the empty booth straight ahead. While I filled Isabella's pockets with tokens, he slid into his seat.

A dark smudge ran under Isabella's left eye like Indian war paint. I licked my thumb and rubbed it away before she could protest. "You want me to come with you?"

Of course I already knew the answer. She required my assistance at Chuck E. Cheese's as much as I required hers at Pier 1. She mumbled something I couldn't make out and left.

Craig held up the hand the staff had stamped when we'd entered. "Invisible ink—how cool is that?"

I watched dirty white socks emerge from the end of the tube slide, followed by the little boy who wore them. When his gaze met mine, I wiggled my fingers at him. Sheepishly he looked around, jerked his hand halfway up, then ran off. "Bella thinks everything about this place is cool."

Bells rang, whistles blew, and children all around us shrieked. Craig looked around and shook his head. "This place is like Vegas for kids."

I set our small plastic number in the center of the table and grabbed the cups. "C'mon, let's go get our drinks."

Craig followed me to the fountain machine, his eyes darting from preteens riding mock Jet Ski video games to the little boy pedaling like mad on a bike that rose on a pole from his efforts. An Asian girl zinged by, nearly toppling Craig. He caught her right before she plowed into him. Muttering an apology, she tore away, chasing after a blonde girl about the same age.

He glanced around. "Where's Bella?"

I held a cup against the Hawaiian Punch lever, watching ice cubes bob in the rising red liquid. "She's around. I don't worry too much here. You can't leave without matching numbers. She'll be fine. Besides, hawkeyed mothers lurk everywhere."

I filled my own cup with Sprite and Craig got himself a Coke. I snapped a lid on each, and Craig came behind me, stabbing in straws.

Just as we set our drinks down on the table, Isabella popped up in front of us like a jack-in-the-box, took a sip of her punch, slapped three rows of paper tickets she'd won on the seat, and raced off again.

Craig squinted at me, dimples sinking into his blond scruff.

"What?"

"What what?"

"Why are you grinning at me? Do I have something on my face?" I patted my fingertips around the corner of my mouth.

"Just a nose."

"Then stop looking at me like that. You're making me nervous."

Dropping his gaze to his hands, Craig ran a thumb over

his knuckles. "You know I never got what you saw in Preston. He was such a geek."

My first thought was that Craig had been a bigger geek than David—overweight, acne-prone, and shy—but I decided it wouldn't be particularly kind to say so. "I guess I clung to the first guy who showed me attention. I was really starving for it back then."

"You, starving for attention? That's hard to believe. You were the prettiest girl in school."

Looking into his eyes, I saw my reflection. In it I looked lovelier than I felt. Mama Peg had told me long ago that I would know a man loved me when I could see myself in his eyes. It was nonsense, I knew that, but my stomach still fluttered nonetheless. Pulling my gaze away, I took a sip of soda. I felt the coldness of the liquid slide down my throat all the way to my empty stomach. "So how in the world did you end up living at my dad's house?"

"I'm sure you remember my mom left us when I was little?"

I didn't but nodded just the same.

"So it was just me and Dad. He did nothing but work, drink, and have an occasional pajama party with a bleach blonde. I pretty much raised myself. When I dropped out of college, he started charging me rent, so I left."

An infant cried behind us. I snuck a glance over my shoulder at the father scooping her from the mother's arms. I turned back around. "What's the difference if you pay rent to your father or mine?"

"My dad was trying to charge me more than he was paying for the mortgage."

"Nice," I said, thinking it was not nice at all.

"It was his way of trying to force me to go back to college, I think, but I didn't want to. He thought if I didn't get a degree, I'd end up just like him. I guess that was the last thing either of us wanted. Anyway, I got to thinking about you one day. Wondering what you were up to, I drove to your house, hoping maybe you had broken up with Preston and . . ." His cheeks flushed crimson. "As Providence would have it, there was a For Rent sign on the saddle barn.

"So I didn't get to see my friend Jenny, but I did get a decent place to live that cost about a third the price my old man was charging. Your dad's the one who talked me into starting the landscaping business. That's how I lost the weight, by the way. Who needs a gym when you're shoveling dirt and hauling tree limbs all day? I love your dad and Mama Peg. They've become the family I wish I had. I know someday I'll have to move on, but I just can't imagine leaving them."

I cleared my throat, feeling defensive. "Yeah, well, someone might feel the same way about your father, not knowing the whole story."

When his callused finger brushed mine, I found myself liking his touch more than I should. "Easy. I'm not judging you, Jenny. I know there's a lot that's happened that I don't know about."

The waitress picked up the number from our table and replaced it with a pepperoni pizza and a stack of paper plates.

As she walked away, Craig lifted a steaming triangle from the pie and placed it on a plate in front of me, then took one for himself.

I scanned the perimeter for Isabella and found her at a toddler's version of a video game. She clapped her hands, then ripped off a row of tickets sticking out of the machine like a paper tongue.

"So whatever happened between you and David?"

Trying to keep my pain from showing, I leaned back in my seat. "Well, basically, he told me he didn't love me."

Craig shook his head. "Wow."

Wow was right.

"Was that before or after he fathered your child?"

"Take a wild guess."

He picked at a piece of pepperoni. "You really loved him, didn't you?"

"I did."

"Has he been a part of her life at all?"

I shook my head, feeling miserable.

"Man, what a jerk. If I had you two, no way I'd ever—"

"He didn't know," I whispered.

Craig's eyebrows shot up.

I tore off a piece of napkin and began to roll it between my fingers. "I'm guessing he knows now. My father told his father last night."

"Didn't you want him to know?"

"I wanted to tell him myself." I took a small bite of pizza.

Isabella's cheeks blazed red as she plopped next to me

and sucked down a gulp of her drink. I laid a piece of pizza before her.

"Mommy, I have a new boyfriend."

"Oh, really?" I took another bite.

She spoke around a mouthful of cheese and crust. "Uh-huh, his name is Jimmy. We're gonna get married."

Craig stared at her with such a disapproving expression that I couldn't look at him without wanting to laugh. I focused instead on Isabella, trying to make it at least appear as if I took her engagement seriously. "Well, congratulations, sweetness."

As Isabella inhaled her slice, Craig gave me a look that asked what I intended to do about this situation. When I said nothing, he crossed his arms. "You're a little young to be into boys, don't you think?"

She reached over and grabbed a piece of pepperoni off his half-eaten slice.

My mouth dropped open at her rudeness. "Bella!"

"Pepperoni's fattening anyway." Craig patted his stomach. "Go ahead and take them all."

Without missing a beat, Isabella picked off the remaining two circles. "Mommy, are you going to marry Craig?"

My daughter had been obsessed with marriage lately, so the question didn't catch me off guard. "No, honey, Craig and I are just friends."

"You're never gonna get married!"

Craig's gaze fixed on her as he sipped his Coke. "Why do you think your mother is never going to get married?"

"Because she doesn't have any boyfriends." Isabella planted her fists on her waist and rolled her eyes. "You need a boyfriend to marry you." She gave him a look that screamed *duh*.

I picked at my cheese. "Don't be rude, and not everyone needs to be married, Bella. Not everyone needs that to be happy."

"You're not happy."

I faked a cough. "I'm happy, silly."

"No, you're not. You cry too much."

I dared not look at Craig as Isabella exposed me. "Hey," I said, keeping my tone light, "we're going to be leaving in about twenty minutes. Do you want the rest of your coins?" She shoved the last bite of her crust into her mouth and held out her hands. I dumped the remaining tokens into her palm. "Put them in your pocket with the others."

Isabella hurried away as Craig studied me with a load of pity that was nearly unbearable. "I really don't cry all the time."

"You want to talk about it?"

"You ask that a lot."

His pinkie touched mine. "Do you want me to stop?"

"I'm dying," I whispered.

His impassive expression told me he already knew. Oddly enough, I felt no betrayal, only relief. "She told you."

"She was really broken up. She needed to talk to someone."

Until then I hadn't imagined how hard the secret must have been on my grandmother. "How did she take it?"

"It brought her to her knees."

I closed my eyes.

"That's okay, Jenny. That's where we all need to be anyway."

"You sound just like her."

"Thanks. So are you going to let me take you out somewhere nicer next time?"

His question left me speechless.

"Well?"

"Have you lost your mind? I'm dying, Craig. I have a year max, probably much less."

"Have you gotten a second opinion?"

"Yes. A second, a third . . . a fifth. The cancer's already spread to my liver, my bones, and my lymph system. There's no cure at this point. They could prolong my life by a few months, but I'd just spend the extra time flushing the contents of my stomach and clogging the drain with gobs of my hair."

He glanced at the braid draped over my shoulder. "Is it the same kind of cancer that took your mom?"

I smiled bitterly. "You'd think so, but nope. She had a brain tumor. Mine started as skin cancer. I ask the doctor to check out a mole on my shoulder and suddenly I'm getting biopsies, blood tests, bone scans, and being told I won't live to see another birthday. No, Mom's and my cancers are completely unrelated, like two members of the same family getting hit by bolts of lightning on opposite ends of the world. Lucky, eh?"

He leaned in so close I thought he intended to kiss me. His breath warmed my lips. "Do you like sushi?"

My heart beat double-time. "Listen, Craig, I appreciate the pity date, but honestly the only thing on my mind now is making sure Bella's going to be taken care of after I'm gone. The last thing either of us needs is to complicate anything. What's the best that could come of us seeing each other? We fall in love and then your heart gets broken when I die? Is that what you want?"

"You falling in love with me? I can think of worse things."

"I've got a rule against dating masochists."

He leaned back. "Hey, I'm not talking about complicating anything. I just like your company. I always have. None of us knows how much time we have, Jenny. If you want to get out of the house now and again, I'm not a bad guy to hang out with. Make hay while the sun's still shining; that's all I'm saying."

When I glanced down, I noticed his thumb stroking his knuckles again. His emotions were easier to read than a children's picture book. I didn't want to hurt his feelings, and if I weren't dying, I'd go for him in a heartbeat, half a heartbeat, but—

Before I could finish the thought, he sprang up as though something had bitten his behind. He ran over to Isabella, who was swinging frantically, trying to hit the heads of plastic moles. She always swung a second too late, just missing them.

Craig took her hands in his, winked at her, and guided her into smashing every artificial rodent that dared show its face. Isabella squealed in delight as tickets churned out at the end of the game. I sat watching them, a smile playing on my lips, letting myself imagine what life could have, should have, been for us.

CHAPTER NINE

ISABELLA AND I lay in bed, nestled against one another under several layers of blankets. I wore light flannel and she, a long cotton nightgown. The evening temperature felt more fall than summer, so my grandmother and I decided to give our Freon reserve a break and open the windows.

The coolness of the room reminded me of childhood camping trips—the way the crisp mountain air made the warmth of my sleeping bag a sanctuary I never wanted to leave.

Isabella laid her palm on my cheek. "Mommy, thank you for taking me to Chucky Cheesits."

"You're welcome, Bells. Glad you had fun."

Raising her finger before her eyes, she admired the trinket she'd cashed her tickets in for—a purple spider ring. She looked up at me through long lashes. "Next time I'm going to save for something bigger."

She said that every time, but the temptation always proved too great when it came time to choose. "I know you can do it."

She hugged me tight. "Beautiful Mama."

I kissed her forehead. "Beautiful Bella. I sure do love you."

"More than anything?"

"So very much."

She bent her neck to look at me, her eyes now little more than slits.

I hugged her middle and pulled her closer. "Bella, do you like Craig?"

"Uh-huh. Maybe I'll marry him 'stead of Jimmy."

"He's really nice, isn't he?"

She nodded. "Is he my daddy?"

"No, sweetness, not your daddy."

"He might be."

"Trust me on that."

"Do I have a daddy?"

"God."

"I mean a people daddy."

"Yes."

"Does he love me?"

I closed my eyes and buried my face in her curls. "He would if he knew you."

"I'd love him too," she whispered in a tone so vulnerable it was all I could do not to cry.

My conscience pointed its judgmental finger at me once again. I had deprived the person I loved most in the world of the one thing she wanted more than anything—a daddy. Until now, I hadn't understood why the Bible said the sins of the father were visited on the son. I thought it unjust of God to charge the innocent for their parents' sins. Now I realized it wasn't a threat, but a warning.

"How about if we read a story?" I managed around the lump in my throat.

She reached up and rubbed my earlobe between her thumb and pointer finger just like she had done as a toddler. "*Goodnight Moon.*"

I leaned over the side of the bed, pulled the backpack from underneath it, and retrieved our worn copy of the classic. A strip of silver duct tape ran down its spine, loose threads poking out like a well-worn hem.

I pulled the blanket up and tucked it around her shoulders. She pushed it back down to just above her waist and laid her cheek against my breastbone. My heart pulsated against her as I opened to the first page and read.

As soon as I said "two little kittens," her eyelids fluttered like butterflies, then closed. I shut the book quietly and recited the rest from memory, pausing where I knew the pages would turn.

As I did, my mind wandered to David, replaying that morning's awful events. He had overreacted, no question about it, but then so had I. The difference was that I had known what was at stake—or rather who—and still I took the low road. He, at least, had been walking blind.

As Isabella drifted deeper into slumber, I crawled out of bed, onto the carpet and my knees. I rested my forehead against the mattress and waited for divine advice regarding my dilemma.

※

Eight hours later, I awoke shivering, with a sore neck and stiff legs in lieu of an answer. On Isabella's side of the bed lay a crumpled afghan. I made my way down the stairs, following the melody of her laughter. As I came to the landing, I found her riding Craig like a horse, kicking her heels into his side and yelling for him to giddyap.

I wondered how long his poor knees had been enduring the hardwood.

Isabella waved at me, causing her to lose her balance and tumble to the floor. Her face scrunched into an angry ball. "You made me fall!"

"I *made* you?"

Though her anger was often misdirected, it never burned longer than it took to blow out a match. Instantly her scowl evaporated. "Did you see me, Mommy? I'm a cowgirl!" She ran to me and hugged my legs.

Her enthusiasm made me smile. "I saw."

Craig stood and brushed off his legs.

My gaze glided over his flannel shirt, half-tucked into faded Levi's. "Thanks for entertaining her."

My father emerged from the kitchen, coffee mug in hand, and stood beside me. He took a sip, wrinkling his nose, apparently no more pleased with the decaf than was Mama Peg.

I gave him a weak smile. "Hi, Dad. Feeling better?"

He sighed and glanced at Isabella. "I tried to give her a ride like I used to give you, but my knees are shot, I'm afraid."

"I don't remember you ever doing that."

He jerked his head back. "Are you kidding me? From the age of five to eight, I was your one-man rodeo. Funny how the mind stays parked while the body hightails it down the fast lane." He took another sip. "Your dad's getting old, Jenny."

Isabella went to him and took his hand in hers. "It's okay, Cowpa. I still love you."

He lifted her up and she straddled his waist. They looked so familiar, as though she'd spent her whole life in his arms, and I knew at that moment she'd be okay. He did love her and she loved him.

From my periphery I caught Craig watching me. "You're doing it again," I said.

He blushed. "Sorry. You're a hard woman not to look at."

Isabella wiggled in my father's arms, wanting to be let down. When he lowered her, she ran to Craig. "Can we go now?"

I gave him a questioning look. "Go where?"

"Swimming."

"Why don't we let your mommy get some breakfast first," my dad said.

These days, nothing held less appeal for me than the thought of eating. On those rare occasions when I did have an appetite, it was usually accompanied by nausea. "Forget breakfast. Let's swim."

Deep lines of concern creased my father's forehead as his gaze traveled down me. "Jenny, you're getting way too thin."

My stomach sank. I was thin, but not terribly so. If my size-five frame worried him now, how much more would my size two, six months from now. "I'm okay, Dad." Maybe after church I'd swing by the supermarket and pick up some Ensure. If I was going to feel sick every time I put something down my throat, I might as well get the most nourishment and calories for my buck.

"Are you turning anorexic?"

Shock and embarrassment stole my words. I couldn't believe he just blurted that out in front of Craig and my daughter. I was thin, had always been thin, and yes, in the last few months my lack of appetite had cost me another ten pounds, but I was hardly a skeleton.

"I'm fine," I said coldly. "C'mon, Bells, let's get ready for church. We'll swim this afternoon. Promise."

Isabella in a polka-dot one-piece and I in a less flamboyant solid black stood side by side on the patio, looking out at the most beautiful piece of real estate to be had in Duncan County.

Centuries-old pine, oak, and sycamore trees framed Lucas Lake on three sides, with the fourth being cleared to serve as our downward-sloped backyard. A fifteen-foot dock parted the water. Tied to one of its posts bobbed a weathered canoe.

The streams of sunlight cascading over the rippling water brought to mind golden scarves fluttering in a breeze. In the distance, hazy blue mountain ridges stretched along the horizon.

When I was younger, my father and I had argued about whether the body of water in our backyard was really a pond or a lake. We never did come to a solid conclusion, which resulted in our referring to it alternately as Lucas Lake and "the pond out back."

I inhaled a lungful of the fresh valley air, while Isabella wiggled her pink toenails and bit her bottom lip. Her eyes were wide with anticipation. "We're going to swim in that giant pool?"

"That's a lake."

Without another word, she took off running. Her beach towel, which had been draped over her shoulder, hit the ground as her curls bounced against bronzed shoulders. I threw mine on top of hers and raced after her. Two summers of swimming lessons had made her fearless but had just the opposite effect on me.

Before I could reach her, she splashed into the water, getting only to her shins. I tried to call out, but her name stuck in my throat. She shrieked, turned toward me with alarm, then ran back out.

I hurried to her, heart thumping. "What's wrong?"

She looked on the verge of tears. "Something icky's in the pool."

"Did something touch you?"

She pointed down. "On the bottom. It's all yucky, like melted ice cream."

I relaxed. Rocky Road, no doubt. "Honey, this isn't a pool; it's a lake. It has a mud bottom, and fish and other creatures live in here."

Her cold, wet arms became a tourniquet around my leg. She looked at the water as if she'd just learned it was the home of the Loch Ness Monster.

"It's okay. Everything in there is harmless. They're God's creatures." Her grip became tighter. "It's just like swimming in a giant aquarium." I rubbed her back, wishing I could always be there to comfort her this way.

Her chest rose and fell in rapid succession, and I knew tears were soon to follow.

I looked over at the porch, where Mama Peg and my father were rocking. The screen door squealed open, and Craig stepped out wearing a pair of aqua swim trunks. I tried to keep my eyes off the muscles in his shoulders and the hair on his chest. Wow, he had changed.

"Hey, ladies, watch this!"

Isabella jerked her head up as Craig ran full speed down the yard. He grabbed the rope hanging from the thick oak branch stretching over the lake, swung Tarzan-style over the water, and let go.

A loud splash filled the air and a swell rose where he'd gone under.

Isabella's mouth dropped open. "Did you see that?" she asked without taking her eyes off the ripples.

Craig's head pushed through the water, his hair pasted against his skull like a blond swim cap. Trickles ran down his grinning face. "Try it, Bella. I'll catch you."

"She's scared—," I started to say, but Isabella took off running. When she reached the rope, she stopped and grabbed the end of it, slowly walking it back as far as she could. Clutching tight, she made a run for it, swinging herself out toward Craig.

"Bells, don't!" I yelled, but it was already too late. She was airborne.

"Catch me!" she screamed, absolutely fearless, utterly delighted.

Her legs kicked in the air as though she were pedaling an imaginary bike, and Craig lifted his arms for her. I held my breath, unsure whether to scream or laugh.

I glanced back at Mama Peg and my father, who had both stopped rocking and watched, their faces lit as they shared her pleasure. Suddenly their grins died and dread filled me. When my father bolted up, I knew something was wrong. I spun around and saw neither Craig nor Isabella. A plea formed on my lips. "Dad?"

As I stood frozen, my father tore past me. Before I pulled together the horror of what had happened, he dove in. When I saw Craig come up for air without my daughter, blood trickling from his nose, panic flooded me with adrenaline. I raced across the pier. As terrified as I was, I still had the clarity of thought to realize I stood a better chance of spotting her from land.

Why hadn't I stopped her? What was I thinking? As the ripples began to smooth on the surface, I nearly lost my mind.

Both my father and Craig surfaced . . . again without my daughter.

My heart stopped, and the only sound I could hear was my own labored and quick breaths. "Bella!" I scanned the water but saw only waves caused by Craig and my father flailing around searching for her.

"Jesus. Oh, Jesus, help." Mama Peg's frantic prayers rent from her throat on a wail, echoing my soul's plea. I didn't turn to look for fear that if I turned away, I would miss her. If I turned away, I might never see her again.

The lake, serene just moments ago, was suddenly ominous—dark and deep. Seconds felt like hours. My soul screamed, *My baby is drowning!* Everything seemed to happen in slow motion except, of course, the passing of time. Each second that flew by meant one more breath Isabella should have taken but hadn't.

With wide eyes, I moved my head back and forth looking for a shadow of her just under the surface, a few air bubbles . . . anything. If she were anywhere near the top, I'd be able to see a flash of her colorful suit, but I didn't. I couldn't just stand there dry and safe on the pier as my daughter's lungs filled with water.

Something brown moved across the water, making me think I had caught a glimpse of her hair, but it was just a twig. My nails dug into my palms as I stood, helpless, searching for her. Craig yelled something, but I couldn't discern his words. Animal instinct took over and I dropped to my knees, screaming her name. What was I thinking, letting her . . . ?

Irrational or not, I had to do something. I crawled to the edge of the pier and dove in. As fast as my arms would fly, I swam to the center of the lake and dove beneath the surface. The shock of the cold water only added to my panic. Though I kept my eyes open, I saw nothing but murky brown. Frantically, I combed the water for her with my fingers. When I grasped something about the size of a small arm, I clung to it with all I had and shot to the surface.

I burst through the water and sucked in a breath as the sun hit my eyes. I looked at the arm I'd grasped and nearly fainted when I saw it was nothing but a tree limb. I was about to duck below the surface again when my father emerged holding a heap of something I couldn't make out. I hastily swiped the water from my eyes.

It was a small body. *Isabella!*

I held my breath as I searched her pale face for signs of life. Her eyes didn't open and I feared the worst . . . until I heard her cry.

For the second time in my life, it was the most beautiful sound I'd ever heard.

CHAPTER TEN

ISABELLA HUGGED MY neck as though clinging to a buoy. I enveloped her inside the beach towel draped over my shoulders. Her legs lay limp atop mine, her cheekbone pressed hard against my beating heart. She felt cold and damp against me, but still I couldn't hold her close enough. Her tears had finally dried and other than being shaken, she seemed no worse for wear. I, on the other hand, would never be the same.

Craig sat on the top stair, looking out at the lake with a balled washcloth pressed against his nose. Several times his solemn gaze moved from the rope Isabella had swung from to the spot they'd gone under. When he finally turned to face us, Isabella clenched her eyes and turned away.

"Bella, honey, I'm so sorry." It was at least the tenth time he'd apologized.

She buried her face in my sternum. I thanked God for her warm breath against my skin.

Her muffled voice vibrated against me. "You said you'd catch me."

She was speaking to him now at least, but his expression only darkened as he wiped fresh blood from his face. "I meant to. It's just—your foot nailed me."

"I tried to swim, but you hit me," she whispered.

He looked at me, not a man, but a vulnerable little boy. I found myself wanting to make room for him on my lap. To cocoon him beside Isabella, inside my beach towel wings. To hold him as he'd held me in the basement.

I kissed Isabella's forehead. "You know he didn't mean it. When your foot hit him, it hurt. His body just reacted to that."

He stared at the back of her head. I felt his pangs of contrition as if they were my own. "Craig, we all know it wasn't your fault. She'll—"

"It was so his fault," my dad said as he pushed open the screen door, grasping a sweating can of RC. "And by hook or crook, he'll pay for it too."

Isabella looked up. With Mama Peg sitting to our right, Dad took the rocker to the left of us. "I saw the whole thing from here. You told him very plainly to catch you and he very plainly did not."

Isabella's bottom lip pooched out as she nodded.

Mama Peg, who I thought had fallen asleep, lifted her head and started rocking again. "Not only that, but he bit you."

Isabella's eyes bulged. "He bit me?"

"I saw that too." Dad nodded.

Craig wrinkled his face in confusion.

I winked at him. "Bit your nose right off!"

She touched her face. "But it's still there."

"That's only because you had the good sense to grab it from him and stick it back on."

"I did?"

"At first you put it on your forehead." I scrunched my nose up. "It looked really weird there, but then you fixed it." I wanted to smile but kept a serious expression. "When you tried to swim to shore, do you know what he did? He waited until your little fingertips touched grass, then snatched you by the leg and flung you back to the middle of the lake."

"Don't forget the laugh," my dad added.

I nodded in his direction. "Oh yes, he laughed all the while."

Mama Peg shook her head at poor Craig in feigned disgust. "A maniacal laugh. The most horrible cackle I've ever heard. It made my ears bleed."

Isabella turned and gave Craig the evil eye.

He didn't know our game or its purpose but was wise enough to keep quiet.

Mama Peg continued to rock, the maple runners tapping

her oxygen tank with each pass. "Then a friendly sea turtle came and tried to give you a ride on its back, but that rapscallion smacked him right out of the water."

Isabella shook her head. "You shouldn't hurt animals, Craig."

"No," he said soberly, "I shouldn't."

Her gaze lingered on him a moment; then she turned to my father. "And a whale asked if she could help me, but Craig poked her eyes right out!"

Craig grimaced. "I guess I'm a pretty mean guy."

"Very mean," she agreed.

"What else did I do?"

She tucked her lips in as she considered it. "Then a one-legged man with a three-legged dog tried to help me, but you threw them in too."

Craig quirked an eyebrow at her. "A one-legged man with a three-legged dog?"

Isabella crawled off my lap and sat next to him. He snuck a half smile over his shoulder at me.

"And then Cowpa reached in to save us both and you threw her in the pool too."

Craig shook his head in a show of mock dismay at his own horrid behavior. "Her oxygen tank made her sink right to the bottom, but I just laughed and laughed."

Isabella leaned into his shoulder. "Just like a creepy supervillain."

Mama Peg winked at me, while my father grinned at the lake.

Craig squeezed Isabella's shoulder. "You know, I really didn't mean it, Bella."

"I know," she said.

"Will you forgive me?"

She said nothing, or if she did, I didn't hear it. She kissed his elbow. "I'm never going swimming again."

Craig tapped his fingertips together diabolically. "Then my ee-veel plan has worked."

We all sat silent for a long time gazing out at the lake that had tried to steal my daughter. The liquid surface mirrored the now-menacing sky. Clouds appeared to float atop the water until ripples scattered them, sending rings lapping at the shoreline. I hadn't realized Isabella had fallen asleep on Craig's arm until he picked her up, cradling her like an infant. I stood and held the door open for them.

"I'm going to lay her down." Isabella's arm dangled from his.

I kissed her head as they passed by and thanked him.

Mama Peg stood and grabbed her tank's handle. "It's about time for my nap too, if no one needs anything." She laid her hand on my father's shoulder. "Are you okay, Jack?"

He looked up at her. "As well as I can be after almost losing the granddaughter I just learned I had."

She gave his shoulder a pat and followed Craig inside.

When the door banged shut, I wondered if my dad would excuse himself too. But he turned to me. "I didn't realize how much I loved that little girl until we almost lost her."

It occurred to me then. Now was the time to tell him about my diagnosis. It would be inexcusable later when he recalled this conversation and remembered that I'd remained silent. Besides, I knew that once I had, my burden would lighten considerably, and concrete plans could be made for Isabella's future. I stopped rocking and picked at my nails. "Daddy?"

"Jenny?" His tone was light and playful.

My insides liquefied. "I have something to tell you."

"You're not pregnant again, are you?"

"Very funny."

"Not really."

"No, not really," I agreed.

"What is it?"

"We've been through a lot."

He watched the lake instead of me. "We sure have."

"I'm sorry for leaving home the way I did."

"I'm sorry you felt you had to. I thought I'd done better than that."

"You did fine."

"You never could lie to save your life."

I breathed in the moist air. "Okay, maybe you could've done a little better."

"That's my girl."

A spine of steel was what I needed, but mine felt more like aluminum foil. How could I tell a man who'd already lost his wife that he was now about to lose his only child as well? It was just too cruel.

"If I had it all to do over again, Jenny, I'd have been the kind of father you could say anything to."

The words shot from my mouth like a bullet aimed at his heart. "I'm dying."

His expression hardened and his lips disappeared into a thin line. It was almost as though he'd been expecting this moment to come. "What do you have?"

"Cancer, Daddy."

He closed his eyes. "The same as your mother."

"Not the same."

"Did you get a second opinion?"

"Five diagnoses. All the same."

"There must be something they can do. Some treatment, surgery . . ."

"It's too far gone."

"Chemo, radiation . . ."

"It's already stage IV," I said, remembering how not that long ago he'd said the same words to me, describing my mother's prognosis. "I'm sorry, Dad."

He leaned his head back against wood, glaring up at heaven as though challenging God. "How long, Jenny? How long do you have?"

"Months."

Slowly he nodded. I marveled at how well he was taking it . . . until he slipped from the chair like a rag doll. His knees hit the porch with a thud. My first thought was that he might be having a heart attack, until he howled in anguish.

If anyone had been watching us, they'd have seen the tears

spilling over my cheeks as a natural reaction to my father's grief. There were tears of pain, yes, but as horrible as it may sound, there were tears of joy too. For the first time in my life I knew—really knew—my father loved me.

He loved me.

CHAPTER ELEVEN

WITH MAMA PEG and Isabella napping and Dad in his cave translating grief into watercolor, I found myself alone on the back porch, considering my fate. The future, to me, was nothing but a circling vulture waiting to pick apart my flesh. How I wished I could forget for a day or two that I was dying. Forget that my daughter would soon be motherless, my father childless, and my body spiritless.

The sky cast an ominous hue, making the normally vibrant greenery look washed-out, like a photograph left too long in sunlight. Though wildflowers bloomed, the scent of earth and moss hung in the air, bringing to mind not summer, but autumn. I wondered if I would live to see it.

Unwelcome visions slunk through my mind—brown and yellow leaves fluttering onto my lowering casket. My daughter weeping all the while, in the black dress I'd already purchased for her.

A raven cawed, jolting me from the graveside back to the living. I scanned the area and spied it perched beside a rotting tree stump. It blinked its unsympathetic eye at me, then turned toward the trail leading into the woods—the trail I had worn into existence.

I pushed myself up, brushed my gritty palms against my cotton shorts, and started down the path, wondering if this would be the last time I would walk it.

Ahead, a patch of ferns marked the place where David and I had veered off to steal kisses and, later, far more. As I stepped through the plants, their serrated leaves brushed my legs, giving me the sensation of insects crawling on my skin. I hurried through them, pausing to rub away the icky feeling.

When I reached a towering oak, I laid my forehead against its craggy surface, recalling a time not so long ago when I had leaned my back against this very spot as David's soft lips pressed against mine for the first time. Next to the birth of my daughter, it was the happiest day of my life. The boy I loved, loved me . . . or so I thought.

Back then, David had been my rock. The only person in my life besides Mama Peg who hadn't let me down. Every time my father or anyone else had hurt me, he was there, a sympathetic ear and a strong shoulder to cry on. Cool and collected, nothing ever knocked him off his game. He was everything I was not—self-assured, calm, and dependable.

I suppose being as in love with David as I was, I just assumed he felt the same about me. Nothing could have been further from the truth apparently. Lindsey did more to ignite his heart in a few months than I had in the three years we'd dated. To think he'd gone off to college, met Lindsey, and married her in less time than it took for me to bear his child still stung.

I ran my hand along the perimeter of the tree. My fingertips trailed over bark until they dipped into a groove. I looked down to find the heart I had carved as a teenager. *GL + DP.*

The sound of twigs snapping echoed nearby. I turned to find Craig behind me, holding two sweating bottles, Sweet Pea in tow.

Craig handed me a Coke. "I saw you come out here and thought maybe you'd want some company."

Cool plastic met my warm palm. "Company would be great."

Sweet Pea meowed at me, feigning innocence. "You don't fool me," I said.

His ears flattened as he leered at me.

Craig's gaze darted between the initials on the tree and me. "Is that what I think it is?"

"Hey, that was a long time ago." I took a sip.

He stared hard at the initials, then turned to me. "I could have that thing mulched within the hour if you want."

"That would be tempting," I said, "but it's not the tree's fault."

He took a swallow of his drink. "I'll bet you didn't know a bunch of us used to hang out here."

Back in high school, David and I often found pop bottles, beer cans, and cigarette butts littering the area but had never caught anyone in the act. "I knew someone had."

He held his hand out to me.

I hesitated, not wanting to encourage any romantic notions he might have. Finally, I gave in to the overwhelming desire to be touched.

As we walked, I took in my surroundings, feeling a familiar peace at being close to nature. Craig rubbed his rough thumb over my ring finger again and again, studying my profile as though he were an art enthusiast and I a Monet. He squeezed my hand. "You look a million miles away."

"I was just thinking."

"About?"

"Nothing worth the words."

He leaned into me. "Can I ask you a question?"

I raised my eyebrows.

"How does it feel to . . . ?"

"To be dying?" I offered.

His expression saddened as he slowly nodded.

I could have kissed him for being so direct about the subject everyone else avoided, but which I so desperately needed to talk about. "I'm afraid," I said.

Craig's gaze lingered on the path of decaying pine needles. "Walking down streets of gold sounds nice."

"Sometimes . . ." Shame held my tongue.

When he looked at me, something in his eyes told me he wouldn't pass judgment no matter what I said. "Sometimes, I wonder if heaven is real or if I'll just . . . you know . . . cease to exist."

"There's a heaven, Jenny."

I warmed at the certainty in his tone. "Most days I know that."

As we walked along, the clouds above rumbled but shed not a drop of rain. I began to hope they were nothing but bluff and bluster. Craig paid them no mind as he guided me along. He stopped abruptly and gathered up my other hand so he now held both. If I hadn't felt like I'd been mentally slogging through quicksand, I would have fled this intimacy, but I was too drained to do anything but stand there.

"What is it?" I asked.

He focused on my hands. "I had a bit of a crush on you back in high school."

"Really?"

He attempted a smile. The queer combination of strength and frailty in his eyes further thickened the fog in my head. "I think I still do."

I hated that I couldn't reciprocate, but it would be far crueler to lead him on. "Nothing like waiting until a girl's on her deathbed to confess your affection."

"I always was a little late on the draw."

"You're more than a *little* late, David."

His face elongated and I realized my mistake. Heat flooded me. "Craig. I'm sorry."

"It's okay."

I knew it wasn't by the sadness in his eyes. A cold drop hit my face. Both Craig and I looked up.

He wiped the water off the bridge of my nose, then took my hand again. "We should be getting back."

We started on the path again, ignoring the occasional droplets falling on our heads.

A gnat flew laps around Craig's head. He swatted it away. "If I knew I only had a few months to live, I think I'd try to cram in everything I've ever wanted to do."

"For instance?"

"For starters I'd watch a Braves game from behind home plate while eating a big pile of gooey nachos."

"Don't wait until you're dying." The intensity of my tone surprised me.

"Jenny?"

I turned to him, not slowing my pace.

"I hate that you're sick."

"Me too."

"If you weren't . . . ?" He gave me a tender look that finished the question for him.

I leaned my shoulder against his as we hurried along. "I'd be on you like . . ."

"White on rice?" he suggested.

"I was going for something a little less cliché." My foot caught on a root.

He grabbed my arm, steadying me. "Pink on Barbie?"

I chuckled. "Yeah, just like that."

The sky opened suddenly, drenching us. Instead of running for the house, which I knew we should do, we stopped and stared at the sky, letting water run over our heads and down our skin. I was cold, wet, and shivering, but all I could do was smile, though I had no idea why.

I turned to face Craig, feeling like I had stepped out of reality into some made-for-TV movie. We just stood there looking at one another as if there was something that needed to be said before the moment passed forever.

The rain darkened his hair, while his button-down clung to him like plaid saran wrap. "We should get you back to the house before you get sick."

"We should," I agreed.

"Have you ever danced in the rain?"

"Never."

He flashed a mischievous grin. "Make hay while the sun's still shining."

"The sun's not shining."

"You know what I mean."

"Is this the same man who told a woman with end-stage emphysema that she can't have a cup of real coffee?

He hung his head in exaggerated defeat. "Point taken." He peered up through his wet, blond lashes. "Genevieve Lucas?"

"Craig Allen?"

"May I have this dance?" He held his open palm to me.
Once again, I took it.

CHAPTER TWELVE

Sunlight stabbed through the window. Shielding my aching eyes, I tried to lift my head, but it refused to budge. My cotton pajamas felt more like burlap against my sensitive skin. Even my hair hurt. Perspiration rolled down my temples as I buried my face deeper into the damp pillow. Why was it so hot? Touching my burning forehead, I realized that the room wasn't sweltering. Just me.

My first thought was of Craig and me dancing in the rain. We shouldn't have been so careless. Then I recalled the oncologist's warning of the symptoms I might soon experience: high fevers lasting a few hours to a week, fatigue, shortness of breath, itching, pain, jaundice, weakness, swelling, infections . . .

And so it begins.

What if I'd waited too long to talk with my father about raising Isabella? What if I died right here in this bed without securing her future? There was so much I still needed to teach her, so much more to say.

With rising panic, I forced my boulder of a head up and opened my mouth to call for help. My parched lips stuck together and my skull felt like it was being kicked repeatedly by steel-toed boots. I dropped back to the pillow. Unable to do much more than blink for what seemed like hours, I simply lay there. Isabella's laughter echoed through the house. Again and again she called for me. I tried to answer but managed only a hoarse whisper.

At last, the patter of small feet made its way up the stairs. She flew through the doorway wearing a pink sundress with curls springing about her head. She grinned at me. "Morning, beautiful Mama!"

I tried to smile back, but pain caused me to grimace instead. Her expression filled with alarm and she ran from the room. Moments later, she returned, pulling my father by the hand. I squinted, trying to force him into focus. His face remained a blur.

"Jenny?" He laid his cold hand across my forehead, then yanked it back. "Dear God."

I meant to say, "It's okay." Instead I mumbled something about a blue train. *I must be dreaming,* I thought. *Or dying.*

I knew it had to be the latter when the strong arms of

God lifted me into the clouds, up, up into heaven. But the moment I submitted to death, I was cast down from my serene cloud into a shockingly frigid ocean. Icy waves rolled over my body, while a waterfall washed over my head. I tilted my neck back to drink from it.

When I looked up, I saw not the King of kings staring back at me, but my father's worried eyes. I looked down, surprised to see myself bathing not in angelic waters but in my own claw-foot tub. My father held a plastic cup over my head and dumped it. Cold water ran down my head and over my clothed body. I shook violently. He dipped the cup into the shallow water and once again held it over my head.

I buried my face into my bent knees and pleaded through chattering teeth. "Please, Daddy, no more."

Water sloshed from the full cup as he set it on the floor. He picked up the towel draped across the sink and held it open for me.

I pushed myself up and stepped out of the freezing tub into warmth. As I rubbed away goose bumps, I noticed Isabella crouched in the corner of the bedroom, crying.

Opening my eyes to darkness, I lifted my head, relieved to find it neither heavy nor throbbing. The clock on the dresser read nine, which meant it had to be nighttime. I groaned, realizing I had slept the entire day away.

I considered the satin nightgown that now clothed me.

When had I put it on? I stroked the smooth lavender fabric, remembering the last time I'd worn it.

"Take that off!" The sting of my father's angry tone shocked me.

My mother, barely able to stand, grabbed his hand with surprising agility. "Jack, no."

"She rummages through your things as if you're already—"

"She's my daughter. She's doing what all daughters do. Stop assuming the worst of everyone."

My father looked at me and frowned. I stared back defiantly, refusing to cry, refusing to care. I had done nothing wrong.

As he sat on the bed beside my mother and me, the mattress sank. He reached out to touch me, but I pulled away, clinging to her instead— smelling her sickly sweet breath, feeling her heart pounding through her rib cage.

"Jack, it's okay." Her voice sounded like gravel. "You're just upset. She understands. Go have your pipe and let me talk with our daughter."

He kissed her so tenderly that embarrassment forced me to turn away.

As his footsteps descended the stairs, she laid her hand on my cheek and began humming the nameless tune she'd sung to me since infancy. I tried not to cringe at the touch of her bony fingers that were even more yellow now than my chain-smoking grandmother's.

The song ended. "Jenny, you take care of your dad. He loves you more than you can fathom."

I rolled my eyes. "You'd never know it."

"Someday you'll have a child and you'll understand just how much we both do."

I ran my teenage hand through her thinning hair as though she were the child and I the mother. My hand emerged with a clump of brown strands. I wanted to throw it down and run screaming from the room. Instead I laid my cheek against hers, ignoring the nasty bouquet I clutched, and hummed the song back to her. . . .

Something stirred in the corner of the room. My hand flew to my chest and I gasped.

"It's just me, sweetheart." My father turned on the lamp beside him. Soft light filled the room. He wore not a neat pair of creased pants and a button-down shirt, but a wrinkled white T-shirt and pajama bottoms. The gray scruff on his cheeks and chin told me more time had passed than I first thought.

"How long did I sleep?" I asked, feeling suddenly disoriented.

He studied me with a look of concern. "Day and a half."

As I considered this, sadness pricked at me. Losing even one day when I had so little time was too much.

When he leaned forward, the lamp cast golden light across his face, bringing to mind angels and my fevered hallucination.

He scratched his chin. "I wanted to bring you to the emergency room but your grandma put up a fit."

"I don't think I would have survived three hours in a waiting room."

"That's what she said, plus she had a good point about there being a lot of sick people there. Probably not the best place to be for someone with a compromised immune system." He rubbed his palms against his eyes the way he always did right before retiring to bed. "We called Urgent Care. They had us give you liquid Tylenol and promise to bring you in if your fever didn't come down in a few hours. Between the bath and the Tylenol it did, thank God."

"How long have you been sitting here?" I asked.

He stood and walked to me, laid the back of his hand on my brow, and sighed. "Awhile." When his eyes glistened with tears, a wave of love rose up within me.

He pulled away. "I made you an appointment with the cancer center next Tuesday—9 a.m. That's not too early, is it?"

I stared hard at him. "Why would you do that?"

"Look, Jenny, I know that you said you got a few opinions."

"Five. And they all agree that I'm dying."

"So what's one more? This place might have some newer treatments, something experimental that might help."

I exhaled my irritation. "Or it might make the last few months of my life even more miserable."

"Who knows? They could extend your life by weeks or even months."

"At what cost?"

"It might not be as bad as you think."

I crossed my arms, feeling like a child again. "I'm not going."

He stood, pointing at me as anger morphed his features. "Stop being so selfish, Genevieve. It's not just about you. What about us? What about that little girl? She needs a mother."

I pushed his finger out of my face. "No matter what I do, I'm going to die. I don't want her last memories of me to be like mine of Mom's—a bald skeleton crouched over the toilet."

He turned his back, watching me now from the dresser mirror. "You don't know it will be like that. You owe it to us to try."

A fury rose from deep within me. I trembled as I stood. "I don't know? Are you kidding? If anyone knows, it's me. You act like I didn't watch Mom die. You always talk like she died gracefully, but she didn't. She didn't want the treatments. I heard her tell you that more than once, but you didn't care. It was you! You hounded her until she got them. She spent the last month of her life leaning over the side of her bed, puking into a wastebasket. She had no hair. She was nothing but skin and bones. Do you know how scary that was for me? Do you? My daughter isn't going to suffer through that just so—"

The creak of floorboards cut off my words. We both turned to the doorway. Mama Peg couldn't make it up the stairs, so it had to be Isabella. In the silence I could clearly hear the shuffle of her small feet. She emerged in the doorway, clutching Cocoa, her stuffed koala. She wore cotton footed pajamas and a crease on her cheek. "You guys are too loud."

I forced a smile. "Sorry, sweetness."

My dad wouldn't look at me as he left the room but stopped to kiss the top of Isabella's head. "Night, sweetheart."

CHAPTER THIRTEEN

So often in life we do things not because they make us feel better, but because others think they ought to. I did a little of both as I read *Jane Eyre* while forcing down a swallow of liquid nutrition. A truer description of the promised creamy vanilla flavor would have been *chalky vitamin*. At least the book was good.

Mama Peg called to me. "Jenny, you have a visitor."

I turned my novel over on the couch, set the can down on the end table, and made my way to the entryway.

I found Lindsey Preston standing by the front door, glancing around nervously, Coach bag draped over her narrow shoulder. My breath caught at the sight of her. By Mama

Peg's puzzled expression, I knew she wondered who exactly she had just let in, while I wondered what.

"Lindsey, what a surprise." I pulled my hair over my shoulder and walked over to greet her. It had been two weeks since my father had confronted Dr. Preston, revealing Isabella's existence. I had figured that if David hadn't staked a claim by now, he wouldn't. Maybe I was wrong.

Lindsey tucked her hair behind her ear, revealing an emerald stud shimmering from a dainty earlobe. I wondered if David had bought her the earrings and how many other jewels he might have given her over the years.

She glanced at me, then the floor. "What a lovely home."

Mama Peg raised her bushy brows in my direction.

"Mama Peg, this is Lindsey Preston, David's . . . Lindsey, this is Mama Peg."

They exchanged a polite nod.

I addressed my grandmother, who seemed to be a shade grayer than she'd been a moment earlier. "We'll be out back."

I offered Lindsey a drink, which she declined, and led her through the house to the back porch. Along the way, she made little comments about the beauty of this piece of furniture or the fragrance of that floral arrangement. Her sweetness soured me all the more.

We stepped outside into a tepid breeze. Four identical white rockers sat in a row on the porch, facing Lucas Lake. The treetops stretched toward the crystalline sky.

The wood porch groaned as we sat. She stared at the

lake, clutching the purse resting in her lap. "Wow, what a view. Do you know how lucky you are to look out on this every day?"

Crossing my legs, I followed her line of vision to the mountain ridges. "Lucky, that's me." I nodded to the purse she hugged. "I won't steal it. Promise."

Her skin flushed. "Oh, I'm not worried about that. I'm just really nervous." She set the bag by her feet.

"Despite the wallop I gave your husband, I'm really pretty gentle."

"I hit a guy once."

My gaze glided over her Olive Oyl physique in disbelief.

"The guy I dated before David. He tried to take what I didn't want to give."

Sympathy finally thawed me. "I can't imagine how horrible that must have been."

Her eyes grew large. "Oh, gosh, no, nothing like that. He wanted me to give him a twenty. I'd had quite enough of his mooching. I told him to get a job. He grabbed my wallet and started rummaging through it. So I hit him." She looked away shyly. "The next day his eye was blacker than coal. He lied and told everyone he'd gotten jumped. He lost me, but I let him keep the lie as a consolation prize."

"What a jerk," I said, feeling frigid once again. All I could think of as I looked at her was that she spent her nights lying on the love of my life's chest. Maybe for a better woman that wouldn't have been an insurmountable obstacle to friendship. It was for me.

Sweet Pea jumped onto the porch and sat at Lindsey's feet, meowing at her.

She reached out to pet him. "Hey, sweet kitty."

I wish I could say it didn't cross my mind not to warn her, but it did. "I wouldn't do that if I were you," I said dutifully.

"Why not?" She stroked his fur anyway as he purred and leaned into her touch. After she gave his ear a scratch, she tried to pull her hand back. Sweet Pea clawed her.

She winced and drew back. "Hey!" Her hand had several fresh lines of red streaking across it. She looked at it and scowled at him.

I almost felt bad. "That's why not," I said. "Are you okay?"

She rubbed her hand and nodded. "Serves me right, I guess, for not believing you."

We sat silent for a moment as Lindsey crossed her legs, then uncrossed them. She stared at the lake, opened her mouth to speak, and closed it again.

It was time to put her out of her misery. Unlike her, I had no problem addressing the issue at hand. "I'm guessing that you know about Isabella."

She drew in a deep breath, her small chest rising and falling as if she needed all the courage the air could provide. "Can I tell you something personal?"

Though there was nothing I wanted less, I nodded, praying she wouldn't share a Hallmark rendition of how she and David had met and fallen in love.

"I've lost two babies in the last five years."

Surprise struck me. David had told me he never wanted children. I guess he just meant with me. I opened my mouth to say something appropriate, but no words came. The anguish brewing in her eyes told me an "I'm sorry" wouldn't begin to cover it.

She struggled to maintain eye contact, then gave up and stared at her wedding band instead, twisting it back and forth on her bony finger. "One of my babies made it all the way to the third trimester. His name was Gabriel. Gabriel Matthew Preston. I held him as he took his last breath."

She closed her eyes and cradled the air. I felt like an intruder, a voyeur of the worst kind, as I watched her grieve her phantom child. David's son.

"Jenny, he was so tiny. So complete." When she looked up, her pain seemed to melt into resolve. "The other died in the second trimester. His name was Joseph. Joseph is the patron saint of unborn children. Did you know that?"

I shook my head.

"I gave him that name before I knew that. He was my first." Tears moved down her face, clearing a path through her blush. She wiped them away, looking embarrassed at her own weakness.

There we were, me not knowing what to say, and her sitting inches, miles, away. After a few moments, the silence became too heavy and I decided to unload it. "You know, Lindsey, this doesn't seem to be any of my business."

She looked back at the house. "Can I see her?"

My blood ran cold. "My daughter?"

"When I learned you claimed to have a child by my husband—"

Claimed? "I don't *claim* that David is her father. David's her father."

"I think I'll be able to tell for sure by looking at her."

My face caught fire as I bolted up. "I think you should go. I may be a lot of things, but a liar isn't one of them."

"I'm not saying that you are." She reached out to touch me.

I jerked away. "Do you want a DNA test?"

She stood, slipping her purse over her shoulder, looking maddeningly calm. Her chair continued to rock as though she still occupied it. "That wouldn't be a bad idea, Jenny. For her sake."

I ripped open the door, willing her to walk through it. "Only my friends are allowed to call me Jenny."

She eyed the open door but made no move toward it. "I think you're making a mistake. Even if she's not his, she needs a father. It's—"

I felt my fingernails dig into my palms as every muscle of my body tensed. "Get out of my house. Isabella *is* David's daughter. She's a beautiful, loving, charming child. And over my dead body will you or David ever get your hands on her."

A slamming car door sounded from the driveway.

Lindsey turned toward the sound. "That's David. I asked him to give me a few minutes alone with you before he came back."

Unsure of what I should do or how I should feel, I put

my hand over my mouth and closed my eyes. Maybe when I opened them, this would all be over. They'd be gone.

"Honey," I heard Lindsey say, "it's not going well."

I opened my eyes.

David had rounded the house and was marching toward me like a soldier on his way to battle. His hair hung uncharacteristically tousled, and anger flashed from his eyes. A rush of pain overwhelmed me.

"Thanks for telling me I'm a father."

Contrition sealed my mouth.

"We want to see her." It wasn't a request, but a demand.

"It's not that easy, David. I'll need to prepare her for—"

"She's my daughter, right? That's what you and your father are saying. I have a right to see her if she's mine."

He said a lot of things after that, but I heard nothing after *if*. It was one thing for Lindsey to question it, but David knew the kind of girl I was. He knew I'd been untouched until him. How dare he!

I expected to lose control of my emotions just then. Instead calmness settled over me. "Lindsey, David, thank you for coming. It was good to see you both again. I apologize, but I really need to be excused."

With that, I walked inside, or tried to. Isabella stood, eyes wide, blocking my entrance. Two gasps rose behind me and I knew David's paternity would never be questioned again. She was, of course, her father's spitting image. Even a man as blind as David couldn't deny it.

Without a word, I took her small hand in mine and led

her inside, hoping she hadn't been standing there long. But when she looked up at me with wonder and joy shining from her sleep-crusted eyes, I knew that she had.

CHAPTER FOURTEEN

WE SAT FACING the television—Mama Peg in the chair, Craig on the floor at her feet, Dad alone on the love seat, and I on the couch with Isabella nestled on my lap. While everyone else stared at the screen, I studied the flickering shadows dancing on the walls. I had no desire to watch beautiful people with their whole lives ahead of them competing in a stupid talent competition.

When the phone rang for the second time in five minutes, everyone looked at me expectantly. I glanced at the caller ID, unsurprised to see David's name once again.

Mama Peg and Craig agreed that I would have to deal with him. The sooner the better. Of course that was easy for them to say. Though my father remained silent on the matter, the sneer he directed at the phone spoke clearly enough.

While Isabella had asked about David countless times since their encounter that afternoon, she didn't seem to realize he was the person whose calls I was avoiding. Though it was hard to tell sometimes what did or didn't register with her.

As the phone continued to ring, Isabella leaned into my chest, eyes fixated on a handsome young Latino singing Stevie Wonder's "My Cherie Amour." I rubbed a lock of her silky hair as I stared at the screen, pretending to be absorbed.

"Oh, for pity's sake." Mama Peg thrust the remote up, muting the show. She turned on the floor lamp beside her, bathing the room in light. "You can't ignore him forever."

I buried my face in Isabella's curls and inhaled the comforting scent of her strawberry shampoo. "I can try."

Preparing for his evening smoke, my father pressed tobacco into his pipe. "This is between them, Mom."

She glared daggers at him. "David shouldn't have to pay for what his father may or may not have done."

He slapped his pouch of tobacco down on the end table, scattering flecks of brown over the tiled top. "This has nothing to do with that and you know it."

She spoke between coughs. "I know . . . no such . . . thing."

The shrill ring of the phone finally fell silent. Relief washed over me . . . until I looked down to see Isabella holding the receiver to her ear, face bright as New York City. My heart pounded as I grabbed it from her and hung up.

"That was my daddy!" she cried.

It rang again. I snatched it up and pressed it against my ear, wincing from more than just the sharp pain of my earring back digging into my neck.

"I want to see her," David said.

Isabella stared at me with eyes that managed to accuse and plead at the same time. How could I make her understand that he would never be the man either of us needed him to be?

"I'm sorry I reacted the way I did." Despite his words, his tone held not a hint of remorse.

"Are you?"

"Don't make this any harder. I screwed up, okay? But, Jenny, you screwed up far worse. Why didn't you tell me?"

"She's sitting on my lap listening. Now's not the time."

"Time's running out," Mama Peg mumbled.

David's breathing echoed heavy in my ear. "Lindsey wants her to come over and spend time with us."

My grip tightened on the receiver. "She's not Lindsey's daughter—she's mine."

"You mean ours."

"So now you believe me?"

"She looks just like me and you know it."

Isabella's heart thumped against me. I stood her up and motioned to Craig. "Would you take her outside?"

He started to push off the floor.

Mama Peg set her shaky hand on his shoulder. "Don't you dare. This conversation concerns that little girl more than anyone. She has a right to know her father."

Exasperated, I stood and turned my back on them all. "I'll let you see her, but it needs to be just you. It's nice Lindsey's interested, but Bella should get to know you first."

"Can she come here?" His tone was softer now, almost pleading.

I cringed at the thought of going back to David's house and facing once again the perfect life he'd made without me.

"Please?" His tone had descended to the plane of genuine humility.

An overwhelming desire to ask him how it felt to want something he couldn't have came over me. How delicious it would feel to break *his* heart for a change.

I opened my mouth to say something that would hurt him as much as he'd hurt me, but something inside me whispered, *Look at your daughter.*

Slowly I turned around. The light shining up at me from her eyes cast out the darkness that had seeped into my soul. Once again I was reminded that it didn't matter an iota what I wanted. It was her future at stake, not mine. I held my hand over the receiver and squatted next to her. "Bella, do you want to go to David's house and spend an afternoon?"

She squealed so loud the windows should have shattered. Dejected, I stood again. "I guess you heard that?"

His laughter sounded as melodic as a hyena's.

"You can pick her up tomorrow around noon." As soon as the words left my mouth, I regretted them.

Before I could hang up, Isabella flung her arms around my legs. I scanned the faces watching me. The look of approval in Mama Peg's and Craig's eyes, combined with the blinding joy shining from my daughter's, told me I had made the right decision. My aching heart told me something entirely different.

My father grabbed his pipe and stalked out of the room. Seconds later, the back door banged shut.

Isabella's grin threatened to split her face, which only made me feel worse. What was wrong with me? I was her mother. I should be happy for her.

Mama Peg studied me a moment, then turned to Craig. "Why don't you read Bella her bedtime story? I think Jenny needs to get some fresh air." With that, she aimed the remote at the television, filling the room with cheers from the television audience.

Craig stood.

"You don't have to," I said, though I hoped he would. Listening to my daughter prattle on about David as I tucked her in was more than I could handle at the moment.

"It's the least he can do after nearly killing you both," Mama Peg said flatly, not taking her eyes off the tube.

Craig grabbed the small of his back. "She knows just where to plunge that knife, doesn't she?"

I shook my head at her sick sense of humor.

He took my hand. "I really am sorry I kept you out in the rain."

"So you've said a hundred times. And like I've said, I'm going to get sick whether I dance in the rain or live the rest of my days in a bubble. It was worth it."

He smiled.

Mama Peg cleared her throat. "Might as well jump out of an airplane without pulling your cord since we're all going to die someday anyway."

Craig shook his head as my fingers slipped from his grasp. He turned to Isabella, who sat on the carpet cross-legged, excitedly rocking back and forth. "Let's go pick out a book, Sleeping Beauty."

Craig disappeared up the stairs with Isabella bouncing at his heels. Mama Peg muted the TV again and turned to me with an expression that suggested a lecture was imminent.

Without giving her the chance to speak, I said, "You were right. I do need some air." With that, I slipped out the back door to join my father. For once he was bound to be more sympathetic.

As I stepped into warm night air, a chorus of crickets serenaded me. Dad threw a glance my way as he dipped the lighter's flame into his pipe bowl. He sucked, causing a small ember to brighten and grow.

A plume of smoke wafted my way as I sat. I inhaled the intoxicating mixture of vanilla and apple that tinged his favorite blend.

He rocked back and forth in his chair, speaking around the stem of his pipe. "She's a good girl."

"The best thing I ever did," I agreed.

"That's just what I used to say about you."

I eyed him. "Really?"

He pulled the pipe from his mouth. "Don't act so surprised. You think the love you feel for her your mother and I didn't feel for you?"

A breeze rattled the azaleas and sent my father's pipe smoke trailing in the opposite direction. The wind died as my dad leaned his head back on the rocker and blew an oblong ring of smoke into the air. "It doesn't thrill me to know I'm going to be sharing my granddaughter with that man."

I feigned interest in my cuticles. "Dr. Preston is more the *grandfather* type than the *cowpa* type. Besides, just because she might love him doesn't mean she'll stop loving you." I realized I was speaking more to myself than to him. "You know, Dad, you're going to need to get along with him for Bella's sake."

"I can't do it, Jenny. He's the reason your mother's not sitting here with us."

I continued to focus on my hands rather than him. "You're going to need to forgive him."

"Are you going to let David raise her?"

At last I looked up, relieved to find his eyes fixated on the lake rather than me. "I don't know. He's her father. You see how she pines for him."

I longed for some fatherly wisdom—some truism that might make the pill of losing not only my man to Lindsey, but possibly my daughter as well, easier to swallow. My father took a long drag of his pipe and nodded.

I drew my legs up onto the chair and squeezed them against my chest. "What if she loves him better than me?"

"Love *him* better than *you*?" He made a face as though I'd asked the dumbest question ever. "He may be her father, but he's still a Preston."

I laughed at his joke but also at the surprising freeness I suddenly felt. I'd come home to find Isabella a family, and maybe I had succeeded. She wanted her father, and it seemed he wanted her too. The only problem was the feud between my dad and Dr. Preston. For Isabella's sake, it needed to end.

"Dad?"

"I don't have the answer," he said.

"You don't even know what I was going to ask."

"Doesn't matter. I don't have any answers. I thought I did when I was younger, but the older I get, the more I realize just how ignorant I am."

"I have to ask you something, and it's no small thing."

"Whatever it is, I'll do it if you promise to go to the cancer center."

I huffed. "This again? Haven't we beat that dead horse long enough?"

"Just one consultation. That's all I'm asking."

Anger rose within me but was quickly replaced with the sadness it tried to mask. "Each time I go to a new doctor, even though I tell myself I'm not going to hope, I do anyway. I begin to think maybe, just maybe, this doctor could be hoarding some secret cure." I hugged my knees tighter. "Dreams for my future—the future I'm never going to have— seep into my mind, but each time I'm left with my hopes crushed and a brochure for hospice care. I can't go through that again. I can't, Dad."

My father's neck was bent so far down, I couldn't see his face. I went to him and wrapped my arms around his now-trembling shoulders. He gathered me onto his lap like when I was little.

I laid my head against him and listened to his heartbeat— the steady, comforting sound of a drumbeat, which in my childhood had lulled me to sleep. The smell of pipe tobacco mingled with his Old Spice deodorant and the fabric softener Mama Peg used on his clothes. It was, to me, a heavenly combination.

I pushed all worries from my mind and surrendered to childhood as he rocked me just as he'd done years before. Deep within my soul, I could almost remember that time when I felt safe and secure in my little protected world full of hugs, hope, and a complete lack of responsibility. I picked my head off his shoulder and looked him squarely in the eyes. "Dad, promise you'll at least try to get along with the Prestons."

He ushered me from his lap. "Jenny, even if my life depended on it, I don't think I could."

I don't know why his stubbornness surprised me so. He'd always been this way. "But if you do not forgive others, neither will your Father forgive you. Your life does depend on it, Dad."

He glared at me. "So we're going to throw Scripture around? 'Hypocrite! first get rid of the log in your own eye; then you will see well enough to deal with the speck in your friend's.'"

The crickets grew louder, and my head began to throb. "Even around this log, I can see that you've got far more than a speck in your eye. Keep ignoring it and one day you'll go blind."

He stood and snatched his pipe off the armrest. "I wish I would."

CHAPTER FIFTEEN

ISABELLA AND I sat side by side on the front porch steps, waiting for David to arrive. The midday sun poured down its happy golden rays over her, while a cloud of gray seemed to hover over me alone. I raised my glass to my lips and took a sip. Cold liquid hit my tongue, accosting me with a taste both rancid and sweet. Though I knew it was my disease-altered taste buds causing the sickening flavor rather than the tea itself, I still couldn't make myself swallow. I leaned over and spit it into the hydrangeas.

Lately, everything managed to offend my palate. This symptom, which I hadn't anticipated, had become even more of a thorn in my side than the ever-increasing fatigue. Nausea rose within me as I eyed the ice cubes floating in the remaining liquid, whose hue reminded me of campground toilet water. Rather than have to look at it, I dumped the rest into the mulch. I watched it disappear into the thirsty ground and turned back to Isabella.

Her right knee bobbed like a jackhammer as she stared hard down the gravel road and clutched her stuffed koala.

I guided her face toward me. "What's my cell number?"

She pushed the bear in front of my eyes and pointed to the numbers I'd written on his tiny T-shirt in laundry marker.

"Just in case you lose Cocoa . . ."

She pressed him tight against her chest. "I won't lose him. He's my friend!"

Despite how miserable I felt, her response still managed to draw a smile out of me. "I know that you won't *try* to lose him, but just in case you do, David has my number and I'll see you at three no matter what."

She looked through rather than at me.

"Bella, are you listening?"

Her gaze slid from me back to the deserted road. "What time is it now, Mommy?"

"Two minutes later than the last time you asked."

"You think he forgot me?"

"Who could forget you?"

The sun reflected off of her white sundress, casting a golden halo all around her as she leaned over to pick a scrap of mulch from her sandal. She looked like a little bride waiting on her groom. I could almost see the woman she was to become and wondered if God would let me watch her wedding from heaven. I would give anything to do that.

A visceral pain gnawed at me. "Remember, you call me if anything goes wrong. If you feel uncomfortable or scared or—"

She heaved a sigh.

"He's going to come, baby."

"I know." A blush colored her cheeks as she brushed a wrinkle from her skirt. "Do you think he'll like my dress?"

I ran the back of my hand across her soft cheek. "Beautiful Bella, even if you were wearing a potato sack, you'd be lovely. Besides, people who love you love you no matter how you look."

She went cross-eyed as she swatted something in front of her nose that only she could see. With her preoccupied, I snuck another glance at my watch. David was now officially late. I picked up the phone from the step beside me and flipped it open. No missed calls. If he let her down . . .

Above us, movement caught my eye. I looked upward. A glass globe dangled from the porch overhang. A hummingbird fluttered beside it, dipping its narrow beak into the glistening red liquid. I started to point him out, but Isabella screamed.

"He's here!" She jumped up, sending the stuffed koala tumbling face-first into a pile of wet mulch.

The same Infiniti Coupe I'd seen parked in David's garage tore forward, spraying gravel and dirt. He stopped the car at the end of the driveway and honked his horn twice, just like he used to do when we were dating. For the first time, I understood why the gesture used to infuriate my father. I waved David out of the car.

As he slammed the door, Isabella ran for him as though she had known him all of her life. The smile she wore was the biggest I'd ever seen on her. Not a trace of fear or trepidation glinted in her eyes. "Daddy!"

He held his arms out to her and she jumped into them. He kissed her forehead while I tried not to wince.

After a moment, Isabella turned to me. "I love you too, Mommy."

My face warmed with embarrassment. Apparently, my jealousy and insecurity were obvious even to my little girl. "Oh, sweetness, I know you do. It's okay. You have plenty of love to go around."

David balanced her on his hip. "Thanks, Jenny. We'll see you around four."

I crossed my arms. "I think you mean three."

The devilish grin that met me would have made my heart flutter a few years ago. Not now. "I mean it, David."

Isabella scrutinized our exchange with such intensity that it slapped the scowl off my face and the negativity from my tone. "You have fun, sweetness." I kissed her cheek and turned to David. "Do you want her car seat?"

He scrunched his nose against Isabella's, making her giggle and me cringe. "I don't think so. We're good. Aren't we, princess?"

She looked at him adoringly and nodded. "I'm not a baby, Mom."

What happened to *Mommy*? "The law says that she needs a booster."

He set her down and smoothed his khaki pants. "Well, I guess I need it then."

"It's for her safety."

His nostrils flared. "Did I say it wasn't?"

It took everything I had not to respond to his defensiveness. He arranged her booster in the middle of the backseat and strapped her in. As I watched the two of them pull away, it felt as though David were driving off with my very heart in the backseat of his car.

I lifted my arm to wave good-bye to my daughter, but she was looking ahead, not behind her. It was a healthy response to life that would serve her well in the coming months. That didn't mean it didn't hurt. What happened to the days when she would allow no one but me to hold her? when she would scream bloody murder when I left her with the sitter to go to work?

I looked down and noticed Cocoa lying on the ground. I bent and picked him up. I started to call for Isabella, but David's car had already turned out of sight. I brushed dirt off the bear's nose. "I'll bet she'll be missing you before the hour's up." His blank eyes stared back, looking as unconvinced as I felt. Hugging him to my chest, I inhaled her scent, which lingered on his fake fur.

I carried the bear back to the house and noticed a small

blob of gray lying on the bottom porch step. As I got closer, I saw a pointy nose and whiskers attached to it. Shivers ran across my shoulders, making them shimmy. A dead mouse. Our biannual gift from Sweet Pea. He meowed at me from the sidewalk.

"Thanks for the carcass," I told him. "You know, you sure have a funny way of showing affection."

The cat took off toward the lake, and I went inside.

The phone rang only once before someone picked it up. Mama Peg yelled from the kitchen, "Jenny!"

Isabella. I jumped up, letting the journal I'd been writing in fall to the floor. Something was wrong. I knew it. I never should have left her with him.

Before I could reach the phone, Mama Peg pulled the receiver from her ear and hung up. "That was David. He's bringing Bella home."

I checked my watch. It was only two. "What happened?" I stared hard, trying to read her body language.

She hesitated. "He didn't say, but I could hear her crying."

Adrenaline rushed through me. "Whimpering or wailing?"

"She sounded pretty upset."

"Upset or frantic?"

My grandmother's eyes answered me before she had even opened her mouth. "Inconsolable."

My stomach dropped as a million possibilities sped through

my mind, each one more horrible than the last. "Well, is she hurt? Did he say what made her—"

"He said that she's okay, just shook up. She's on her way home."

From the front of the refrigerator, I snatched the scrap of paper with David's number on it. I picked up the phone and dialed as fast as my fingers would fly. Lindsey answered.

"Put my daughter on."

"Jenny? They're on their way."

"What happened?"

"I don't know. We took her to the pool—"

My heart stopped. "You did what?"

"David wanted to teach her to swim."

"No," I pleaded as if it hadn't already happened.

"He just tossed her in the shallow end. She could have stood up but she panicked."

My eyes refused to blink away the tears blurring them. She must have been terrified. My baby. My poor baby. "Is she okay?"

"It's really not as bad as it sounds. He pulled her right out."

Lindsey's calmness fueled my anger. "She almost drowned two weeks ago."

Silence met me.

I began to tremble. "She almost died!"

I heard only her ragged breath.

"He had to know that she was scared."

Lindsey's voice dropped to a whisper. "He wanted her to learn how to swim."

"She already knows how to swim. Didn't she tell him?"

Mama Peg laid her hand on my shoulder. "Sweetheart, you're yelling."

I shook her off.

"We didn't know, Jenny. I'm so sorry. We didn't know," Lindsey said through sniffles.

I wanted to reach into the phone and grab her by the neck. "You knew that she didn't want to go in, right? I know she told you."

"When you fall off a bike, you need to—"

Red flashed before my eyes and I heard nothing except the rapid pounding of my pulse. "I haven't even been able to give her a bath since it happened, you idiot. You—"

Mama Peg lifted the phone from my quaking hand. While I shook with fury, she spoke into the receiver. "Lindsey, I know whatever happened wasn't on purpose. Jenny's just upset."

I snatched the phone from her, growled into it, and slammed it down.

Minutes felt like hours as I waited for David to bring my daughter back. My mind played out all kinds of gut-wrenching scenarios. Isabella clinging to the father she trusted so readily as he pried her little fingers off his shoulder, her pleading with him to stop . . .

Thinking of my daughter being terrified knocked the wind out of me, and I clutched my stomach. What kind of people would force a child to do something that petrified her? Not anyone that needed to be parents. What kind of future would she have with them? That behavior was inexcusable. Unacceptable. Absolutely unacceptable.

I threw open the screen door and hurried to the front lawn to wait for them. It had been two weeks since it last rained, and the grass showed it. It crunched under my feet as I paced, trying to spend my anger before they arrived. The more I marched, though, the more upset I became. I couldn't believe he had done what he'd done. I kept picturing my little girl, flailing and frantic, until I felt as though I were the one drowning.

Would she suffer lifelong trust issues now? She would definitely be scarred. *I've spent her whole life trying to protect her, and he undoes it all in one afternoon. Falling off a bike? What a ridiculously stupid analogy.*

Before David's car had come to a complete stop, the back door opened. Isabella jumped out and ran for me. David called for her, but she didn't slow. She threw herself into my arms, nearly toppling me. I held her as tightly as I could, but it wasn't nearly tight enough. I wanted to somehow again merge her with me, as we had once been, and protect her from the world.

David got out of the car and stood before me. "Is she always so over-the-top?"

All the blood in my body shot to my head the instant I looked at him. My temples pounded and my eyes felt like they had been replaced with laser beams set on annihilating him. "She almost drowned two weeks ago, you moron."

"She said something about that."

"And you threw her in anyway?"

"She just needed a little confidence. The same thing happened to me at that age and—"

"Shut up," I snapped.

He reached out to touch Isabella, but she buried her face in my chest. For the first time, David actually looked hurt instead of prideful. Good.

He leaned against his car. "How did you know what happened?"

"Lindsey." I kissed the tears off Isabella's lashes before it dawned on me. "Why was she there?"

"What?" he said.

I rested my chin on Isabella's curls. "Why was she there? You promised me that it would only be you."

"She's my wife, and I didn't promise."

I shook my head at him in complete disgust. "I used to be able to trust your word."

When I turned to leave, he grabbed my arm. I glared at him until he let go.

"I never once lied to you," he said. "Lindsey came because Isabella begged her to. Ask her if you don't believe me." He stared at Isabella's back with a sad expression. "I didn't mean to scare her."

Isabella wiggled to get down. I set her on the ground, and without turning to say good-bye to her father, she ran inside.

"I would never hurt her on purpose, Jenny."

Isabella disappeared into the house. The door slammed shut and David winced.

I pressed my fingers to my forehead, trying to force my racing thoughts into words that made sense. I looked up. "This isn't going to work, David." I headed for the porch.

He called after me, "Don't do this, Genevieve."

I turned. "You did this, not me. You're trying to treat her the same way that you treated me. We both deserved better."

His expression changed him into a man that I no longer recognized. "She's my daughter and she *will* be part of my life. Don't fight me, Lucas. You won't win."

Without answering, I turned back around and headed inside, leaving him alone with his threat.

CHAPTER SIXTEEN

THE SMELL OF sweat and cedar passed under my nose right
before something touched my arm. I opened my eyes, surprised to see Craig squatting next to my bed.

His hazel eyes crinkled at me. "You should see your
hair."

I shielded my mouth, hoping that my breath didn't smell
as bad as it tasted. "That good, huh?"

"Let's just say you probably wouldn't win the Miss North
Carolina title."

"I don't think I stood that great a chance even on my best
day." I sat up the rest of the way, glanced at the alarm clock,
and groaned. It was nearly dinnertime. My one-hour nap had

somehow turned into three and still I could have easily slept a few more. "Why are you here?"

He sat, sinking one side of the mattress. The intensity of his gaze sent an unexpected thrill through me, and I found myself smiling at the ridiculousness of it. How in the world had I managed to develop a crush in the midst of dying? Only me.

"Wow," he said.

"Wow, what?"

"Even with your Medusa hair, you still manage to look beautiful."

I crossed my arms and looked him over in return. He wore a John Deere T-shirt, shorts, and grass-streaked tube socks that peeked up through crusty work boots. I started to say something smart about the way he was dressed but stopped myself. The truth was that he looked exactly the way a man should.

He winked. "Even looking as raggedy as you do, I'd share a mattress with you any day."

I felt myself flush. "That's enough."

He covered his mouth and fake-coughed the word *prude*.

"I'll take that as a compliment. The last time I laid down my prudity, I ended up with Isabella."

"That's not a word," he said.

"Isabella?"

"No, *prudity*."

"Yes, it is."

"Oh, come on . . . *prudity*?"

"It is so," I said, trying to sound certain.

"You wanna bet?"

I combed my fingers through my tangled hair. "First, you compromise my reputation by being in my bedroom unchaperoned, and now you want me to gamble?"

He bent over to pick a pillow off the floor. I found myself at eye level with his bottom. It was a fine butt, small and round, which I had no business admiring. Heat rose in my cheeks. I looked away as he straightened.

"Listen, Mother Teresa, I'm not trying to take advantage of you or cause your backslide." His smile faded. "I'm not David, Genevieve."

My hands clutched the blanket. "What's that supposed to mean?"

"I actually care about you."

My heart grew heavy. "He cared once too."

Craig opened his mouth as if to argue, then closed it again.

After a moment of silence, I gestured to his feet. "How in the world did you get past Mama Peg in those filthy things?"

He looked down at his boots and then at me. "Crud, I forgot why I even came up here."

"Which was?"

"I'm supposed to let you know that Ted's down there waiting to talk to you."

I knew only one Ted, and the thought of him in my

house gave me the same Alice-in-Wonderland feeling I got the first time I ran into one of my teachers at the grocery store. "*Uncle* Ted?"

"He ain't my uncle, but yeah, that's the one."

"What does he want?"

"My guess is it has something to do with his nephew's daughter."

I sighed. Apparently David and Lindsey weren't going to be the only Prestons I was going to have to contend with. I didn't know why it hadn't occurred to me until then that Isabella wasn't just inheriting David, Lindsey, and Dr. Preston . . . but Ted, his wife, and the rest of the Preston clan. I flopped back on my pillow and yanked the blanket over my head.

Craig tore it off.

A gust of air hit my legs. "Go away."

He grabbed my ankles and pulled my feet to the floor.

I batted his hands away from me. "Okay, already. I'm up."

Eyeing my upright position, he nodded smugly and sauntered out. Perspiration had soaked the back of his shirt in the shape of an upside-down heart. He started to close the door behind him but paused and peered back at me. "I wouldn't take too long if I were you. Your father's down there reading him the riot act about his brother."

My stomach cramped at the thought of what could be going on downstairs between these modern-day Montagues and Capulets. After changing into a clean lace-rimmed T-shirt, pulling my hair into a ponytail, and speed-gargling some Scope, I hurried down to intervene before blood could be shed.

As I made my way to the landing, Isabella's laughter fluttered in from the yard, and I wondered if Ted was entertaining her. The thought neither warmed nor disturbed me. He was the type who would offer a kid a sucker, then expect a quarter, but at least he didn't have a god complex like his brother.

When I reached the bottom of the stairs, I saw him sitting on the couch, looking as out of place in my living room as a vulture in a bluebird nest. He wore white work pants with a Ted's Café silk-screened shirt tucked into them. His bald head gleamed more than usual, making me wonder if he had shined it up special for the visit.

My father stood, arms crossed, leaning against the doorway between the kitchen and the living room.

Ted's gaze fell on me. He jumped up. "Jenny, long time no see."

I gave him my best what-pray-tell-are-you-talking-about look. "I just saw you two weeks ago."

My father cleared his throat.

Ted's small eyes darted between him and me as he laughed nervously. "What are you talking about? I haven't seen you since you left town. How many years has it been now?"

I blinked a few times, wondering which one of us was the crazy one. I decided it was definitely him. "We're not exactly hiding from the Mafia, Ted. What can I do for you?"

My father's eyes narrowed at Ted's lie. No wonder the

guy was about to sweat a river. Jack Lucas's icy glare could unnerve the devil himself.

Ted glanced at Dad. "I've never been a great-uncle before."

My father snorted. "This entire godforsaken town calls him 'uncle.' You'd think he'd gotten his fill of it."

"Stop being rude, Jack!" Mama Peg yelled from the kitchen.

My father said nothing in his defense, but the scowl on his face deepened considerably.

Perspiration beaded fresh on Ted's brow. He pulled a balled-up handkerchief from his pocket and blotted his forehead. "Jenny, mind if we talk private?"

My dad's eyes further narrowed into slits. "Blood is thicker than water, Genevieve. Don't you ever forget that."

I shook my head at his infantile behavior.

With a black look on his face, my father plodded into the kitchen, leaving us alone.

Ted sighed with relief, then gestured to a grease-stained brown sack resting on the coffee table. "Are you hungry? I brought you some burgers."

I was surprised my stomach didn't lurch at the mention of food. "A little, thanks. How much do we owe you?"

He gave me an incredulous look. "I'm not asking you to pay for them."

Shocked, I stuttered my thanks.

"I know I've got a reputation for being cheap, but I'm not *that* bad."

I quirked an eyebrow at him. "It's common knowledge that not even your family gets their meals for free."

His face turned crimson. "Good grief. I lay a bill in front of my nephew once or twice to prove a point and people are still smarting off about it."

Hunger began to gnaw at my stomach. I was anxious to get some calories in me before the urge to eat took another two-week hiatus. "What is it that you want, Ted?"

He sucked in his bottom lip and chewed on it before speaking. "I'll bet you didn't know your little one is the only grandchild in the family. The only one." Fresh beads of sweat formed on his brow. "We—I—would like the chance to get to know her."

"If Isabella wants to get to know her Preston relatives when she's grown, that will be her choice, but for now . . ."

He looked even sadder than the night the café was robbed. I felt sorry for him, but I couldn't base my decision for Isabella's future on feelings—his, mine, or anyone else's. Still, he *was* her great-uncle and an okay guy despite his last name.

I needed time to think this through, list the pros and cons, maybe talk it out with Mama Peg and Craig. I wanted to do what was right, but I suspected that the right thing for the Prestons wasn't going to be what was right for Isabella. She had to be my utmost consideration. I rubbed at my temple, trying to clear my mind. It didn't work. I couldn't think straight with him watching me. "Ted, thanks for coming. I know you're interested in Isabella, but I need some time to consider this."

He wiped his forehead again. "Jenny, this family feud has gone on long enough. I know my brother messed up with your mom. I understand your daddy's anger, but that little girl, she had nothing to do with any of that. She deserves to know her family. All her family."

"I'll be in touch." My words sounded strange and distant.

Ted laid his palm on my arm. "There's something else you need to know. David's talking about suing for custody."

I reached out for something to hold on to but my hand grasped only air. "What?"

"I tried my best to talk him out of it. I told him we should settle it among ourselves. That once it went to court, any chance of reconciliation would be lost forever."

A cloud exploded in my mind. "*Full* custody?"

"Don't worry, Jenny. He won't get it, I don't think. No judge worth his spit would take a little girl from her mama."

No, I thought, *but if the mother was dying . . .* The air no longer seemed to contain adequate amounts of oxygen. I breathed faster, but the more air I tried to suck in, the faster the room spun. "He would really try and take her away from me?"

"I think he just wants to share . . ."

Ted said something more after that, but his words swirled around my head as jumbled as alphabet soup. The ground rolled under my feet. I wanted to ask if he felt it too, but no words would come. Ted's mouth opened wide as he reached out to me . . . a second too late. I heard a thud as the floor slammed my head, and the room faded to black.

CHAPTER SEVENTEEN

THE COMBINATION OF bleach and alcohol was almost pungent enough to drown out the smell of disease and misery clinging to the air. Chatter laced with medical jargon, intermingled with banging cabinets, clicking heels, and squalling monitors, returned me to a place I'd never have come willingly—to replay memories I'd give anything to erase.

My father leaned into my mother and pressed his pink, healthy lips against her cracked and pale ones. "Hang in there, honey. There's a clinic in New Mexico I just heard about. You get past this episode and we'll—"

She winced as she struggled to raise her hand to his cheek. "No . . . more." The words dribbled out, barely a whisper.

He turned his tear-soaked face toward me. "Jenny, tell your mom the promising things we heard about—"

"Stop it," I hissed. "Haven't you put her through enough? Look at her!" I stared him down, not bothering to hide my resentment.

My mother had been given a patient-controlled analgesic pump filled with morphine that could alleviate her suffering—if my father hadn't kept it just out of reach. Instead he insisted on a daily dose of healing massage—though she found even the slightest touch painful. Classical music playing through the night, every night—despite her request for peace and quiet. Enough was enough.

Mama Peg stood by the foot of her bed, breathing heavier than Darth Vader. "Jack, tell her it's okay to go. I think she's waiting on your permission."

My father and I jerked our heads in my grandmother's direction. Just because I hated the militant approach he used to battle Mom's cancer didn't mean I wanted her to stop fighting altogether. I wanted her to beat this, but on her own terms.

Her skeletal hand reached out toward me.
I flinched and pulled back. Anguish glinted
in her mustard-colored eyes, maybe from the
rejection, maybe from pain. A nauseating smell
like rotting fruit permeated the room. I turned
away as I tried in vain not to inhale the stench,
hating myself for feeling revulsion toward my
own mother.

"Jenny," she whispered, reaching out her
bony fingers once again. This time I let her
hand make contact.

"Tell her it's okay." Mama Peg stepped
toward the bed, leaned down, and kissed Mom's
forehead. "You fought the good fight, Audra.
It's okay. I'll take care of them. Me and Jesus.
Don't you worry, love. Don't you worry."

I thought I'd cried so much over the past few
weeks that my well had long since dried up, but
tears still managed to spring anew.

Tell her, my conscience whispered. *Tell her!*
it screamed.

I closed my eyes and laid my head on her
now-flat chest. Through the thin hospital gown,
her jutting ribs pressed against my cheek. "Mom.
Mommy. It's okay. I'll be okay." I'd always been
taught that it was wrong to lie. I wouldn't be
okay without her. None of us would. But telling
the truth right then seemed like the bigger sin.

Her chest rose and fell fast. Then slow. Fast. Then slow. Shallow, then shallower. The breaths grew further and further apart, each one so solitary, it seemed as if it would be the last—each new straggling gasp for air a surprise. I counted between each rise and fall of her chest, thirty seconds, forty, one minute, then two . . .

My mouth felt desert dry. I tried to lick my lips but my tongue stuck to the roof of my mouth. I opened my eyes, unsurprised to find fluorescent lights beaming down on me. A brunette dressed in navy scrubs hung a bag of fluid on a pole next to my hospital bed, then glanced at me and gasped. I doubt she could have looked more surprised if I'd strolled out of the morgue with a toe tag still attached. She hurried into the hall and soon returned, followed by my father.

"Thank God," he said as he made his way to my side. Dark bags hung under his eyes.

I pushed myself up and winced at the IV catheter poking the bend of my arm.

He motioned to me. "Jenny, lie back down."

I couldn't stand the thought of any man, anyone, telling me what to do, how to live, and especially how to die. I would not spend my last days like my mother, no matter how uncomfortable it made him or anyone else.

I draped my legs over the side of the bed.

His eyes widened in horror. "Please, Jenny. You're d—"

"Dying? Yes, I'm well aware."

His Adam's apple rose and fell as he swallowed. "I was going to say *dehydrated*."

"Oh," I mumbled, feeling like an idiot. "Is that why I passed out?"

"Probably, though Ted thinks it was shock."

Memories filled me with dread. "He wants Isabella."

My father's brow furrowed, making the fine lines on his forehead turn into full-fledged wrinkles. "Ted?"

I almost laughed. "Now there's a scary thought. He'd slap a bill down next to her bowl of morning Cheerios and tell her gratuities not included."

He smiled wearily.

A pink plastic cup filled with ice chips sat on my bedside table. I drank the melted water in the bottom. Nothing had ever tasted so good. "No, David. He's suing for custody."

My father sat beside me, making the bed sink under his weight. His gray eyes were veined with red. I waited for him to say something about David being unfit for parenting or some other Preston-related insult, but he said nothing.

"Who throws a terrified child into a pool?" I demanded. "What kind of father would he make?"

"I'm not arguing with you." He took the cup from my hand. "Jenny, please lie back down."

I nodded to the bag of fluids flowing into my arm. "How many of these have I gotten so far?"

He squinted at it. "I've seen them change at least three. Of course I left a couple of times to check on Bella and your grandma, so it may have been more."

Isabella. She'd already seen more than I'd intended, and the worst was yet to come. I wanted to hold her so badly. "How's she doing?"

"Bella? She's scared, but we reassured her you'd be home soon."

Of course she was scared. She'd never so much as seen me with the sniffles. Now here I was, passing out and spending hours in bed, incoherent from fever. I couldn't even begin to imagine what must be going on in that little mind of hers. Things were going to get much worse before it was over. I needed to do a better job of sheltering her from my illness, though I had no idea how.

I motioned to the IV catheter in my arm. "They pull the needle out of these things after they put them in, right?"

He answered slowly. "Yeah, I watched them put it in."

I pinched a corner of the clear, filmy dressing covering the site and before he could protest, yanked, pulling it off and the tiny plastic tube out of my skin. His mouth dropped open, and he was actually stunned silent for a moment. A drop of blood beaded on the bend of my arm where the tube had been. Liquid meant to flow into me now leaked onto the floor, forming a small puddle.

I signed myself out of the hospital against medical advice, and within the hour, I was kissing Bella's cheek and enduring another familiar round of cold stares from my father.

CHAPTER EIGHTEEN

SOUTHERN TOWNS ARE generally known for their quaintness and hospitality, particularly small Southern towns. Tullytown was all of those, with its rolling pastures, dogwood-lined Main Street, and giant sign reading, "Home of the world's finest sweet potato pie. Come and getcha some!" But to the residents who lived here, what really set us apart wasn't our friendly smiles or country colloquialisms. It was the unique ability to spread gossip faster than warm apple butter.

So it was no great shock to see David's car pull into my driveway less than thirty minutes after I'd gotten home from the hospital. I believed my father when he said he hadn't told Ted about my diagnosis. Nonetheless, David had managed to find out. Whether Dr. Preston had read my chart, someone had overheard nurses talking, or something else entirely had happened really didn't matter. The damage had been done.

At the kitchen table, Isabella played Go Fish with Mama Peg while I slipped out the front door. Humidity better suited for a steam room stole my breath—that and David Preston standing close enough for me to smell the spearmint on his breath.

Sadness glinted in his eyes. "Why didn't you tell me?"

I studied him, trying to decipher whether he was really grieving the news or just putting on a convincing show. I came to no conclusion. "What does it matter?"

He gathered up my limp hand. "So it's true?"

It was pointless to answer. He probably had more information on my diagnosis than I did. I slipped my fingers from his grasp.

He studied me a moment. "I'm sorry."

When his hand cupped my cheek, my weak emotional barrier cracked and affections not buried nearly deep enough began to seep out. My breath quickened and I leaned into his touch . . . until I remembered Lindsey. I stepped back. "What do you want, David?"

"You know what I want."

"Why would you try to take her from me?"

He looked at me questioningly as if he honestly didn't know what I was talking about.

With his flagrant attempt to deceive me, anger instantly

sealed the breach in my wall. "Ted told me you're filing for custody."

He snorted in disgust. "Can't live in Talkytown without the world knowing your every move."

I shook my head at him . . . and at myself for almost believing that he actually cared. "You're a piece of work."

"What choice are you giving me?"

We stood silent before one another, David staring at me, while I stared at a bowing dandelion in the yard. If it weren't for the tapping of a woodpecker in the distance, the silence would have been deafening.

"If anyone should be mad, it's me," David finally said. "When were you going to tell me that you were dying? before or after Isabella showed up on my doorstep with her suitcases?"

I peered at him. "She won't be showing up on your doorstep."

"You need me to raise her."

"No, David, I don't. I don't need you to do anything."

"You're not putting my child into some kind of foster care."

"Mama Peg and my dad are going to raise her."

His mouth gaped and he turned toward the front door as if wanting to ask it, *Can you believe her?* He turned back to me. "Your grandmother probably has less time than you do."

"My father should be around to see her to adulthood."

His cheeks and neck mottled. "She's my child. *My* child!"

My gaze shot to the window. "Keep your voice down. She's inside."

His fists were balled at his sides, his lips pressed so tightly that they disappeared. He glared at me, all signs of fury barely contained. I wondered if Lindsey ever made him this angry or if I alone had that effect. The thought gave me a sense of power over him that I'd never had when we were dating.

"I *will* be raising her after you're gone," he said.

David never had learned to come at me from the side where I could be safely approached. If he had broken down and told me he loved her, or that he was sorry for hurting me, or that being a father scared the daylights out of him, or anything that made him vulnerable—human, like me—I would have softened and things could have been amicable between us. Instead, he charged at me head-on, declaring that this was a battle only one of us could win.

"I'm her father. I have rights."

"You're nothing more than a sperm donor."

"You made me that."

"You threw a child who had almost drowned into a pool."

He yanked at the knot of his silk tie. "This again? I said I was sorry. How many times do I have to say it? I'm sorry, Jenny. I'm sorry. I'm sorry. I'm so stinking sorry!"

"You never said you were sorry, but you certainly are."

His eyes narrowed. "You haven't changed a bit."

I knew I shouldn't have said what I had but figured if I apologized, he'd just throw my line back at me. I studied the polish chipping off my big toe.

With his index finger, David pushed my chin up so I'd have to look him in the eye. "I'm not the reason she's terrified of water. If that's anyone's fault, it's yours. She was under your care, not mine, when she nearly drowned. And it's your fault I wasn't around for her. She's mine and I *will* get her."

I smacked his hand away from my face. "She's not a possession. That little girl may look like you, but she's all me. If you hate me, you might hate her. I can't die without knowing that she'll be okay. Without knowing if everything she does makes you as mad as I do. Not knowing if you're going to get sick of her one day like you did me."

Despite my anger, despite wanting to be strong and not give him the satisfaction of seeing me upset yet again, tears came.

His expression softened and he placed his hand on my wet cheek. "Jenny, I don't hate you and I didn't get sick of you. We just weren't right for each other. Lindsey and I—"

I turned from his touch. "You're no father, David."

His expression hardened once again. "Unfortunately, I am."

Unfortunately?

His eyes grew wide. "I didn't mean it that way."

I glared at him.

"Why does everything with you have to be so dramatic?" He looked over my shoulder, eyeing the front door. "I want to see her."

I stepped to the side, blocking his entrance. "We can discuss visitation later."

"Visitation?" He laughed. "Oh, I'm getting more than just visitation. She's my daughter as much as she is yours."

"No," I said. "Not as much."

"My dad says you'll be lucky to make it through the summer. She needs parents. Lindsey wants to be a mother. I want to know my daughter. What's the problem? I'll let her stay with you until you're gone, but we need to start transitioning her to a life with Lindsey and me."

My daughter having a life without me was something I'd begun to come to terms with, but the thought of her calling another woman *Mommy* made my jealousy over David dim in its glaring light. But my resistance to letting them have her wasn't due to jealousy. It really wasn't. It was simply wanting the best for her. "You can have visitation, but she's going to be raised by my family. My mind's made up."

He grabbed my arm. I tried to pull away, but his fingers only tightened. "You unmake it, Genevieve. I'm trying to be fair, but if you want to play hardball, you know I'll win. I always do."

My cheeks grew hot enough to fry bacon. "She's not a trophy. She's my daughter."

"Save your platitudes. You either start making me out to be the good guy in her eyes and let Lindsey and me start keeping her some so it's not such a shock when you die, or I'll force you to do it. You know that my dad and Judge Hendrickson practically shared a crib. That's who'd get the case, you know. Force my hand and you'll lose her now."

"You wouldn't." Even as I said it, I knew that he would.

"Lindsey and I will be by to pick her up tomorrow at nine. You have her ready, Jenny, or so help me—"

"Don't you threaten me."

"It's a threat I intend to make good on."

"Get off my porch."

"Nine o'clock, Lucas. You have her ready."

CHAPTER NINETEEN

SOFT RAYS OF moonlight ignited the mist rising above Lucas Lake, making it appear enchanted. Standing on the dock in my bare feet, I pressed my toes against the smooth, timeworn wood and gazed out over the water. A warm breeze combed through the hair draped over my shoulders and caused my skirt to flutter against my ankles. From a distance I must have looked surreal standing there—like a fairy-tale maiden waiting for her lover to return from some ill-fated quest . . . and like her, I felt completely lost and alone.

I wondered whether—if I prayed hard enough, hoped intensely enough—maybe, just maybe, Jesus might walk on water once again. As the full moon cast a perfect path of gold over the lake, I could almost imagine Him moving along it toward me, arms outstretched—ready to lead me far, far away from the worries of tomorrow. Then it dawned on me that someday soon, He really would.

I looked over my shoulder at the house and thought I glimpsed Isabella's bedroom curtain twitching. The longer I stared at it though, the more convinced I became that it was just my imagination. As I turned back, I noticed how silent the night stood. The uncanny quiet made the squeal of the back door opening sound like an ax crashing through tranquility. I did not turn to see whose company I would soon be in. Maybe if I ignored whoever it was, I'd be left alone to sort out the labyrinth of emotions and questions I was lost within.

David would be at my doorstep tomorrow morning, and still I couldn't decide whether I should let Bella go with him or risk a court battle. If I gave in, was it out of worry that I'd lose my daughter completely? I couldn't let fear be the motivator. Couldn't let it cloud my mind—not with so much at stake. But if I refused to let her go, was it because I honestly thought he would hurt her? Or was it, as Mama Peg suggested, my way of getting even with him for rejecting me? I didn't think so, but doubts still lingered.

I yearned to do what was right. I wanted that so much. The decisions I made now would be written in ink, not pencil. If I made the wrong decision and David turned out to be as fickle with my little girl as he had been with me—loving her one moment, indifferent the next—I wouldn't be around to set things right.

Ignoring errant strands of hair that tickled my cheeks and neck, I closed my eyes, letting the warm air stroke my face . . . and prayed. I prayed for clarity. I prayed for grace. Mostly, I prayed that I would make the right decision for my daughter, regardless of what it would cost me.

Strong hands grasped my waist, startling me. I turned and found myself nose to nose with Craig. A hint of the red wine he had sipped over dinner still lingered on his breath. I waited for him to say something, but he simply kept his hands planted on my sides as though we were getting ready to share a dance. "You look like an angel in this light."

I gently pulled away from him and felt myself blush. "Thanks."

He took my hand and lifted it to his face, brushing my palm against the scruff on his cheek. His eyes riveted on me, he leaned into my touch. It was at that moment it really hit me just how intensely Craig had begun to feel for me. The depth of emotion etched on his face caught me completely off guard. I had no more clue what to do with Craig than what to do about David.

I withdrew my hand, walked to the edge of the dock, and sat. Pushing myself forward until my toes dipped below the surface of the tepid water, I half hoped he'd sit next to me and half hoped he'd go back in and leave me to my misery.

His arm brushed my elbow as he sat beside me. He curled his fingers around mine and laid our conjoined hands on his leg. I did nothing to encourage or resist. I simply stared at the lake.

A breeze rippled the surface, dispersing my golden road.

Replacing it were tiny flickers of moonlight, which resembled hundreds of fireflies dancing near the water's edge.

Craig turned to me. "What are you thinking about?"

I told him.

He followed my line of vision. "You've got quite an imagination."

I took the opportunity to study him while he looked away. His hair appeared a pleasant reddish blond under the light of the orange moon, his expression contemplative. "What are *you* thinking?" I asked.

He looked down as though he'd been exposed. After a few seconds he glanced up at me. "Honestly?"

Regretting the question, I nodded.

"About when to try and kiss you."

I tried to decide how best to respond. "Craig, I—"

He barricaded the rest of my sentence against his lips. Just for a moment I tasted the possibilities that would exist if I weren't dying. Feeling warm and chilled at the same time, I yanked back.

He grinned at me like a child.

My heart pounded. "Don't do that again."

His smile remained. "Oh, I'm going to."

Before I could object, he made good on his promise. The moment he leaned in for the kiss, I turned, giving him a mouthful of hair.

He grunted. "You played the hard-to-get thing already, Jenny. This is the part of the story where the guy should get the girl."

I slipped my hand from his and kicked at the water. "What am I going to do?"

"First, you're going to let me kiss you."

I gave him my best I'm-in-no-mood-to-play look. "About David. He's coming tomorrow to pick her up."

He studied me. "And this is bad?"

"He's no father."

I didn't have to see the look on his face to know it was one of disapproval. His tone made his feelings perfectly clear. "Because of the pool?"

My face grew warm. "Yes, because of the pool."

"Easy, I'm just asking."

"Did I sound upset?"

"Every time someone mentions David, you sound upset."

I dipped my toes in the water, watching them poke up and disappear again. After what I thought was an adequate silent intermission, I changed the subject. "So how's business?"

"Wow. That had to be the worst segue ever. If you were an anchorwoman, you'd be so fired."

I drew my feet out of the water and wrapped my arms around my bent knees. The breeze died, causing the surface of the lake to become as smooth as a mirror. My path of gold was back, leading right to where Craig and I sat. Could it be an omen from God? If so, I failed to comprehend the significance.

Craig pushed his shoulder playfully into mine. "Okay, you want a change of subject, you got it. Business is great. I probably need to hire another guy or two to keep up."

I tried to sound enthusiastic. "That's great."

"Yeah, but I'll tell you, the responsibility of having nearly a dozen guys under me kind of freaks me out." He unfastened his sandal strap. The rip of Velcro must have sent frogs diving because a half-dozen plops followed. He slipped his sandals off and lowered his feet into the water. "Knowing that these guys are depending on me for their bread and butter is overwhelming. More than half of them are married with kids. If I mess up, they're out of jobs. No job, no food, you know?"

I put my feet back into the lake and nodded.

Craig drifted ever closer to me until our hips touched. He slid his shin under my calf and rubbed his foot against mine. Feeling exceedingly self-conscious, I studied the design on my T-shirt.

"I guess being a mom, you know all about responsibility."

Did I ever.

His big toe traced mine. "You ever mess up really bad with Bella?"

I thought about it a moment. "Oh yeah."

He gave me a half smile encouraging me to tell.

"Okay, but you're not allowed to think I'm horrible."

He grinned. "Too late."

"Okay, when Bella was an infant, she had colic. She screamed nonstop for hours every night. I had a baby swing that was too big for her, but it was the only thing that would quiet her. The straps were way too long. She would fall sideways if I didn't prop her up real good with rolled-up blankets. Anyway, besides the swing, I thought maybe we'd both get some relief if I Ferberized her."

Craig looked lost.

"You know, not pick her up right away when she cried. You're supposed to wait five minutes before going to comfort the crying child, then ten, and so on until they sleep through the night kinda thing."

"That sounds harsh."

I shrugged. "You'd think differently if you were the one listening to it. Anyway, I was desperate. I'd have dipped myself in gold paint and mimed a lullaby for her if I thought it would have helped."

Craig chuckled.

"So," I continued, "she starts crying in her swing. I'm in the kitchen and decide I'm not going to get her right away this time. And so I watch the clock, listening to her scream her head off for the longest five minutes of my life. Finally I go into the living room, and . . ." I paused as my stomach clenched and shame filled me. "She had slipped down under the tray. The straps had caught under her armpits and she was being swung from the outside of the swing."

Craig let out a bray of laughter, but I did not.

He looked at me. "Oh, c'mon. That's funny."

I understood how he found humor in it, but I still couldn't. "The strap could have just as easily caught her throat," I said. "I could have killed my daughter just like that."

He stopped laughing and laid his arm across my shoulder. This time I leaned in and laid my head against him, taking in his warmth and familiar smell.

"Jenny, we all make mistakes. Not a single one of us is perfect."

I noticed then that, though more muted than normal, the lake's symphony was indeed playing. The frogs' baritone voices spoke to each other, the crickets softly chirped, and I thought I could even hear the cattails whistling in a distant breeze. I wondered if it had been there all along and maybe my anxiety had managed to drown it out.

"What time do you have to get Bella ready?" he asked.

I turned to him in surprise. "I didn't say she was going."

He gave me a perplexed look. "Why wouldn't she?"

I realized then what had taken place. He'd managed to get me to admit I was no better a parent than David. I wondered if it was by design and if there was any way to undo the conclusion now hanging in the air as blatantly as the moon. It was obvious that I could no longer use the pool incident to justify myself. Craig's expression told me I had come to the conclusion he had wanted me to.

"Clever boy," I said without humor.

"Clever man," he responded with a wink.

"I hate you."

"No, you don't. You love me."

"*Love's* a little strong."

Wriggling his eyebrows, he said, "It's a lotta strong."

He leaned into me again. I felt his breath on my lips as he stared at me for the longest time. Hazel eyes hypnotized me as the anticipation of our kiss sent an unexpected thrill through me. The longer we paused, the more intense my desire grew.

Finally I could stand it no more. I parted my lips and met his. A wave of longing washed over me so strong it stole my breath.

His lips made their way from my mouth to my throat. I leaned my head back, reveling in his attentions. He devoured me and I wanted him to. I wanted to wrap myself around him. To be as close as humanly possible. I wanted him and it was obvious by the passion in his kiss that he wanted me too.

As his hand softly traced my neck, I realized that I had faced a moment just like this one once before—and just like then, I had the choice to either succumb to temptation or flee. Without giving myself a chance to justify my weakness, I pushed him away and bolted up.

The bewilderment and disappointment on his face was unmistakable. "Jenny, stop running from me."

I hugged myself. "I have to run. You should be running too."

He grabbed my hand. "Why don't you want me?"

I tried to smile but couldn't. "I do want you. Wow, do I want you."

"I don't understand."

"My flesh is weak. I'm so very weak, Craig."

He stood and cupped my cheek. "Marry me."

My breath caught. "What?"

"It's not a sin if we're married."

A strange combination of alarm and amusement came over me. "I'm not going to marry you just so we can—"

"It's not just for that. I'm falling in love with you, Jenny."

His words hung in the air for an uncomfortably long time while I tried to regain my senses. "I like you a whole lot, but—"

"I'll take it." He sank to one knee and reached for my hand.

This was too much. My brain was already overloaded with everything else. I simply didn't have room for another issue. I said as gently as I could, "This isn't going to happen."

Undaunted, he continued as if I hadn't already refused. "Genevieve Lucas—"

"I'm not marrying you."

With a look of dejection, he stood. "What are you afraid of, divorce? If we can't keep it together for the time you have left, we've got serious issues."

"Oh, we have serious issues all right," I said.

He sat down and put his feet back in the water. "Well, I tried. There are worse places to die than in my arms, you know."

Relieved by his good-humored tone, I laughed. "On the toilet, for one."

He reached up and took my hand, encouraging me to sit again. "Yeah, that would be worse, but just slightly. Behind the wheel would be a worse place too. Think of all those pedestrians and other motorists, not to mention your passengers."

Biting back tears I could never let him see, I took my place next to him and rested my head against his shoulder.

Again he put his strong arm around me. "Are you letting Bella go with her daddy tomorrow morning?"

I sighed. "I guess it's the right thing to do."

"It is," he said. "I really think so."

I'm not sure how long Craig and I sat there or when we made the ill-fated decision to lie down and close our eyes. I only know that the next morning it felt muggy and uncomfortable. Mosquitoes had made me their breakfast and the hard wood of the dock pressed against my side. Craig's chest rose and fell under the weight of my head.

I squinted, disoriented when I saw not my ceiling fan, but the sun glaring back at me. I heard two quick blares of a car horn. By the time I registered where I was and what the sound meant, it was too late. David's car was peeling out of the driveway.

CHAPTER TWENTY

WHEN I CALLED David's house to explain, I was met with an arctic "I'm done playing with you," followed by the receiver slamming in my ear. My hand trembled as I set the phone back in its cradle and leaned against the kitchen counter.

Craig watched with a pensive expression, his hair bending to the left like grass in the wind. His shirt lay half-tucked in and half out. A five-o'clock shadow darkened his chin and cheeks. "He'll get over it once he realizes you overslept."

I ran my tongue over gritty, unbrushed teeth. "I don't care if he does." My words rang false even to me. Of course I cared. My daughter's future was at stake. "This just proves why he shouldn't be a father."

Craig opened the fridge and pulled out a carton of Tropicana. He gave it a quick shake, then set it on the counter next to an empty glass. "Jenny, remember the conclusion you came to last night. Nothing's changed."

But it had. I'd been reminded of the Preston family's cold, unyielding nature. This anxiety eating a hole in my stomach was not a feeling I wanted Isabella to live with for the next twelve years. "Let us have our day in court if that's what he wants. I doubt he'll win anyway. Friend of the family or not, no judge is going to take a child away from a dying mother." I hoped to God I was right as I looked out the window and watched Mama Peg and Isabella taking turns smelling a stalk of lavender.

Craig glanced at the wall clock. "I can stay if you need—"

"Go," I said. "I've made you late enough."

He touched his forehead to mine. "For the record, that was the best night of my life. It would have been even better if you'd accepted my proposal."

Feeling an overpowering urge to kiss him, I picked up the carton of orange juice, filled the glass, and handed it to him.

He swallowed it down and set the glass in the sink. "Anything I can do for you before I go?"

"Say a prayer."

"Already have."

Lying on the couch, I transferred my worries about Isabella's future and my own onto the pages of my journal. The squeal of the front door opening was echoed by my daughter's familiar shriek. With a basket overflowing with garden flowers swinging from her pudgy arm, Isabella ran to me, leaving a trail of petals and leaves. Rolling her oxygen tank behind her, Mama Peg followed, stopping every few feet to pick up debris.

"Look, Mommy!" Bella thrust her basket onto my belly. I set my journal on the coffee table and examined her bounty. An orange flower with petals outlined in lemon rested on top. I picked it out and held it before her. "This is called a—"

"Marigold," she blurted.

"Wow, little miss smarty-pants."

"Mama Pig already told me."

My grandmother gave Isabella a strange look as she went into a coughing fit.

"*Who* told you?" I asked just to hear her say it again.

She spoke slow and loud as though I were old and deaf. "Ma-ma Pig."

I gave my grandmother a smug grin.

Mama Peg furrowed her bushy brows at my daughter. "For the last time, it's not *pig*; it's *Peg*." She turned around and motioned to her polyester-clad bottom. "Do you see a curly pink tail here?" Her milky eyes moved from Isabella to me.

I chuckled. "I don't see a tail, but your panties do appear to be in a bunch."

Mama Peg turned back around. "Keep it up and I'll sic Sweet Pea on both of you."

"You're the one who wouldn't let her call you Cowpa. You

brought this on yourself, pork chop." I tucked the flower behind Isabella's ear, placed a hand on each of her shoulders, and made a show of admiring her. "There. Now you look just like a fairy princess."

Her eyes widened as she looked to Mama Peg for affirmation. My grandmother nodded.

A grin spread across Isabella's lips. "I wanna see!"

My heart swelled with love for her. "You've got a mirror on your dresser."

After a half second of consideration, she tore up the stairs.

Mama Peg pointed to the afghan across my legs. "It's at least eighty degrees. You can't be cold."

I fingered the multicolored crocheted yarn, feeling unreasonable shame. "I am."

She waved her hand as though she could shoo my chill away. "Well, no wonder. You don't have an ounce of insulation on them skin and bones of yours. Why don't I make us some eggs?"

My stomach turned. "I already had a can of Ensure."

She adjusted the tubing around her ears. "You can't live on that."

Tired of having this conversation over and over with her, my father, and Craig, I sighed loud enough to get my point across.

She wheeled her tank toward the kitchen. "Well, at least eat a banana."

I mentally test-drove the fruit on my lips and found it

didn't make me want to hurl. "I'll try." I pushed back the blanket and, feeling less than enthusiastic, followed her.

She pulled an unblemished banana from the wire basket and handed it to me. "You want some coffee with that?"

I worked the peel. "I don't think I could keep it down."

She cradled my cheek with her soft, quivering hand. "Jenny, it's my job to fuss over you since your mom isn't here to do it, but only you know what you need. It's your job to stand up for it."

She withdrew and hit the Start button on the coffeemaker. Steaming brown liquid trickled out, along with the aroma I used to love and now could barely tolerate.

My eyes narrowed at her. "Is that decaf?"

She thrust her chin up defiantly. "Depends."

"On what?"

"On whether or not you're going to give me a hard time if it isn't."

"Naughty girl."

"Don't tell Warden."

"Hey, it's my job to ask since your mother isn't here to do it, but only you know what you need."

A small bulge moved under her closed lips as she ran her tongue across her teeth. "Someone's full of herself today." After a few minutes, she pulled the glass pot out and the brown stream stopped flowing. Glass clinked against ceramic as she poured herself a cup.

Mug in hand, she turned around, made her way to the table, and sat beside me. "It's nice to see your smile again."

She dipped her spoon in the sugar bowl and withdrew a heap. "I heard David's infamous two-horn beep this morning while you and Romeo were asleep on the dock."

I nodded but said nothing.

She stirred her coffee. "He peeled wheels out of the driveway."

"I know."

"You should also know that he's not going to let this go. You sure you don't want to reconsider letting him raise her?"

I broke off a piece of banana and popped it into my mouth. "I'm not sure about anything."

"I can't say I think you're making the right decision."

I broke off another piece. "I'm not asking."

Her eyes didn't leave me as she sipped from her cup. "Fair enough."

We sat in silence a moment, I finishing my banana and she sipping on java. Finally she asked, "What happened with you and Craig out there, or don't I want to know?"

A smile besieged my lips. "He proposed."

She peered up from her coffee.

"Why don't you look surprised?"

She set her mug down on a closed book of crossword puzzles. "That boy's clearly in love with you. Too bad he didn't realize it a few years ago."

"It wouldn't have mattered anyway," I said.

Her face scrunched up in obvious disgust. "Of course not. You were so blinded in love by Horny Horn Blower, you couldn't see the forest for the trees."

"Horny Horn Blower?"

Her laugh, even mixed with hacks, was a melody to my ears. Always had been.

"So what did you say?"

I reached across the table and cradled her warm cup in my hands. "I said no."

"Why?"

"It wouldn't be fair to make him a widower, for one."

She opened her mouth to say something, but I kept on. "Besides, I like him a lot, but love takes time, which of course I don't have." I let go of the mug. "And anyway, look at all the confusion over Bella's custody. If I married him, he might be able to throw his hat in the ring. The waters are murky enough." I paused. "Why are you looking at me like that?"

"I've never seen your face turn the same shade as a pomegranate before, that's all."

I had nothing to say in my defense, so I simply oinked at her.

She shook her head and pried her cup from the flimsy book cover. It left behind a ring of brown.

"What are you going to do today?" I asked.

She looked out the window. "I thought I'd teach my great-granddaughter about roses."

I remembered her leading me through the same garden decades earlier, explaining the difference between a hybrid tea rose and a polyantha. The thought of Isabella getting the same loving lecture brought me unspeakable joy. "Thanks."

She laid her hand on mine and gave it a gentle squeeze. "My pleasure, kiddo. What about you?"

"I'm going to visit Mom."

She took her hand back and cradled her cup. "I hate to be the bearer of bad news . . ."

"Very funny," I said. "Will you be okay with Bella for a while?"

"Sure, but do you think she might like to go and see her grandmother's grave?"

My chill returned. "I'm not ready to talk to her about death."

"Jenny, you're going to need to soon."

I pushed up from my chair. "I will, just not today."

CHAPTER TWENTY-ONE

Arlington Cemetery was located at the end of a wide road lined with magnolia trees. My car tires crunched over their giant seedpods as I slowed to a stop and parked to the right of the colossal iron gate.

I'd told Mama Peg that I was here to visit my mother's grave. That was the truth, but not the whole truth. The main purpose was really to visit my own. I didn't know if it was normal to want to see where my body would ultimately rest, but normal or not, I was curious to lay eyes on the plot I'd purchased for myself.

Even if the visit was a bit morbid, it did force me to get outside, which I figured wasn't a bad thing. Fresh air might

lift my spirits and give me a shot of the energy I desperately needed. Plus, I reasoned, sunshine was supposed to be
a natural antidepressant. Even if it didn't make me feel any
happier, it would leave some healthy color on my cheeks,
which might at least lift my family's spirits.

I shut the car door and turned around. It seemed I was
spending more time these days trying to appear well than
actually feeling that way. I had anticipated eventually having
to mask the severity of my illness for Isabella's sake, but never
did I dream I'd be faking it this early on for my grandmother's
and father's benefit. I wondered how often my mother had
done the same.

I set out down the snaking asphalt road. As I wound
about various graves, I squinted against the glare of sunlight, trying to make out the dates on the tombstones, some
as old as the town itself. It occurred to me for the first
time that I would soon be in the presence of Christians
who had lived throughout the ages. My gaze fell on a row
of old, white headstones lined up like dominoes. Within
months, I could be sipping tea with Queen Esther and
Mary Magdalene while one of these Confederate soldiers
recounted his life story to us.

I smiled before remembering what my mother had to
endure before reaching heaven. Like her, I would first have
to suffer physical death. Heaviness settled over me as notions
of how it would feel to have my soul ripped from my body
whirled through my imagination like a tornado, making my
heart beat faster and my head swim.

Closing my eyes, I succeeded in shutting out the death surrounding me. After a moment, I was able to divert my thoughts back to why I had come. I gazed across grassy knolls in the direction of my mother's grave. The trek there would give me a chance to clear my head and consider the many possibilities of stone markers, urns, and inscriptions I had to choose from.

I wanted my epitaph to say something profound, different—but not too different. Something that would make people who read it know that I had loved and had been loved. Something to indicate I had been a real person with hopes and dreams. Most importantly, something to point to the God in whose hands my soul would ultimately rest.

I wanted beautiful, poetic words, but a writer I was not. Mama Peg could come up with something exceptional if I set her to the task. I hadn't told her yet that I had bought myself a spot as close to Mom's as possible, but still not as close as I would have liked.

As I trudged along, I came upon something I'd never noticed before—a family plot guarded by a miniature replica of the larger fence surrounding the perimeter of the cemetery. It was an odd sight, this graveyard within a graveyard, and I stopped to consider it.

Countless winters had taken their toll on the black metal fence, but the peeling, weathered surface only added to its mystery and charm. Within these iron slats lay four tiny graves, each marked by a stone angel.

Elizabeth Munroe, 1876–1877
Jonathan Munroe, 1878–1880
Julia Munroe, 1884–1884
Caroline Munroe, 1881–1885

With a heavy heart I read the dates again and again, trying to absorb the magnitude of this family's loss.

As I pushed open the small gate, remnants of spiderwebs tickled my fingertips. The hinges screeched in protest at their thrust from hibernation, while flecks of rust sprinkled the ground. Part of me wanted to leave this morbid parcel and erase the misery contained here from my memory, but something drew me forward.

I traced the grooves of each child's engraved name, grieving as if I'd known them. I wondered what could have caused such catastrophic loss within one family. A genetic disease for which we'd since found the cure? Surely it wasn't related to financial hardship. Their parents obviously had money to afford such elaborate markers.

The cherub statues watching over each small grave were more than mere tributes. They were masterpieces of art. One blew an intricate horn, announcing the child's arrival to heaven. Another raised his chubby arms as though releasing his charge's soul. The third held a dove above his curly head, encouraging it to take flight, and the last angel simply clasped his hands together in mournful prayer.

In the center of the four plots lay a carved angel collapsed upon the ground. Her stone arms lay draped over a headstone, her face scrunched and sobbing in utter defeat. Though the artwork was amazing, the sight itself was wretched. I moved in closer to read the words engraved upon the grave of Betsy Anne Munroe, 1858–1902.

Here lies the mother of four deceased children. No woman has known as much misery. Her existence was filled with nothing but heartache. Her husband died in a foreign land. Four of her six children were taken from her before their time. Death was the only mercy God ever showed her.

I stood dumbfounded. I'd never read such a dark epitaph. Surely there had to have been some joy in this woman's life. God was not so cruel. What of her two remaining children? Besides their love, she must have experienced the beauty of autumn, the splendor of a sunset, or the sweetness of a kiss. I felt the clutch of her depression clawing for me and I fled. When the latch of the gate clicked shut, relief filled me.

A cloud slid in to dull the sun while fatigue crept back into my bones. If I hadn't been so close to my intended destination, I might have abandoned my mission and returned home to bed . . . but just ahead I spotted my mother's grave.

I knelt on the grass, ignoring the lumpy ground pressing into my bare knees. Though some found it sacrilegious to set foot on a grave, let alone sit atop it, to me it was as close to my mother's lap as I'd get on this side of heaven.

Half a dozen white roses, no more than a few days old,

rested in a cement urn set against her headstone. My father, who'd seldom given her flowers when she was alive, made sure she had a steady supply in death. It was surreal to think he might do the same for me.

I fingered a blade of grass and peeked around to make sure I was alone. "Hey, Mom." I felt silly speaking to her when I knew she wasn't there. Bones did not hear. I turned my face toward the sky. "I'm going to be with you soon." A smile crept across my lips as I really digested that these were more than mere words. Soon I would hold her hand. Feel her kisses. Did spirits hold hands? Of course they did. What kind of heaven would it be without affection?

I could hardly wait to tell her about Isabella and all the stuff I'd sworn she was wrong about growing up but found to be right once I became a mother myself. I don't know how long I knelt there, daydreaming about our reunion, but after a while my neck began to ache. I looked back down to her headstone.

Here lie the remains of Audra Ann Lucas, beloved
wife, mother, daughter, friend. Do not mourn her,
for she lives.

As if I hadn't seen these words a thousand times, I stared, amazed at the profoundness of them. I closed my eyes, letting sun rays soak into my anemic flesh. They felt as nourishing to my soul as Isabella's kisses or Mama Peg's touch. The simple joy of breathing fresh air, feeling the sun, and being among the green God created filled me with amazement. I scanned the trees with their heavy limbs, the grass cushion under me, and the wisps of white sailing on a sea of blue above. The simple grandeur of it all took my breath away.

Placing a hand over my heart, I marveled at such beauty— so familiar and yet it felt new. I'd had all this at my disposal my entire life, but I'd never really appreciated it. I realized then that it was only the tip of the iceberg of what I'd been taking for granted.

The thought saddened me, but I figured I could spend my time either regretting the past or enjoying the present, but not both. I opted for the here and now. Though there were times that fear of the unknown crushed me with panic, at that very moment, surrounded by sunshine and warm thoughts, I found myself actually welcoming death.

I wished I could have bottled that rare feeling of peace so that when I found myself in the throes of depression or gasping for one last breath, I could drink of it. There was nothing to fear, and yet so often I had . . . and knew I would again.

I stood and brushed flecks of dirt from my knees. Looking over my shoulder, I eyed an unmolested hill. My hill. The place where my body would lie. I would be the first to break the seal of that new ground, unless some unfortunate soul beat me to the finish line. I tried to remember the bearings of the plot I'd bought for myself.

Like a pirate searching for treasure, I stood in front of the pine tree landmark and walked ten paces to the right.

I stopped on the spot that would be my final resting place. My breath caught as a feeling came over me, so foreign I could no more assign words to it than describe the color of a smell. I was standing on my own grave!

I wasn't sure why, but I felt a sudden compulsion to lie down. With a brief scan of the area for witnesses, I caught only a blur of color from a distant pedestrian not close enough to worry about. I laid myself down in the direction I assumed my body would be buried, ignoring twigs and uneven earth jutting into my back.

Grass tickled my cheek as I turned my face to the right and considered the smooth stone mausoleum standing there. I looked to my left at the tree, watching a squirrel scurry up it, disappearing into greenery. Then I looked to the sky because I figured that's how I'd be planted, facing upward, unless they dropped my casket when they lowered it and didn't bother to fix me. But I didn't guess that was likely. The bizarre thought made me laugh. *I'm lying on my own grave,* I thought, laughing like a lunatic. This made me laugh even harder.

So there I lay for a while, feeling strangely pleased about my purchase and my view. I wasn't far from my mother's grave, and though I had wished it was closer, I was now glad they weren't side by side like the misfortunate family.

I closed my eyes and covered them with my palms, trying to experience it in utter darkness, though under the direct sun, my eyelids still glowed with red. I heard the soft patter of footsteps and realized that I probably looked more than a little nuts lying there on the ground in a cemetery. Still,

I chose not to get up. Impending death has a way of making a person not care quite so much what others think.

A familiar smell passed by and I turned, trying to get a better whiff. Slowly I opened my eyes and nearly jumped out of my skin when I saw Craig bent over me. "Interesting spot you've chosen for a nap. Very gothic."

I jumped up and brushed grass from my legs. "Don't scare me like that! What are you doing here?"

The smile left his lips. "Mama Peg asked me to come. Jenny, David called. He's really doing it. He's asking for full custody."

If Craig hadn't embraced me then, I might have collapsed. His strong arms loaned me the strength I needed to stand. I leaned against his chest, listening to his heartbeat, until he at last pulled back.

"He won't get it," he said. "But you know, he probably is going to be awarded custody when you . . ." He looked down, then looked back up with a solemn expression. "This is yours, isn't it?"

I nodded. The reality of my condition seemed to hit him then because the color drained from his face.

This time it was my arms reaching out to him.

CHAPTER TWENTY-TWO

WE STOOD IN the wide, marbled vestibule of the largest and busiest law firm in all of Duncan County. David's attorney had asked us to come to see if we couldn't work out "this whole mess," as he called it, rather than leaving it to a judge who didn't know what was really what in our lives. As angry as I was with David, the thought of taking my chances with Judge Hendrickson didn't leave me feeling as confident as I would have liked, and so I'd agreed to at least listen to what they had to say.

Well-groomed men and women came and went as we waited to be called into the office. Hushed chatter whirled around us, intermingled with the clicks of heels and an occasional cough. Isabella's fingers wriggled restlessly in my grasp. My father sat by my side. With his charcoal suit, silver hair, and wire-rimmed glasses, my father still looked every bit the lawyer, but he would not be representing me today. He'd instead hired an up-and-coming hotshot his ex–law partner had recommended. A lawyer who apparently was quite popular, as he kept running into old friends. At that moment, he had left us to walk a pretty redhead to her car.

"Dad, thank—"

"Genevieve, there's nothing I wouldn't do for you." He checked his watch for the umpteenth time.

I might have argued that there'd been plenty he hadn't done for me. Instead I said, "I know you hate being here."

"Not as much as you do, I'm sure." He glanced at me, pity glinting in his eyes.

It was a look I'd come to hate almost as much as the cancer itself. When I turned away, my gaze fell on David and Lindsey, who occupied two chairs on the opposite side of the waiting room. He wore an expensive-looking three-piece suit and an expression that hinted he had better things to do with his time. In contrast, Lindsey appeared meek and mild with her hair pulled neatly back. Her pink dress was patterned with checks. Over it she wore a matching cardigan. Cashmere no doubt. Probably a gift from her doting husband.

When hatred filled me, so did shame.

Her doe eyes looked everywhere but in my direction. Her bony fingers clutched her husband's arm. I hated that she clung to David, *my* David, as though she were being thrown around in an angry sea and he alone could save her. Of course, I had done the same, but when our storm came, he simply pried my fingers off and swam for shore alone. It seemed I'd been treading water ever since.

My father gave his earlobe a rub. "Now, remember, we're just here to talk. See if we can't decide outside the courtroom what's best for Bella . . . which of course is staying with us. "

"I get it, Dad. Honest. What if they won't compromise?"

"Then a judge will decide."

My heart ached. "Judge Hendrickson?"

He didn't answer.

Isabella yanked my arm in an attempt to escape. I knew she wanted her father, but I just couldn't let her go. "Bella, knock it off."

She scowled as her hand went limp in my grasp. I addressed my father again. "I'd like to get this thing settled today. The last thing I want is for him to win custody after I die. She'll be traumatized enough."

Isabella jerked her head toward me and I realized what I'd done. I was thankful when she voiced no questions, though her expression made it clear she had them. The knots in my stomach tightened with the realization that I could no longer postpone our talk.

My father crossed, then uncrossed, his legs. "I'll be glad when this whole thing is over. If I never have to hear the name *Preston* again, it'll be too soon." The name dripped from his lips like venom.

Isabella's troubled expression moved off me onto him. It

dawned on me that she was 50 percent Preston and knew it. So when my father bad-mouthed them, he was—in her eyes—also putting her down.

I cleared my throat and gestured in her direction, hoping he'd catch my drift. Instead, he pulled a cough drop out of his jacket pocket and tossed it at me. Rolling my eyes at his pathetic sense of perception, I handed it back.

Down the hall, a door opened and a tired-looking man wandered out of it. Strands of white dragged from the tattered hem of his well-worn jeans. Lindsey turned to watch, giving me a view of the back of her head and the mother-of-pearl combs securing her simple braid.

Isabella tore her hand out of mine and pointed in her direction. "Hers is different!"

Lindsey and David turned toward us at the same instant as though the response had been choreographed.

Heat crept up my neck as I pushed her pointing finger down. "Not so loud. What's different?"

She patted the back of her head. "Mine's fat! Hers is skinny." She tore at her hair, disheveling the braid I'd fixed for her that morning. I grabbed her hands to stop her. My face broiled. With today's meeting throwing off our routine, I knew my normally sweet child might be having a hard time, but even I was caught off guard when she howled as though someone had struck her.

"Stop it," I whispered, squeezing her hands and wishing for a vortex to be sucked into. Of course she'd have to have a meltdown today of all days, right in front of them.

Her hair stuck out wildly as she shook her head like a lunatic. "I want to look like Lindsey! Fat braids are ugly. I look ugly! Ugleeeeeee . . ."

Frantic to quiet her, I pleaded, "Shh . . . I'll fix it. Just be quiet."

She stopped yelling, though the scowl on her face only deepened. I squatted behind her, clamping her narrow hips between my knees to keep her still and me steady. Combing through her hair with my fingers, I went to work. Lifting my arms felt more like lifting fifty-pound barbells as I tried to create the type of inwardly woven braid that Lindsey wore.

Ignoring my aching muscles, I gave it my best but just didn't have the skill to make it work or the energy to keep trying. With my last bit of strength, I fashioned the only type of braid I knew how—one identical to the one she had just yanked out.

My arms fell to my sides. "There," I said, trying to sound confident.

She reached behind her to feel, but I guided her hands back down. "Don't touch or you'll ruin it."

"Does it look like hers?" she asked.

I turned her around to face me and gave a weak smile. "It's beautiful like you."

When her lips tightened and eyes narrowed, I knew she'd called my bluff. Before I could react, she thrust her hands back and felt my failure.

Her face contorted. I braced myself for the inevitable tantrum, but just as she opened her mouth, Lindsey's skinny legs appeared before me. Feeling compromised in my squatting position, I stood.

"I'm sorry, Jenny. I couldn't help . . . I, um, wasn't eavesdropping or anything. . . ." She wrung her hands as she mangled an attempt to spit out whatever it was she was trying to say.

My father's expression hardened as he positioned himself between us. "Mrs. Preston, it is completely inappropriate for you to initiate dialogue with my—"

I sighed. "Dad, please."

He glared at me, paused, and stepped aside.

Lindsey gave Isabella a shy smile. "I could fix her hair like mine if you want me to."

Just like that, apparently all was forgiven because Isabella beamed at her. I wanted to say something horrible and scathing to Lindsey. Something that would make her slink back to David humiliated, but of course, my conscience wouldn't allow it. "Thanks, Lindsey, that's kind, but I'll take care of it. She's just tired because—"

"Oh, I don't need an explanation." She fingered the strand of pearls that lay against her collarbone. "I know how kids are."

I wasn't sure what it was in her words that flipped my switch—the presumption that Isabella was like all other children, or just raw jealousy—but on it went. "You might know how kids are, but you don't know how *Bella* is."

She blinked at me, looking not angry or hurt, but confused. For some reason that fueled my irritation. Why wouldn't she take the hint? I wasn't being cryptic about my desire for her to leave us alone.

I pointed across the hall. "I think David wants you."

She turned to look at her husband, who glowered his obvious disapproval.

Isabella batted her lashes at me. "Please, Mommy?"

My chest felt as though someone were sitting on it. "I told you I would fix it, and I will."

When Lindsey walked back to David, I once again knelt behind my daughter. I had no idea how I was going to accomplish something I'd already proven I couldn't do. It was crazy, and I knew it. I should've just let Lindsey fix her stupid braid. But in my mind the inability to do this equated with my inability to take care of my daughter and ensure her future. Lindsey had already proven she was more worthy of David's love. Now she was about to prove she was also more worthy of being my child's mother.

Isabella crossed her arms. "Why don't you want me to be pretty?"

Her question and the bitterness in her tone caught me off guard. "What? Why wouldn't I want you to be pretty? That's silly. I can do this. You'll see."

With everyone's eyes on me, I felt like I was performing onstage naked. I separated her hair into sections and tried to reverse my usual braiding process, though I doubted that would accomplish the desired result. My arms trembled and ached. Not only did the braid I was fashioning bear no resemblance to Lindsey's, it bore no resemblance to a braid. Hot tears of frustration leaked down my cheeks.

I covered my face, conceding defeat, and sobbed into my

hands. After a moment, I peeked through my fingers at my daughter.

"It's okay, Mommy. I like this braid. It's pretty."

Her troubled expression looked just like the one she had worn while crouched in the corner of my bedroom when I was racked with fever. I hated that.

She tilted her head and laid her soft palm on my cheek. "I don't need a skinny braid. Don't worry, Mommy; I won't go with Lindsey. Okay? Don't cry."

I willed my tears to stop falling and faked a smile, determined to do a better job of sheltering her innocence. "Bells, you should have a beautiful braid and you should be able to go say hello to your daddy." I lifted her small hand from my cheek and kissed it. "Go visit with them."

She hesitated, but I ushered her forward.

I felt like Scrooge standing next to the Ghost of Christmas Yet to Come as my father and I looked on. Isabella went right up to Lindsey and sat on her lap as if she'd known her all her life. And as though nothing had happened between them, she talked David's ear off while Lindsey plaited her hair with ease.

I sagged against the wall, paralyzed. The three of them had become a family despite my attempt to keep them apart. It was clear that they were already tattooed on each other's hearts and would remain so, regardless of whether David and Lindsey cared for her one weekend a month or every moment of every day.

I considered the contrast between the fear in her eyes a

moment ago and the carefree joy on her face now. A five-year-old shouldn't be forced to witness her mother's slow and painful decline. It had almost killed me to watch my mother's grueling last days and I'd been much older than Isabella. I couldn't even braid her hair, for crying out loud. Soon I wouldn't have the strength to kiss her good night. She deserved better than that. She deserved a mother and a father. She deserved them even if they didn't deserve her.

An office door opened and a suited man poked his head out. He held up his hand and waved for Lindsey and David to come in.

My father gave my shoulder a squeeze. "You'd better get Bella. He'll speak to them privately for a few minutes and then call us in too."

Feeling as though I had a millstone around my neck, I trudged over to David and Lindsey. Instead of retrieving my daughter, I forced out the words, "She'll live with you. Just give me tomorrow to say good-bye."

David's mouth hit the floor.

Lindsey furrowed her brow. "Jenny, it doesn't have to be all or no—"

I raised my hand to silence her. "It's what's best."

She shook her head and opened her mouth to say something else, but David cut her off. "Honey, Jenny knows what she's doing."

I glared at him, then, forgetting my weakness, attempted to lift Isabella from Lindsey's lap. Thankfully she stood before I could drop her.

I intertwined my fingers with Isabella's, more aware than I'd ever been of the shape of her fingers, the feel of her skin. "C'mon, sweetness. I've got a surprise for you."

CHAPTER TWENTY-THREE

Isabella slept during the two-hour drive to the ocean while I watched the median strip transform from grass to sand. My car vibrated along a poorly paved road as houses no bigger than closets blurred past. Normally, I'd have every window open, relishing the feel of my hair whipping about me, carrying a burden no heavier than a beach blanket.

Today my baggage was far more cumbersome. In lieu of carefree thoughts of sand castles and sunshine, memories I wished I'd never made weighed heavy on my soul. I should have thrown them off, focusing instead on how I would break it to Isabella that her mother probably wouldn't live long enough to wish her a merry Christmas. Try as I might, though, the only conversation my thoughts would entertain was the one which put a period in my life where there should have been a comma. Again and again my mind replayed the moment I learned that I was going to die. . . .

Dr. Frederick sat across from me in his small office. His voice cracked with emotion as he broke the news that the cancer I'd just learned I had, had already spread throughout my body. I was dying. Even if I opted for every treatment available, in all likelihood, I still had less than a year to live.

"Miracles happen every day, Genevieve. Let's not limit God, but just in case yours doesn't come, you might want to start making arrangements for your daughter, getting your affairs in order . . ."

Just in case, I repeated over and over in my head like an autistic prayer, trying to drown out the rest of his words.

"There are treatments that could give you a little more time. Probably very little. Of course, they would also diminish your quality of life. And it's rare for cancer as advanced as yours to respond at all."

Shut up! I wanted to scream. *Why won't you just shut up? I'm not dying!* It was all I could do not to call him a lunatic and a liar and run from the room.

Just in case. Just in case. Just in case.

Just in case what? I should have demanded. *Just in case a meteor doesn't fall from space carrying a radioactive cure? Just in case a statue doesn't blink to life and heal me with its bloody tears? Just in case a scientist doesn't emerge from the Amazon waving a newfound species of cancer-curing root above his head like a banner?*

I knew what the good doctor really meant was, *Just in case you can't make it day to day without hope, here's a shard you can cling to. Don't hold it too tightly, for it's sure to cut.*

I considered using his words with Isabella, to enlighten her to the idea of death without robbing her of hope, but would that be more cruel? Of course, God could heal me if He so chose. He'd performed far greater miracles. But just as I knew He could turn the sun green if He wanted, I still expected it to rise gold. Isabella, however, at five years old, was not the realist self-preservation would need her to be.

I parked and scooped my little optimist from her booster seat. She laid her head against my shoulder without so much as raising an eyelid. My heart filled with love as hers thumped a steady rhythm against my chest. Since the first moment I'd heard the *whoosh-whoosh* of that beating heart on the ultrasound, I'd been under the sweetest enchantment. Leaning in, I inhaled her warmth and strawberry scent, thinking that heaven could not be paradise without her there.

The afternoon air carried the distinct smell of brine, which seemed to calm my nausea rather than add to it. Forecasters had predicted a 90 percent chance of rain, which explained why the boardwalk stood deserted except for a few joggers. The seagulls seemed to know something the forecasters didn't. Instead of moving inland as they normally did before a storm, they spread wide white wings, circling the tumultuous sky and cackling. The ocean answered with an indifferent roar.

As I neared the steps leading from boardwalk to sand, what little strength I had left me. I bent and lowered my daughter to the ground. Her eyes fluttered open and confusion colored her expression. I took her hand in mine and guided her down the plank stairs.

As our steps became weighted from the sand, Isabella rubbed slumber from her face and looked down. After a moment, her gaze drifted up toward the surf. Her eyes turned into saucers as she breathed her thoughts rather than spoke them. "So much water."

It was a reaction I not only expected, but had looked forward to. My daughter had never seen the ocean before.

"It sure is," I said.

"I'm not going swimming in there."

"No, sweetness. We're not."

Waves dove at the shoreline. Circles of foam glided toward us, then retreated, sweeping shells back into the tide. The water's ripples reflected the gray of the sky, as did the glistening sand at the water's edge. Isabella turned toward me, mouth still open.

Though weariness tugged at me, I couldn't help but smile. "It's amazing, isn't it?"

She turned to face it again and whispered, "The water sounds like thunder."

I took my sandals off and helped her do the same. She slid her hand into mine and the two of us ventured to the surf. We inched forward until the foamy water crept over our ankles.

"It tickles!" she squealed.

I laughed as I bent and picked up a scallop shell. Salt water and time had worn its ridges smooth. I brushed off a piece of seaweed and handed it to her. She turned the shell over in her hand, examining it.

"Look around," I said. "They're everywhere."

Scanning the shell-strewn beach, she asked, "Can I have some?"

"Of course."

My daughter and I spent hours identifying what creatures came from what seashells, writing in the sand, letting the water break on our feet, and talking about everything and nothing. The sky never delivered on its threat to drench us. Eventually, Isabella's yawn told me it was time to go. I hated that our perfect day was about to be over and hated even more how it would end.

"Bells, it's time."

She frowned and picked up a broken mussel shell. "I don't wanna leave."

"We're going to have a grown-up talk now."

The black shell tumbled from her hand. "Really?"
I nodded.

"Wait." She poked a chubby finger into the wet sand, drew a stick figure, then looked up with a shy smile. "That's you, Mommy."

I studied her crude artwork. "You forgot my earrings. You know I look naked without them."

She twisted her mouth at me, then jabbed a thumb into each of my sand ears. Next to her picture of me, she drew a small circle, which I knew was to be her head. I'd never seen her draw me without including herself. Before she could finish, the advancing water wiped me out.

I stared at the sand canvas where my portrait had been and thought, *That's just how it will be.* In a few months, I'd be erased from this earth as if I'd never existed at all. Just another empty shell.

Undaunted, Isabella took two steps back and drew me again. After she finished, I laid my hand on her head. "C'mon, sweetness." I grabbed our sandals, walked to the edge of a sand dune, and sat.

I wrapped my arms around my bent knees and watched my daughter do the same, aware for the first time just how often she mimicked my actions. It was through me that she was learning to become a young lady, but it would be Lindsey, not I, who would usher her into womanhood. A debilitating mix of sadness and jealousy seized me.

I should be the one to help her choose a prom dress, to whistle obnoxiously as she walked across the stage to collect her diploma, and to tuck baby's breath into her curls before she lowered her wedding veil. Longing struck me with such force that I felt it physically. My stomach ached as though I'd been punched. That, of course, would have hurt less.

My daughter watched me intently, so I kept my expression as neutral as I could manage. If there was ever a time to keep it together, now was that time. Drowning her in my tears would only frighten and confuse her.

This moment was one that Isabella would remember for the rest of her life, playing it over and over again, whether she wanted to or not. It was my job to make the memory as tolerable as possible.

She scooted closer and I took her hand in mine. It felt smaller than it ever had before, but then so did mine. The clouds shrouding the sun all afternoon began to dissipate, causing the ashen hues that had streaked the water's ripples to be replaced with shades of pink and violet. Isabella and I sat, watching the changing colors reflected on the water. "Where does the sun go at night?" she asked.

For a moment, I considered using the sun setting as the metaphor to describe my dying, but my gaze fell again to the ocean horizon with no end in sight.

"It goes to sleep, just like you."

She laid her head against my arm. "I'm getting cold."

I crossed my legs and pulled her into my lap. I engulfed her in my arms, loving the warm feel of her against me. Though the ocean air chilled me, my palms still managed to grow damp.

Isabella snuggled her shoulder blades tighter against my chest.

"Bella, you know I love you?"

"I know. I love you too."

I tightened my hold on her, feeling her small arms pinned against her delicate frame. She wiggled for breathing room. Wanting her as close as possible, I loosened my embrace as little as she'd let me get away with. "I need you to listen to me."

She pulled from my lap as though she were going to run away, but instead she knelt before me just as I'd done to her so many times. Tears fought hard to fill my eyes, and I fought harder to hold them back. My word, I loved this child. *Take this cup from me, Jesus. Take this cup.*

"Look at the ocean."

She hesitated, her eyes lingering on me as though I might disappear if she were to turn away.

"Can you see the other side?"

She shook her head, making her curls, wild from the breeze and salt water, flounce.

"You can't see the other side, but there is one. Do you believe me?"

She nodded.

"Mommy is going to heaven soon. Heaven is like the other side of this ocean. Just because you can't see it doesn't mean it's not there."

She frowned. "Today?"

"No," I said, "but very soon."

"On a boat?"

I shook my head. "Jesus is going to take me."

She stared at me a moment. "I'll go too."

I ran my fingers over her cool cheek. "You'll cross that ocean someday, but not with me."

Her frown deepened. "I want to go with you."

I took her hand and kissed it. "Your daddy needs you to stay with him. You're going to live with him and Lindsey until we can be together again. They'll take good care of you."

"No!" She ripped her hand out of mine. "I want to go with you."

"God says I have to go without you."

She scowled. "Then God's bad."

"No, sweetness. He's very, very good."

Her face contorted and her lower lip quivered. "I hate God."

I laid my hands on her shoulders and squeezed. "Please don't say that. Remember this, Bella—we don't understand what He's doing a lot of times, but *He* does. We just have to trust Him."

In a stoic move, she tucked in her lips and stared at the sand. I gave it a minute to sink in, letting the crashing waves serenade us.

Finally she looked up. "When will you come back?"

"When someone dies, they don't come back."

Tears spilled down her round cheeks. "I don't want you to die."

I leaned in and kissed them away. "I'm going to heaven.

Be happy for me. It's a beautiful place and nobody ever cries there."

Her shoulders heaved. "I want to come with you."

I held her for a long time, her body trembling with the force of her sobs, until at last she grew still. I pulled back and wiped her tear-streaked face. "We'll just be apart for a little while. Then it will be your turn to cross the ocean and we'll be together again. This time forever and ever and ever."

She stared into my eyes with an intensity I'd never seen, then threw her arms around me and hugged me harder than she ever had before. "Don't go, Mommy. Please don't leave me."

I pulled back to meet her gaze. "I'll never leave you. I'll always be right in here." I laid my hand over her heart and felt its soft thump against my palm. "I'll be waiting for you on the other side, watching you grow . . . and loving you."

Isabella said little as we walked to the car. Now, belted in her car seat, the silence carried over as she stared out the window. Her vacant expression reminded me of a soldier's after a tour of combat duty. As much as I wanted to tell her that everything would be fine, I couldn't change reality.

After some time of staring at the broken white line as it parted the road before me, I looked in the rearview mirror to find Isabella's head lying against glass, her mouth open and eyes closed. Just like that, all her worries melted with unconsciousness.

I'd spent the entire day holding it together for her sake. Now, at last, I felt safe to release all that I'd held back. As I cried, I heard her stir in the backseat. I quickly stifled my tears and glanced back, afraid I had woken her. Her eyes fluttered and then she grew still again. Seeing her so at peace made me long for the same.

Someday soon, I thought, *I'll have that.* Part of me wished that day were now, but the worst of my journey was still ahead of me. I'd have given anything to not have to climb this mountain to my grim summit. I didn't see how I could make it without Isabella by my side, but for her sake, I knew I would. For her sake, there was nothing I wouldn't do.

CHAPTER TWENTY-FOUR

ISABELLA'S LAST DAY slipped like sand through my fingers. A cloud hovered over the house as bedtime drew near. Craig spent the evening in the saddle barn, giving us time alone as a family. Mama Peg, my father, and I wore strained smiles as we lingered about my daughter, playing board games, faking laughter over her silly jokes . . . missing her even before she left us.

Mama Peg tried to make our last night together as special as possible, positioning several vases of her prized roses around the living room. She had my father light a row of candles, which now flickered down the length of the fireplace mantel, casting the room in a soft glow. The atmosphere seemed better suited to a romantic evening for two than a somber farewell.

As Isabella knelt before the coffee table with her face resting in her hands, her glistening lips reflected the candlelight. Chestnut curls framed her face. She was beautiful.

You're doing the right thing, I told myself as I studied her profile. I could still see her anytime I wanted, and when she missed me, I was just a phone call away. As wrong and unnatural as it felt to say good-bye, it was for the best. Or, more accurately, for *her* best. With the proverbial knife piercing my heart, it certainly wasn't for mine.

I consoled myself with the reminder that David and Lindsey had promised to do anything they could to ease Isabella's transition into their care—open-door policy was the way David put it. Of course, I trusted his word about as much as an infomercial promise, but Lindsey was another story. As much as I disliked her, I believed she would use her influence with David to keep him honest.

I tapped my plastic gingerbread man along the Candy Land board while my conscience pointed its accusing finger at me. *How could you, her own mother, abandon this helpless child?*

I took a deep breath, trying to clear my mind. The smell of pipe smoke clung to my father and the surrounding air. I looked at him, hoping to find a glimmer of empathy and strength in my daddy's eyes, but he wouldn't look at me. I wasn't surprised. He hadn't said a word to me since the car ride home from the lawyer's office.

The only thing worse than his silence was the accusation in his gaze when, on the rare occasion, our eyes did meet. He acted as if I were throwing my daughter to the wolves. He had to know I'd rather be skinned alive than leave her, but death was going to steal me regardless of what any of us wanted. Wasn't it better to say good-bye now before I became a gruesome shadow of the woman I wanted her to remember? It was the right decision despite what he thought. It was.

And anyway, I doubted his motivation was concern for Isabella as much as it was competition with the Prestons. Nothing more than a sick little game of selfishness and pride. Isabella was just a trophy he was about to lose. God forbid that Jack Lucas shelve his narcissistic motives for a moment and support his only child on the worst day of her life. God forbid that he act like a father.

Neither Mama Peg nor Craig initially agreed with my decision either, but they at least made an attempt to understand where I was coming from. My grandmother must have asked me a dozen times since yesterday if I was sure about it. It took an explicit reminder of Mom's anguished final moments to convince her that my plan was sound.

Isabella drew a card from the pile on the center of the board and moved her piece to the next yellow square. To help ease her fears about David, I'd spent much of the evening recounting every cute story I could think of about him, which wasn't many.

My father's first words to me in two days were "Listening to you, you'd swear that twerp was some kind of hero."

Isabella slapped her spent card onto the table. "He's not a twerp!"

Mama Peg tried to answer, but a coughing spell rendered her incoherent.

I gave my father a look that told him he'd gone too far. "No, Bella, your daddy's not a twerp. He's a very smart man."

Isabella smirked a *so there* at my father, who rolled his eyes in response. He picked up another card. "Double blue!" He slid his piece to the final square on the board and grinned. "Grandpa wins again!"

Isabella's face scrunched, readying for tears. "You cheated!"

Mama Peg shook her head at him. "You couldn't let her win?"

I kissed my daughter's cheek. "Just because someone else wins doesn't make them a cheater." I eyed my father. "It might make them a jerk, but not a cheater."

"So," my father began, "we're going to fight on my last night with my granddaughter?"

I snorted. "It's all about you, isn't it?"

Isabella crossed her arms and turned her back on us all.

"Just like her mother," my father mumbled.

Mama Peg moved faster than a woman in her health should be able to, reached across the table, and flicked his forehead.

"Ow!" He slapped his hand over the spot. "What was that for?"

She glared at him. "Grow up."

Craig stepped into the living room, dressed for bed in a

white T-shirt and cotton pajama bottoms. "Just wanted to pop in and wish our girl good luck on her new advent—" His smile melted as he browsed our faces. "Why does everyone look peeved?"

I pushed myself off the floor and stood. "Dad beat Isabella at Candy Land." I looked at him with disgust that I hoped he could feel right down to his marrow. "Twice."

Craig raised an eyebrow at him. "That's quite a victory, man."

Mama Peg adjusted her tubing. "Yes, we're all very proud of him, as you can imagine."

My father sighed. "I don't believe in throwing a game. Any game. What would that teach her? Losing builds character even more than winning does."

I snatched the board up and dumped the game pieces into the box. "Well, Bella ought to have lots of character, then, with all she's about to lose." I shoved the lid on.

"That's your doing," he said coolly.

I slammed the box back on the table, making the game pieces rattle. "My doing? Do you think this is my doing? You think I want this?"

Craig leaned into me and laid his hand on my arm. His warm breath fell on my ear. "Not now."

My father pushed off the coffee table. "She shouldn't be leaving us. This is wrong."

"Why is that?" I shook Craig off me. "Because you say so? You're not the expert on what my daughter needs."

"Why are you so angry with me?" he asked.

"Me angry with *you*? You've been angry at me ever since Mom died."

"That's not true."

"No?"

His gaze darted around, taking in everything but me.

I smiled bitterly. "You can't even look at me."

"I can look at you." He forced himself to stare at me for an uncomfortable second, then looked down.

"See! Am I that detestable to you that you can't even stand to see me?"

He mumbled something that I couldn't hear, then walked away. As usual.

We all stood for a moment, silent.

Finally Craig scooped Isabella up and planted a kiss on her forehead. Her pink cotton-clad legs dangled midair. "You are going to have such a good life with your daddy and Lindsey."

Isabella tried hard to suppress a smile. "Will you come to visit?" she asked.

He squeezed her tight. "So much that you're going to get sick of me."

An unabashed grin spread across her face. "Daddy says he bought me a princess bed."

Craig winked at her. "Well, of course. Where else would a princess sleep?"

She bit her bottom lip, looking almost as smitten with him as I was. *We should be a family,* I thought. *Craig, Bella, and I should*— I obliterated the thought before it could finish forming. I was not in a position to dream. Not for myself at least.

I glanced at the clock on the mantel. "It's almost ten. We should go to bed now."

The room fell as quiet as a morgue.

"Kiss Mama Peg and Craig good night."

Each good night was drawn out and morose. I doubted my funeral would be as depressing. I heard the back door open and shut.

"She's just going a few miles away. You're still going to see her," I said.

My father leaned against the doorjamb. "It won't be the same."

Heat flooded my cheeks. "Why do you have to do that? Why do you have to make everything so—"

"He's right," Mama Peg said. "It won't be the same. Just because he's your father doesn't mean he's always wrong."

Her words had a special sting to them when she took his side against me. I was never quite prepared for it. Not possessing the energy needed to argue, I just piled this new hurt on my already-heaping mound. "Bella, kiss Cowpa."

My father knelt before her on one knee as though preparing to propose. He took her cheeks into his hands, brought her forehead to his lips, and kissed it. "You're going to visit us every other weekend regular, but if you want to come home, home-home, if you don't like it there . . . if for any reas—"

"Oh, for pity's sake." Mama Peg rolled her oxygen tank over to him and grabbed his ear.

He grimaced. "I'm just saying, if she's not happy—"

She twisted his lobe, silencing him. "You tell that child everything is going to be okay, that you love her, and that we'll see her soon. And that's *all* you say."

My father looked like a little boy fresh from a spanking as he yanked his ear free and stood. "See you soon, princess."

I could see Craig holding back laughter, and apparently it was contagious because a snicker escaped me before I could contain it. I tucked my lips inside my mouth and turned away.

"It's going to be just fine, everyone." Mama Peg scanned our faces, making deliberate eye contact with each of us. "We're all going to be just fine."

"Come on, sweetness." I put my hand on the small of Isabella's back and led my daughter up the stairs.

She started for her own room. I took her hand, stopping her. "Sleep with me tonight."

She looked down at the ground as if embarrassed. I lifted her chin, forcing her to look at me.

"I want to sleep by myself," she said softly.

Surprised, I jerked my head back. "Since when? You ask me every night to sleep with me."

Her lips disappeared inside her mouth as she looked to the side. I realized then that she might be trying to pull away from me and that this was probably a healthy response, even if it was painful.

"Okay, you can sleep in your own bed if you want, but can we snuggle awhile?"

She paused, then nodded. I turned the tiny knob of the

bedside table lamp, flooding my bedroom in golden hues. I reached over the bed, pulled back the afghan, and patted the cool sheet twice, encouraging her to crawl in. When she did, I joined her.

We wiggled into the covers until they enveloped our shoulders. There I lay, nose to nose with the child from whom I'd never been separated for more than twenty-four hours, wondering how either of us would survive this. It wasn't an issue for me, of course; I was dying anyway. How would she fare? I wondered. Her warm breath puffed rhythmically against me, still hinting of the brussels sprouts we had eaten for dinner.

"Oops," I said. "We forgot to brush our teeth."

She reached to pull the covers off.

I grabbed her hand. "It's okay just for tonight."

She relaxed.

"But brushing your teeth is important."

She blinked at me. "I know."

"And so is saying your prayers. God misses you when you don't talk to Him."

She yawned. "I know, Mommy."

"And going to church. There's so much you need to learn. Promise me you won't give Lindsey a hard time about going. I made her promise that she'd take you."

She yawned again. "Okay."

"That's important, Bella."

"I said okay." She closed her eyes, then jerked them open, looking like she remembered leaving an iron on that might be burning down the house.

"What is it?" I asked, alarmed.

"I need to sleep in my own bed."

With a heavy heart, I ran the back of my hand down her soft cheek. "Oh, okay."

She crawled out of bed and stood over me, her face cast in shadows as she studied me. "I love you, Mommy."

"I know, sweetness."

Her sad little smile looked just like my mother's. "Good night, Mommy."

"Good night, baby. See you in the morning."

She paused in the doorway, turned around, and looked at me for a moment before disappearing around the corner.

I lay in bed for what felt like hours, tossing and turning, fighting unconsciousness. I somehow thought that the sooner I fell asleep, the sooner morning would come, and the sooner she'd be gone. I didn't realize that sleep had overcome me until I was jolted awake by a scream.

CHAPTER TWENTY-FIVE

MY EYES FLASHED open. I squinted at the digital numbers on my alarm clock—5:00. Propping myself up on my elbows, I listened. In my sleepy state I couldn't decide whether the scream had been real or dreamt.

When I heard nothing, I figured I must have had a nightmare. I laid my head back on the pillow. Distant sirens, so muted that I thought I might be imagining them, encouraged my eyes open once again. As the hum grew into a wail, I stopped questioning their existence and slid my legs over the side of the bed.

As secluded as we were from the rest of Tullytown, we seldom, if ever, heard sirens. I planted my bare feet on the cool plank floor, wondering to which of our unfortunate neighbors the trouble belonged.

My father's muffled scream stopped my heart. "Jenny!"

My only thought was that he needed me. I tore down the steps. My ankle twisted on the last stair, sending a burn through my foot. I didn't get my hands up in time to protect myself, and my face hit the wall. Ignoring the pain, I wiped wetness from my nose. Mama Peg stood in the hallway just outside her bedroom, looking bewildered. Her long charcoal hair lay draped across the shoulders of her nightgown. "What's going on?" she asked. "Why are you bleeding?"

"I'm fine. Where's Dad?"

She looked around and shook her head.

I scanned past her to the front door, which stood wide open. Panic seized me. Had we been broken into? Was the intruder still inside? Had my father been hurt, or . . . Acid rose in my throat as I considered the *or*. I held my breath and panned our unremarkable surroundings. "Go in your room and lock the door."

Her eyes grew wide. "I'm not leaving you out here. What's happening?"

Blood trickled onto my lips. I rubbed it against the shoulder of my T-shirt.

The sirens grew louder and louder until they vibrated through the whole house, while flashing lights cast everything in an eerie red glow. They were right outside. One of us was hurt. Dad? Recalling our last words to each other, I cringed.

I charged out the open door. Cool air struck me, along with blinding lights spinning from the top of an ambulance. "She's over here!" Craig screamed in the distance.

She.

The only unaccounted for *she* was Isabella. But she was in bed sleeping.

The deafening sirens fell suddenly silent. Paramedics jumped from their vehicle and ran up to me as if I were the one needing attention.

I touched the blood on my face, shook my head, and stepped back.

My father stood halfway between the house and the pond, looking like he'd witnessed a murder. "Over there!" He pointed toward Lucas Lake.

Beyond him knelt the silhouette of a man. His back moved up and down as though he were doing push-ups. A flurry of confusion, lights, questions, and sobs surrounded me. I couldn't make sense of any of it.

The kneeling man yelled, "Over here!" Craig. It was Craig.

Someone turned on the ambulance's headlights, flooding him in bright white. Drenched, Craig's T-shirt clung to his chest as he leaned down. A soaked, limp Isabella lay beneath him on the ground. Somehow my heart understood before my brain caught on. Isabella's outstretched arms made no sense even as panic raced through me like quicksilver. I heard my breaths come in small, quick pants. Why was Isabella lying on the ground?

When Craig blew into her mouth, I finally understood.

I ran, screaming, toward her.

I fell before my daughter. Craig thrust the heel of his hand up and down into the center of her chest. Water spewed from her mouth. Then vomit. He pushed her on her side. Her arm fell listlessly to the ground. Her eyes didn't open and her chest didn't rise. A medic asked Craig how long he'd been at it, then took over. The other's rough hands pried me off my daughter's shoulders.

"No!" someone screamed over and over.

Me . . . it was me screaming.

Stop screaming, my mind told me. *It's not helping. You're not helping.* They tried to perform CPR around my clutching hands. *Let her go,* I thought. *You're in the way. You're going to kill her.* But I couldn't. She was all I had. She was all that mattered.

The medic pulled my arm. "Get off and let us help her."

I wanted to let go. I tried. I couldn't. Someone grabbed my waist and yanked me backward. Clawing the air, I screamed and tried to get back to her.

Her lips were black.

From a small screen, a television news anchor droned on as the fluorescent lights of the pediatric ICU waiting room flickered above us. Craig sat next to Mama Peg in one of the bolted-down chairs provided, while my restless father stood, sat, and stood again. Feeling no desire for comfort, I occupied the hard floor.

Craig rubbed his eyes with the heel of his hand. The same hand that had saved my baby's life . . . if she lived, that was. The *if* doubled me over in anguish. Everyone was so entrenched in their own grief that mine went unnoticed. When I felt collected enough to speak my first words since the car ride over, I asked Craig to repeat what had happened.

He leaned back and stared at the ceiling. "Something woke me. Sounded like a kid yelling for help, but when I listened, I didn't hear it anymore. I thought I was dreaming." He shook his head. "I should've . . ."

Breathing even heavier than usual, Mama Peg laid her hand on his arm.

He looked down at it but made no response. "Anyway, I tried to go back to sleep, but it kept nagging me. I figured the only way I was getting any rest was if I checked it out. I really didn't think . . . Once I got outside, I heard splashing. I ran as fast as I could." He looked at me with eyes so haunted I couldn't bear to hold his gaze. I wanted to comfort him but had nothing to give.

He let out several deep breaths before continuing. "I saw her go under and went in. It took so long to bring her to shore. I don't know how she got out so far."

It felt like I was moving out of hell into purgatory as numbness replaced grief. I turned to my father. "When did you . . . ?"

He stopped pacing and leaned against the wall. I don't know whether it was the harsh lighting or the circumstances, but he looked so very old.

"I heard Craig cry for help. I ran outside. He told me to call 911. I didn't know what happened." He looked at me then, and I felt that for the first time in a very long time he actually saw me. "I yelled for you, Jenny, but you and your grandma sleep so heavy."

I buried my face in my knees, trying to process it. A picture of my daughter thrashing in the water, panicked for air, played like a horror movie in my mind. It was too much to bear.

Mama Peg slipped one hand into mine, the other into Craig's. "Jack, come pray with us."

Through sobs and whimpers, each of them petitioned God for healing. How many times, I wondered, had they prayed the same for my mother? for me? How many times had I prayed this for myself? And yet I was still dying.

When it came my turn, I did not bother with this seemingly impotent request. One simple plea ascended from the deepest, most anguished part of my soul—*Have mercy.*

Afterward, we took turns speculating why Isabella would be in the lake. My father assumed that she wanted to swim in it one last time. Mama Peg considered that it might be some sort of symbolic baptism into her new life. Craig thought maybe she was rebelling somehow.

It was clear to me that all of these theories were faulty. She was still terrified of submersion. I had only recently coaxed her back into taking a bath instead of a shower. I wondered if, in her childish rationalizations, she thought I was sending her away because she had done something bad, and as a punishment, she made herself do what she feared most.

The possibility sickened me, but it was the only thing that made sense.

We waited at least an hour for someone to tell us what was going on. When my father stopped a nurse in the hall, she said, "We have time to save your granddaughter or explain, but not both."

He let her go.

I sat on the floor, hugging my knees. Mama Peg rubbed my back. "Jenny, please sit up here with me. No telling what kind of funk is growing down there. Think of your immune system."

"Good," I muttered. "I hope I catch something."

Dressed in the ridiculous combination of sweatpants and wingtip shoes, my father paced to and fro. He traced the same path over and over, stopping in front of the TV, then the empty magazine rack. TV. Magazine rack. TV. Magazine rack. TV. Rack. *Click click clack. Click click clack. Click click clack.*

I couldn't take it anymore. "Will you sit down already?"

He continued on as if he hadn't heard me.

I slapped my palm on the seat of an empty chair.

Mama Peg squeezed my shoulder. "Jenny, he's grieving too."

Craig slid off his chair and took a place next to me. He laid his arm across my shoulders. "She's going to be okay," he whispered in my ear.

I looked into his eyes. Red and swollen, they offered no comfort, only a reflection of my own fear.

"If she lives, it's because of you," I said.

He licked his lips. "No. It's a miracle I even heard her."

Just when it seemed we'd rot in that room waiting for an update, a man in a lab jacket with a stethoscope draped around his neck appeared in the doorway. He had our full attention. "I have good news and bad."

Good news: she's alive. Bad news: she's a vegetable.

He paused as he looked me over. "What happened to you?"

I pulled my long hair over the bloodstain on my shoulder. "Bloody nose."

"Do you need—"

"Just tell us," I said.

He looked as rough as we did. He scratched his five-o'clock shadow and took a seat in the one of the empty chairs across from us. He looked at me with eyes that reminded me of a basset hound's. "You're her mother?"

My stomach turned and tightened. "Yes."

"She's a beautiful little girl."

"Just tell us," I repeated.

Like a defendant on trial watching the jury for clues of a verdict, my eyes were attuned to every nuance of his body language. When his shoulders slumped slightly, I wanted to cry. "She's not dead yet, but she will be," I blurted.

He looked at me with a strange expression. "We just don't know. When someone goes into a coma, it can be for hours, it can be for years, or it can be forever. We just don't know."

My father bellowed a visceral sound as he lifted a fist to

the ceiling. "How much can I take? How much?" He covered his face with one hand while the other, still clenched, fell at his side.

Unfazed, the doctor turned back to me. "I can't say I know what you're going through. I'm a parent, but my children are home in bed."

"You hope."

He gave me a questioning look. "Excuse me?"

"She was home in bed too," I said. "Safe and sound."

He looked liked he'd rather be anywhere but there. "I'm sorry."

"Can we see her?" Mama Peg asked.

He studied her with a concerned look. "Are you breathing all right?"

She coughed. "I'm fine."

I noticed then that she was the worst shade of gray I'd ever seen on her. Alarm filled me. "Mama Peg, are you okay?"

Ignoring me, she answered him. "Do y'all have any oxygen tanks you could loan?"

He leaned over hers and checked the dial before looking back up. "How long has it been empty?"

She didn't answer.

He shook his head and hurried out of the room.

"Why didn't you say something?" I asked. "We're in a hospital, for heaven's sake."

She looked at me but said nothing. It was a stupid question.

A nurse walked in lugging a green, metal tank. Filling the

room with clinks and clangs, she slid my grandmother's empty tank out and replaced it with a new one.

Mama Peg exchanged the tubing, turned a knob, sucked in a deep breath, and coughed. "Sweet air, I've missed you."

I stared at her a moment, watching the pink return to her skin. "Don't you do that again."

The nurse picked up the spent tank. "I was going to say the same thing."

Mama Peg nodded. "I won't. Thank you."

"Can we see her now?" I asked.

The nurse glanced at the large round clock hanging above the doorway, then back to me. "In a minute, but understand that when you see her, she's going to look a little frightening. A respirator is breathing for her."

I'd envisioned myself on life support many times, but never in my wildest dreams had I imagined Isabella. But at least she was alive, and where there was life, there was hope.

"What are her chances?" The question came from my father.

Dr. Reid stepped back through the doorway. He mouthed a thank-you to the nurse, who nodded at him and left. "The fact that CPR was initiated so soon improves her chances, but ultimately, your guess is as good as mine."

"Will you pray for her?" I asked.

The look he gave me told me that wasn't within his scope of practice.

I stared hard at him, trying to will him into agreeing. As irrational as it was, I somehow felt as though his prayer, added to ours, might be the tipping point Isabella needed. "She'd pray for you."

He studied the ground.

Anger welled up inside me at this man who, a moment ago, seemed full of compassion but now wouldn't even pray for a dying little girl.

My grandmother laid her hand on my shoulder. "Thank you for everything, Dr. Reid."

He slipped his hands into his lab jacket pockets and looked up. "I'll pray," he said. "I'll say a prayer, for whatever it's worth."

When Mama Peg smiled at him, I realized that she hadn't put in her false teeth. She seemed to realize it too and clamped her mouth shut.

With only two of us allowed to visit at a time, it was Mama Peg and I who followed the doctor through the pneumatic doors into the pediatric ICU—or PICU as he kept referring to it.

It was even brighter than the waiting room. A myriad of bells and alarms sounded from every direction. I wondered how patients got any sleep. My gaze flitted around, searching for Isabella, past walls of glass and nurses. The doctor touched my arm.

I jumped.

He put his hands up. "Didn't mean to scare you. Before I go, I have a question. I got the basic story of what happened from the ER docs, but it didn't make sense to me. Why would a child be swimming by herself at that time of morning?"

I tried to look around him. "I don't know."

He pulled his stethoscope off his neck, letting it hang from his hand. "Do you think it's possible that she might have been depressed?"

His question knocked the wind out of me. I felt Mama Peg's soft hand wrap around my arm and squeeze. "What? She's five years old. You think she *wanted* to drown?"

His face flushed. "Pediatric suicide is rare, but not unheard of. I'm sorry. I shouldn't have—"

"Please," I said, unable to take anymore. "Just show us where she is."

CHAPTER TWENTY-SIX

THE LAST TIME I had seen Isabella in a hospital, she was an infant. It seemed that the moment she was born, the nurses whisked her away for her first bath. Too impatient to wait for them to bring her back, I walked myself to the nursery so I could admire her through the glass. I looked past cribs lined up like train cars until my gaze fell on the most magnificent sight imaginable. A pink card hung above her with "Baby Lucas" scrawled on it between inky footprints. Fleshy rolls covered her arms and legs. She was so fat! I felt a grin, wider than the world, spread across my face. I kept thinking, *That roly-poly thing came out of me?* It didn't seem possible.

When first I held her, her dark hair lay plastered against

her head. But there, lying in the nursery under a warming light, magnificent ringlets sprang from her freshly washed head. My heart leaped and sank in the same instant. Those were David's curls.

I watched her lovely face scrunch as the nurse slipped a thermometer under her arm. Her porcelain skin turned red as she clearly expressed her dislike of the procedure. Oh, she was beautiful! The nurse saw me in the window and picked up my naked baby girl. She held her up to the glass for me to get a better look. Perfect little feet dangled at the end of perfect little legs. She stopped crying and opened her eyes. Her sweet lips pursed as if preparing to nurse. . . .

From those same lips there now protruded a clear plastic tube that led to a ventilator. With each unnatural, gasping sound, air forced its way into her lungs. Another tube snaked out of her left nostril. A catheter drained urine from her bladder into a clear bag hanging from the end of the bed. An IV fed fluid into her arm. Monitors with incomprehensible zigzag readouts beeped sporadically.

I laid my hand over my mouth, my mind unable to grasp the truth my eyes were seeing. Her face was swollen beyond recognition. If it weren't for the curls of brown sprawled against the stark white pillow beneath her head, I might not have known it was her. A layer of what looked like Vaseline glistened over her eyelids and lashes.

I felt as though a boulder had landed on my chest. I could barely breathe. *My baby. My poor baby.*

This is what hell feels like, I thought. *This is hell.*

Mama Peg intertwined her arm with mine. Paralyzed by anguish in the doorway of Isabella's hospital room, we held each other up. A nurse stood in the corner of the room near the ventilator, looking as though she were attending a wake.

"Can she hear us?" I asked her.

"Impossible to know for sure," she said. "We assume that she can and talk to her about everything we're doing. If she comes out of it, you can ask her if she remembers anything. That's the only way to know for sure what she heard."

"*When* she comes out of it," I said.

Her face flushed and she averted her eyes.

Mama Peg stared hard at her. "*When* she comes out of it, we *will* ask her."

I unlinked my arm from my grandmother's and moved to my daughter's side. I picked up her limp hand, placed it in my palm, and kissed it. She felt so foreign, so cold and lifeless. Something tapped against the back of my knees. I looked behind me to find that the nurse had brought me a chair. I sat and laid my forehead against my daughter's shoulder.

I stayed there for some time, brushing curls from her forehead, tracing the curves of her face, and lamenting about all that I should have said but hadn't. All we could have done if I hadn't been so busy with things that didn't really matter. All the dreams I had for her that might never come to pass now.

Someone touched my back and I jerked up, disoriented. As soon as I opened my eyes, bright lights hit me, along with the vague notion that something was wrong—something that I didn't want to remember. I looked at my unconscious daughter and my heart sank.

"Jenny, it's time to go home now," my father said, and I realized it was his touch that had woken me.

I sat up and rubbed my eyes. "I can't leave her."

"Honey, let's go check on your grandma, grab something to eat, and get cleaned up. I'll bring you right back."

I shook my head. "I'm not leaving her. What if she wakes up?"

He laid his hand on my shoulder. It felt so heavy. "Dr. Reid said he gave her medication so that won't happen. She won't wake up while we're gone. I promise. Besides, David's here. He wants to talk to you before he sees her."

I felt shame that I hadn't thought to call him. "Who told him?"

"Mama Peg."

Of course. The only rational one among us. I kissed Isabella's clammy forehead. "I'll be back soon, Bells. Your daddy wants to visit with you awhile. I love you."

David sat in the waiting room alone, slapping a rolled-up magazine against his open palm, staring at a black television screen. Upon seeing me, he stood.

His eyes welled as he opened his arms. "Oh, Jenny."

The tears I couldn't seem to release at Isabella's bedside now spilled freely as I fell into his arms. He held me tight, whispering, "Our girl" over and over. I pulled back and touched his rough, unshaven face. So much was exchanged between us as I met his gaze.

"I'm sorry, Jenny. I'm so sorry for everything."

The wall of offenses I'd constructed against him over the last six years imploded with that apology, leaving me trembling in the aftershock. "I'm sorry too," I said. "David, I stole so much from you."

Flashes of Isabella's first laugh, first word, and first birthday raced through my mind. He had no idea the treasures I had stolen from him.

After a time, he swiped his arm across his wet face. "Any change in her condition?"

I shook my head.

He exhaled and nodded. "I guess I should warn you that my father's on his way."

Though I dreaded having to face Dr. Preston, I said nothing. I figured he had as much right to be there as any of us.

He glanced over my shoulder. "Can I see her?"

"Of course. But, David, she looks bad." Besides Isabella and my mother, I'd never felt so connected to another human being as I did to David in that moment. No one bore the yoke of this burden with me as evenly as he did. There was a strange comfort in that. I placed my hand on his face and looked him squarely in the eyes. "She's going to be okay." I had never wanted to believe anything so badly.

"Of course she is," he agreed.

When we returned from home, showered and fed, my father excused himself to use the restroom while I was left to deal with the Preston clan, who had converged upon the PICU waiting room. My gaze immediately landed on Lindsey. Standing alone in the corner, she wore a warm-up suit that looked like something Mama Peg would wear. She wasn't quite the same delicate creature without makeup and tailored clothes.

Uncle Ted spotted me first. He hurried over and smothered me in an embrace that reeked of cooking grease. Just as nausea began to summon up the contents of my stomach, he released me. "Jenny, how is she? How's our girl?"

Everyone's eyes were now on me. David's relatives studied me with anticipation. "She's in a coma."

"Says who?" a man bellowed from behind me.

I cringed at the sound of his voice, braced myself, and turned around.

A squatty, well-dressed man fixed his beady eyes on me. At five feet five, it wasn't uncommon for Dr. Alfred Preston to be underestimated at first sight, but that always proved to be a mistake. He was in my eyes a modern-day Napoleon. The only person in town who didn't seem to fear him was my father.

He dipped his head at me. "Genevieve."

Too weary for small talk, I simply mimicked his gesture. "Dr. Preston."

"Who said that my granddaughter's in a coma?"

What does it matter who said it, I wondered. "Dr. Reid."

"Since when is he a neurologist?" The way he looked at me made me think he expected an answer.

Unnerved by his gaze, I finally shrugged.

"She's on a ventilator?"

"She is," I said.

He frowned at me. "Who wrote that order?"

I was in no mood for a browbeating from him or anyone else. "You can stop talking to me like I'm your nurse. She wasn't breathing. What did you expect them to do?"

He continued his interrogation as if I hadn't spoken. "Did another doctor talk to you about it? Did they tell you what they were doing and why? Did they consult with specialists?"

I just looked at him. Eventually he'd have to realize the stupidity of this conversation.

He took off his glasses and slid the earpiece into his mouth, looking self-important. "Dr. Reid is a pediatrician, not a pulmonologist, Jenny."

I crossed my arms. How could he not know how presumptuous he sounded? I had the strongest urge to fire questions at him in French, demanding that he answer me. If I had known French, I would have.

He stared at me for the longest time the way David always did when he was on the cusp of finding a solution. Finally he blinked. "How long was she hypoxic?"

I tried to make my annoyance with him obvious by letting out an exaggerated sigh. Why did it always seem that brainiacs were too dumb to realize they were talking over everyone's head?

He raised his eyebrows, waiting for me to answer.

"I guess you could ask Dr. Reid. Excuse me now."

My father appeared beside me, locking eyes with his nemesis. Fear for what scene he might make caused my heart to race.

I turned to him. "When I go back to see Bella, don't you dare start anything."

Dr. Preston trailed his gaze slowly down the length of my father, daring him to defy me.

My father glowered back at him. I was glad I couldn't read his thoughts. Most likely they were homicidal.

Dr. Preston pulled his gaze from my father and addressed me. "Stay here, young lady. I'm going to take care of—"

My father squared his shoulders. "Don't tell my daughter what to do."

Here we go. "Dad, don't."

His face reddened. "You go see your daughter, pumpkin. I'll handle him."

Pumpkin? The last time my father referred to me as *pumpkin*, it was to praise me for learning to tie my shoes.

Dr. Preston looked up defiantly at my father, having to bend his neck back so far it looked like it might break. "You may not like me, Jack, and I might think you're a lunatic, but my granddaughter is lying in there dying, and I'm going to do something about it even if I have to do it over your dead body."

Something snapped in my father—I could see it in his eyes. I stepped between them. "Dr. Preston, if you can help Isabella, then please . . ."

His gaze never left my father even as he spoke to me. "Jenny, I know you don't have any reason to trust me, but you need to in this case. I've studied under the finest pediatric specialists in the world. There's plenty in medicine I wouldn't pretend to know, but this—*this*—is where I excel."

"He killed your mother," my father growled behind me.

"For the five hundredth time, your wife wasn't my patient." Dr. Preston turned to me. "What your father doesn't seem to grasp is that your mother mentioned she was getting frequent headaches and was tired. As a *friend*, I suggested she start taking iron and ibuprofen, thinking maybe she had some anemia, but told her she needed to make an appointment with her doctor. I did not diagnose her and I certainly didn't kill her."

"I know," I simply said.

My father glared at Dr. Preston. "Don't you let him near my granddaughter."

"*Our* granddaughter," Dr. Preston replied. "Your family seems not to understand the concept of fifty-fifty genetics."

I turned and looked at my father. His eyes were as wild as the night he'd learned of my mother's cancer.

I gave Dr. Preston a severe look and shook my head in warning.

Fear seemed to replace impudence as his eyes at last grew wide with understanding. "Let me go find out her condition at least." He hurried away faster than I'd ever seen him move.

Looking embarrassed and unsure, David's family mumbled excuses and apologies as they scattered, leaving us alone.

My father licked his lips. "Jenny, you can't be serious about letting that quack have anything to do with her care."

"If he can help . . ."

He gave me an incredulous look. "He killed your mother."

I thought about trying again to dispel this long-held belief of his, but in his irrational state of mind, the only thing it would accomplish would be to further infuriate him. "Daddy, I know you think he messed up, but you don't get to be chief of staff for no reason. What if he can help her?"

He shrugged. "I don't care what he can do. He's not touching my granddaughter."

The gravity of his words shocked me. Was hatred really a more powerful emotion than love? "Listen to yourself." Unable to stand the sight of him, I walked away.

He stood alone in the hallway, wearing his bitterness like some warped badge of honor.

Down the hall, as far away from him as I could get and still see the doors to the PICU, I leaned my back against the wall and waited for Dr. Preston to reemerge. A custodian rolled a container of murky fluid past me, sending a waft of bleach my way. I bent my arm over my face to keep from smelling it. I hadn't vomited in nearly forty-eight hours and I wanted to keep it that way.

After more than an hour, Dr. Preston strode through the pneumatic doors, accompanied by another man. This doctor couldn't have been much older than I was. His face was almost as red as his hair. The poor thing wore the expression of someone about to face a firing squad. With a hand on the man's back, Dr. Preston guided him toward me. "Dr. McNeal, this is Isabella's mother."

Shaking his hand left mine cold and wet. I looked at my palm, then at him.

"Oh, sorry. Just washed them."

Dr. Preston gestured to his companion. "Dr. McNeal is an associate of Dr. Reid."

"Nice to meet you," I said.

Dr. Preston turned to the redhead. "Tell that child's mother why you have her on a paralytic."

He gave Dr. Preston a questioning look. Dr. Preston simply stared at him.

"Well, Ms. Preston," Dr. McNeal began.

"Lucas."

His face mottled. "My apologies, Ms. Lucas. If your daughter was to wake up and feel a ventilator forcing air into her lungs, that would be pretty frightening, as you can imagine. She would panic and might try to rip the tube out. This obviously would—"

"Wait," Dr. Preston said. "Would you repeat what you just said?"

"Repeat what, sir?"

He bent his head to the side like a confused dog. "The part about *if she woke up*."

"If she wakes up and finds a ventilator—"

Dr. Preston put his glasses back on. "But she's in a coma; that's what Dr. Reid told her mother."

The man furrowed his brow. "You know as well as I do that they can come out of it without warning."

Dr. Preston nodded like a simpleton. "Yes, that's right. That's right. But if she's on a paralytic, how would we know if she started coming out of it, do you suppose?"

Sweat beaded on the younger doctor's forehead. "After a while we'll wean her from the medication and reevaluate."

"Oh, stupid me. I thought that airway pressure release ventilation had eliminated the need for paralytics."

"We're not using APRV."

Dr. Preston's nostrils flared as red crawled up his neck. "Yes, I've been made aware. So we have her on continuous respirations and paralytics. How long are we going to leave her in this forced coma?"

Confusion and alarm filled me. I looked back and forth between the two doctors, but they were focused on each other. "Forced? I thought—"

Dr. Reid stepped off the elevator wearing a wrinkled lab jacket and flew up the hall in long strides, looking as irritated as Dr. Preston.

At the sound of his footsteps, David's father turned. "Oh, look, it's the great Dr. Reid."

Dr. Reid glared at him. "I got your emergency page. This couldn't wait until tomorrow?"

"Oh, I'm sorry, Dr. Reid. Did I wake you from your nap?"

"I've been on call for two days straight. I need to sleep sometime."

"I realize you need your beauty rest more than most, but this is important. You see, someone told this young woman that my granddaughter was in a coma."

He threw me an accusatory look. "She is."

Dr. Preston's eyes narrowed. "A chemically induced one."

Dr. Reid gave David's father a look that could have killed. "As per protocol, Dr. Preston, after I saved the child's life, I assessed her faculties and found her to be completely unresponsive."

Dr. Preston's mouth turned up in a hint of a smirk. It seemed to me a small miracle that he had made it to his age without someone beating the life out of him. "For which we are eternally grateful, Doctor. Thank you for doing your job. I was told that we got her back on the very first shock, but that certainly doesn't take away from your claim to heroism. Now then, since you've been given your proper due, would you please tell me how you'll know if she becomes responsive?"

Dr. Reid's eyes looked like they were in danger of popping out of his head. "We'll wean her and reevaluate."

The redheaded doctor broke in. "That's what I just told him."

When Dr. Preston turned his attention to him, the young doctor looked as though he might soil himself. "When?" Dr. Preston asked.

Dr. Reid's words were sounding increasingly clipped. "I haven't set up those parameters yet."

"The longer she's on the ventilator, the lower her chances of a full recovery, wouldn't you agree?"

My gaze ping-ponged between them. The tension in the air was thick enough to suffocate, but something told me that this exchange might mean the difference between Isabella living and dying. Though I didn't fully understand the debate, I realized they had two very different opinions on what was best for my daughter. I wanted to hear it out.

Dr. Reid tapped his large sneaker against the floor. "I realize this, Doctor, but hypoxemia might also have equally dire consequences if she doesn't breathe on her own, don't you think?"

"I gave the orders to wean her," Dr. Preston said.

They stared so hard and long at each other that I half expected one of them to draw a pistol. It was Reid who ultimately lost the staring contest. "You have no right to do that; she's my p—"

Dr. Preston took a step forward, entering Reid's personal space. "In case your memory is as poor as your doctoring, let me remind you that I'm chief of staff. They're all *my* patients."

Dr. Reid closed his eyes and tucked his lips in his mouth in what appeared to be an attempt to calm himself. "If she wakes up," he finally said, "she's going to be terrified. We are trying to prevent that. I don't call that bad medicine."

"Why isn't she on APRV?" Dr. Preston asked.

Dr. Reid pressed his fingers against his temple. "No matter what I say, you're going to attack it."

Dr. Preston donned a smug expression. "That's the first intelligent thing you've said."

Dr. Reid looked at the ceiling as his foot continued to tap. "I understand that you're going through a stressful time, so I'm going to—"

"You're going to extubate my granddaughter."

Dr. Reid's foot stilled. "You're insane."

"That may be so, but that's the course we're taking. I had the nurses titrate the paralytic. Guess what? Isabella is responding to pain stimuli. She's wiggling her toes. She's trying to open her eyes."

I gasped at the news. As much as I wanted to run to her, I knew I had to stay behind and hear the rest of the conversation.

Dr. Reid jerked his head back in surprise.

A severe expression replaced Dr. Preston's previous smug one. "That's right, Doctor. And after I took her off the archaic continuous respirations you had her on and moved her to APRV, her spontaneous breaths picked up."

Dr. Reid rubbed at his chin. "What are they now?"

"Ten per minute."

"Not enough."

"Not yet, but I believe once the medication wears off completely and we extubate her, her lungs will have to work. I predict that they will."

Dr. Reid's foot started tapping again. "She's not ready."

Dr. Preston took another step forward. "Listen, you sniveling brat, this is my granddaughter. My flesh and blood.

This isn't some spitting contest that you can win with the evil Dr. Preston. I know you, the rest of the doctors, the nurses, and probably even the candy stripers hate me, but it doesn't matter. What matters is that I have earned my position and I'm going to use it to save my granddaughter's life."

Dr. Reid turned to me as if expecting me to intervene. When I didn't respond, he turned back to Dr. Preston. "If we extubate her without weaning her down for a day and she codes, you will not only lose your position as chief of staff, I'll make the case to the board myself that you lose your license to practice altogether."

"If something happens to my granddaughter," my father said from behind me, "he's going to lose more than his license."

CHAPTER TWENTY-SEVEN

WHILE OTHER TEENAGERS had to be prodded and pleaded with to go to sleep at a decent hour, I never had to be asked. I wanted to go to bed early just so I could have plenty of time to lie there and dream of my future with David. Staring at the ceiling, I'd fantasize about what sort of life we'd someday have. I imagined a wedding both simple and elegant.

My bridesmaids would wear champagne-colored silk, while I would be a modern-day Cinderella dressed in a strapless white gown lined with lace and pearls. David would be dashing, of course, in his tailored tuxedo. We would gaze dreamily into one another's eyes, feeding each other cake and promises as our families toasted the beautiful life we were about to embark upon.

Often I imagined David placing a finger over his lips and leading me down the hall to the doorway of our daughter's bedroom. Hand in hand we would watch her sleep, in awe of her sweetness, the love we felt for her . . . and for each other. Somehow I'd always known we'd have a daughter, even though the rest of the details didn't quite work out as I'd fantasized.

Now, years later, my dream had twisted into a nightmare. David's hand clutched mine as we stood beside Isabella's hospital bed, marveling not at her innocence but at her inner strength—hoping it would be enough to see her through. Instead of praying over her future occupation, husband, and friends, my only concern at that moment was whether or not she would live.

Though the PICU guidelines stated only two could visit at a time, Dr. Preston ensured that exceptions were made for us. It was clear from the glares the staff sent his way when he wasn't looking that they resented his interference, but thankfully no one took out their frustrations on us or Isabella.

David and I tried to stay close to our daughter but out of the way, while my father and Mama Peg stood almost flush against the wall. My father never took his glowering eyes from Dr. Preston, and I think everyone understood if there was one death today, there would surely be two.

Dr. Reid occupied the position at the head of Isabella's bed. He held a clear bag with which to pump air into her mouth if needed. At the foot of her bed stood a nurse and a respiratory therapist. Dr. Preston explained he would be the one to remove her tube and if she didn't breathe on her own, it would quickly be reinserted. Though he was adamant that he didn't believe it would be necessary.

Isabella's eyes fluttered open, then closed again. Dr. Preston leaned over her. "Isabella, it's Grandpa. Listen, darling, we're going to take the tube out of your throat now. It's going to feel uncomfortable, but it will be over quickly."

Her mouth twitched.

He gently pried the white tape holding the tube in place from her skin. "When it comes out, you're going to need to take some deep breaths for us so we don't have to put it back in. Okay?"

I heard soft footsteps behind me and turned to see Lindsey slink into the room. With bags under her eyes and strings of disheveled hair hanging loose around her face, she looked like she was in equal need of a nap and a shower. Her weary gaze flitted from Isabella to Dr. Preston and finally rested on David's hand intertwined with mine. When her eyes met his, he dropped my hand and reached for hers.

Feeling cold and alone, I hugged my arms around myself.

"Here we go," Dr. Preston said. He grasped Isabella's ventilator tube. "When I count to three, sweetheart, I need you to hold your breath."

My heart froze as the gasping sound of the ventilator fell silent.

"One."

Lord . . .

"Two."

Please . . .

"Three."

Make her breathe. Oh, please, make her breathe.

Everyone's eyes were riveted on Isabella as Dr. Preston, in one fluid motion, pulled the tube from her mouth.

"Breathe," he commanded.

As seconds passed, her skin took on an unnatural purplish-red color. She made a gurgling sound, but her chest didn't rise. Another second passed. Then another. Panic filled me as I waited for someone to do something, anything. Dr. Reid stared hard at Dr. Preston.

"Come on, child, breathe," Dr. Preston said.

Dr. Reid pressed a clear mouthpiece over Isabella's lips, ready to pump air into her from the bag attached to it.

Dr. Preston pushed him away. "Not yet."

I moved to her side and pleaded in her ear. "Bella, it's Mommy. I need you to breathe. Baby, please, please breathe."

The room stood so quiet that the tick of the wall clock sounded like a drum.

"That's enough," Dr. Reid said to David's father. "Re-intubate."

Everyone came to life as if a director had called, "Action."

"No!" Dr. Preston bellowed.

Everyone froze again.

How much time had passed? I wondered. Had it been one full minute? two? How long could they wait?

My head swam. "Please," I cried. "Someone, please do something!"

No one moved. Isabella opened her mouth as if she wanted to breathe but couldn't remember how. I clamped my eyes shut. *Oh, God, please, please, please . . .*

I heard something that sounded like a tire leak and looked at Isabella. Her chest rose as she sucked in a breath.

"Another one, Bella. Take another one," Lindsey said, her voice the calm center of our hurricane.

Isabella turned her head, fixed her glazed eyes on David, and pulled in another breath.

I counted the seconds between the rise and fall of her chest. *One Mississippi, two Mississippi . . . five . . .*

Breath.

One Mississippi, two Mississippi . . . four . . .

Breath.

The nurse put a nasal cannula like Mama Peg's around Isabella's ears and slid the clear prongs into her nostrils. When Isabella's breaths became rhythmic and regular, everyone clapped while I could only sob.

When Dr. Preston turned around, his eyes were red and wet. It took me a moment before it registered that he'd been crying too. As long as I'd known him, I'd never seen him shed a tear. I wouldn't have believed it possible had I not seen it for myself.

He looked up to the ceiling and exhaled, then addressed the respiratory therapist and nurse. "I'll want her vital signs every fifteen minutes for an hour, then Q two. Get a blood gas and—"

"What are her respirations?" Dr. Reid asked.

The nurse answered, "Fourteen."

"Very good. Her oxygen saturation?"

The respiratory therapist grinned. "Eighty-five percent and rising."

Dr. Reid pulled his stethoscope off his neck and listened to Isabella's lungs. After a minute, he turned to Dr. Preston with a smile. "She sounds most excellent."

"Of course she does, Doctor," David's father said smugly.

Dr. Reid looked at him, then left the room.

I kissed Isabella's damp forehead. "Bella, can you hear me?"

She stirred but didn't open her eyes.

Dr. Preston stood beside me and gently forced her lids open with his fingers. He pulled a penlight from his lab coat and shined it in her eyes. "They're dilating." His tone told me that was a good thing.

"When will we know if she's going to be okay?" I asked him.

He turned a small black wall knob. A tiny ball rose within a clear cylinder as he adjusted her oxygen level. "That's a good question, which I can't answer. This is the one thing that's completely out of our hands. We just have to wait and—"

A horrible raspy sound came from Isabella.

I looked down at her. With the exception of her breathing, she lay as still as a corpse—eyes closed, mouth slightly parted. Dr. Preston and I looked at one another questioningly, then back to her. I fixed my eyes intently on my daughter, refusing to blink so that I wouldn't miss any movement. Her lips moved so slightly I wondered if I imagined it. A thin string of spittle bridged her parted lips. "Maaa . . ."

My gaze flew behind me to David, then back to her.

I leaned over her. "Baby, I'm right next to you. Can you hear me?"

Slowly, she blinked her eyes open, looked right at me, and whispered. Her voice was so quiet and sounded like gravel, but I could still understand every beautiful word. I turned around and repeated what she'd said. "She's thirsty." I started to laugh. "Isabella said she's thirsty!"

"She's thirsty!" David exclaimed as he picked up Lindsey and spun her.

My father slapped Dr. Preston on the back so hard the sound resonated throughout the room. He jerked his hand back as if suddenly remembering their feud.

A nurse left the room and returned with something that looked like a synthetic lollipop. When she slid it into Isabella's mouth, my daughter clamped down so quick and hard that the nurse came close to losing a finger.

"What's that?" I asked her.

"It's a damp sponge. She needs to take it slow at first."

"Oh, for pity's sake," Mama Peg said. "Somebody get that child a glass of water."

The nurse tucked a strand of hair behind her ear and looked to Dr. Preston for direction.

He nodded his approval. "I'd do what Peggy says if I were you. You don't want to tick off a Lucas. They're as mean as bulldogs."

My father's mouth twitched as he fought to repress a smile.

I squatted by my daughter's side. I knew I should give her time to recover, but I just had to know. "Sweetness, why were you in the lake?"

The room grew still as everyone waited along with me for her answer.

She set her palm on my cheek. I slid it to my mouth and kissed it.

The nurse handed me a plastic cup filled with water. I held it to Isabella's lips and she drank. After she'd taken in several sips, I moved it away again. She swallowed and grimaced. "My throat hurts."

"It's from the tube," the nurse said, not looking up as she continued writing on Isabella's chart. "We'll get you some medicine that will make you feel better."

I brushed a curl from Isabella's cheek. "So, sweetness, please tell us why were you swimming all alone."

I squeezed her small hand to encourage her. It felt warm again, as if life had suddenly reentered her.

My daughter looked at me with her golden-brown eyes and gave me a look that seemed to say, *Don't you know?* "I was trying to get to you, Mommy. So we could be together forever."

Her answer left me speechless. As tears streamed down my face, I kissed her sweet lips and turned around.

"I don't understand," David said.

Mama Peg placed a hand over her heart. "Oh, my heavens. She was trying to cross the ocean."

I nodded as I wiped tears from my face.

My father cleared his throat the way men sometimes do to keep from crying. "You used the same analogy your mother used with you."

I nodded again, still unable to form words.

David and Lindsey shared a puzzled look.

The nurse took the cup from my hands and gave sips of water to Isabella, while I explained the metaphor to the Prestons.

When I finished, David said, "Jenny, it's clear she needs more time with you. Take a few more days with her. There's no hurry."

Lindsey yanked her hand from his. Her doe eyes flashed him an intense look I didn't comprehend. "No, David. Not just a few days."

His expression hardened into stone as he crossed his arms. "Lindsey . . ."

"No, you listen," she said. "We have forever with her; Jenny doesn't. That little girl needs her mother right now. They belong together."

David opened his mouth, but a cool look from Lindsey silenced him.

"We have forever," she repeated softly. "Forever, David."

CHAPTER TWENTY-EIGHT

WHEN I WAS pregnant, it was the oddest thing, but my sense of smell became so intensified it was like having a strange little superpower—albeit a useless one. The moment I walked into a grocery store, I'd know they were frosting a cake, steaming shrimp, or giving away samples of granola three aisles down. I don't know if it was hormones causing it or why I should experience that same phenomenon now that I was dying, but suddenly my olfactory abilities could rival a bloodhound's.

This would come in handy, of course, if I were called upon to sniff out smuggled drugs or prison escapees, but the only thing it really accomplished was to render me in a constant state of nausea. Even aromas that used to make my mouth water now only sickened me. I'd get within a hundred feet of most foods and my stomach would begin to churn like a cement mixer.

Today my heightened sense of smell was welcome for a change as it enunciated the stream's invigorating scents of earth and moss. I inhaled it, feeling an overwhelming appreciation for life—both mine and my daughter's.

Isabella and I sat hip to hip on my favorite boulder, watching tiny silver fish dart downstream as we wiggled our toes under crystalline water. Beams of sunlight speared the green canopy above, indiscriminately spotlighting unremarkable stones and piles of decaying leaves. Though Isabella had just been released from the hospital the day before, with the exception of a scratchy voice, you'd never have known she had been through a life-threatening trauma.

As her mother, however, it was obvious to me something was unmistakably different about her. My independent child had become an oversize appliqué. When I napped, she napped. When I needed fresh air, coincidentally, so did she. I couldn't even empty my bladder without her as an audience. I didn't mind her company, of course. I loved having her near me. After all we'd been through, I guess we were both a little fearful of losing each other.

I knew, however, that this clingy behavior could not be allowed to continue unchecked for much longer. Despite the fact that Isabella had lived through her ordeal, I would not be so lucky, which meant that the task of transitioning her to a life without me had to remain my first and foremost goal. How would I accomplish this? I had no worldly idea. I thought maybe inspiration would befall me there at the stream and had intended to come here alone to think, but when Isabella heard the back door open, she was by my side faster than I could say, "I'll be right back."

I touched the plastic hospital bracelet still around her wrist. "You know, you'll need to take that off sometime."

She turned her hand this way and that, admiring the adornment. "I like it."

"It is pretty cool," I agreed.

She laid her head against my arm. "Sarah had a bracelet like this."

"Supercool Sarah from preschool?"

I felt her head nod against me.

"Why was she in the hospital?"

She shrugged.

"Bella, I want you to promise me you'll never try to cross the ocean by yourself again. Or the lake. Or a puddle. Or anything. God says I have to go alone."

With her bare feet, she kicked at the stream and sent a spray of water over the ground. A salamander bounded from under a leaf and, before I could point him out to her, darted up a tree and out of sight.

"I wish you didn't have to go," she said.

"Me too. But God has things for you to do here—important things. When you finally do come join me in heaven, I'm going to ask if you did all the things you were supposed to do."

She grabbed her heel and forced her foot so close to her mouth that I thought she intended to bite her toenails. She examined her foot as if she'd never seen anything quite like it, then set it back in the water without explanation. "What things?"

I pulled her onto my lap and hugged her to me. "Well, I don't know exactly, but I suspect you'll need to go to college, help some hurting people, maybe hike across Europe, become a doctor who finds the cure for cancer, or possibly be the first woman president. I don't know." I turned her face toward me and grinned. "And of course, fall in love."

She opened her mouth and stuck her finger in, pantomiming a gag.

"Where did you learn that?"

She raised her palms and shrugged.

As I laughed, I hoped against hope that she'd forever keep the memory of this conversation tucked away in the recesses of her mind. "The thought of boys won't always make you gag. Someday they might not seem so yucky at all."

She ran her cold, wet foot down the length of mine. "Craig's not yucky."

"No," I agreed. He certainly wasn't.

She blew a curl out of her face. "What else do I have to do?"

I leaned back and studied a pair of blue jays taking turns flying in and out of a small nest. "Only God knows, but I definitely want some grandchildren. I'll need something interesting to watch from heaven in case there's no TV."

"From me?"

"You're the only one who can give them to me."

"How many?"

I laid my chin on the top of her head. "That's up to you and your husband."

"I want forty-two."

She couldn't see me smile. "My, but you'll be busy. Why so many?"

"Then they can do all my work for me."

I chuckled. "With forty-two mouths to feed, you might have a little work cut out for yourself, too. I suggest marrying a rich man with a big libido."

"What's a *lopeto*?"

I hugged her tighter. "Never mind. Do you promise you won't ever try anything like that again?"

She pushed off my lap and slipped her feet into her sandals. "I was really scared."

My heart sank as the phantom memories of her flailing and afraid rushed back to me. "I'll bet you were." I followed her lead and put my sandals back on. "Promise me, Bella." I hooked her chin with my finger, forcing her to look at me.

"I promise."

I knelt down and squeezed her tightly. It was so nice to feel her little heart beat against me. "That's a good girl. So, where are we off to?"

"My daddy shouldn't have done that." She held her hand out to me and I slipped my fingers around hers.

"Done what?"

She led me down the dirt path that would take us past the tree carved with David's and my initials, and eventually home. Pebbles and twigs crunched under my feet.

"He shouldn't have thrown me in the lake."

I stopped walking, causing her to follow suit. "Bells, your daddy didn't throw you in the lake. That was the pool, remember?"

She shook her head. "No, he threw me in the lake. I almost drowned and then they put that straw in my mouth and now my throat hurts."

I studied her a moment, trying to understand why her memory was so garbled. I didn't know if it was childhood confusion, the trauma of her near drowning, oxygen deprivation, or something else entirely, but I couldn't let her believe that David had tried to drown her. "Bells, you're getting confused. He didn't do that. You tried to cross the ocean to get to me, remember?"

She tucked her lips in, considering my words. "I still don't want to live with him."

"Isabella, when I go to heaven, you *are* going to live with your daddy and Lindsey."

Her eyes grew large with a fear I didn't understand. "He'll throw me in again."

"No, sweetness, your daddy would never hurt you. He loves you."

Her expression darkened.

"I promise."

She looked on the verge of tears. "He threw me in the pool."

"That's right, but it wasn't deep. All you had to do was stand up."

She opened her mouth and recognition seemed to wash over her face. "He didn't throw me in the lake. I woke up early and . . ." She searched my eyes as if she could read the missing chapter from her book there. "I wanted to get across and wait for you."

I picked her up and set her on my hip as I did when she was a baby. She was considerably heavier now and I was considerably weaker. Still it felt so good, so right, to feel her weight against my side. "That's right. But now you've promised you won't do that again. You promised me you would do all the things that growing-up girls do, and when you're old and God calls you home, *then* we'll have our very fine reunion."

She laid her head against my shoulder. "That will be a good day."

"A very good day," I agreed.

"Mommy?"

"Yes, sweetness?"

"Do you think Lindsey is pretty?"

Jealousy nipped at me. "Do you?"

"Very pretty."

"Prettier than me?" As soon as the words left my mouth, I knew I shouldn't have uttered them.

"Mommy?"

"Yes?"

"Do you love Daddy?"

I took in a deep breath. "Yes."

"Does he love you?"

A pain, far too familiar, stabbed my heart. "He loves Lindsey."

She gave me a look of pity, then kissed my forehead. "*I love you, Mommy.*"

Me too, a voice whispered behind us.

I turned, expecting to see Craig, but there was no one there.

"Did you hear that?" I asked her.

Head heavy against my shoulder, she peered at me through slits. "What?"

I took one more look behind me but saw only a squirrel scampering around the base of tree trunk.

"I'm losing it," I told the squirrel.

Thankfully he didn't answer.

CHAPTER TWENTY-NINE

IF LOOKS COULD kill, Isabella would soon be fatherless. Eyes ablaze, she slammed her Barbie onto the rug and torched David with a fiery glance. "Stop staring at me!"

David sat on our living room couch next to his wife, considering Isabella with a perplexed expression. I could see his wheels turning the problem around in his mind, searching for a logical solution to her irrational emotions.

Isabella was supposed to be visiting him and Lindsey at their home, but when they came to collect her, she refused to go. I wasn't at all surprised. No matter how many times I reminded her that David had not tried to drown her in the lake, and no matter how many times she recounted what had actually happened, her heart refused to believe what her mind knew.

Distracted by the tension, I had read the same sentence of my novel a half-dozen times and still didn't register its meaning. Giving up, I folded the corner of the page, set it on the coffee table, and addressed my daughter. "Bella, be nice."

Mama Peg sat across from me in her recliner, flipping through the *TV Guide*. The sound of paper rubbing against paper was magnified by the silent pause. "Someone needs a nap," she said.

Isabella twisted her face into something that reminded me of a gargoyle. "I do not!"

I tried to give her the same look my mother used on me to send shivers down my spine. "Don't you raise your voice, young lady."

It didn't have the same effect on my daughter. She dismissed it with a shrug.

I gestured to David. "Can I speak with you a minute?"

He looked at Lindsey as if needing her permission. She gave him a benign glance, then went back to watching Isabella play. At last he stood and followed me.

The kitchen still smelled of the balsamic vinaigrette Mama Peg had served with lunch, although the scent of lemon dish soap now nearly eclipsed it. Still dressed in church clothes, Craig had his hands buried in a sink full of water. Suds clung to the blond fuzz on his arms. He glanced over his shoulder at me, then nodded at David. "Hey, man."

David just looked at him, then back to me. "What?"

I rested my hand on the grooves of the doorjamb. "I know this is going to sound crazy, but she holds you responsible for almost drowning."

He studied me a minute, then narrowed his eyes. "What exactly did you tell her?"

My eyes narrowed back. "What do you mean, what did I tell her?"

"Why would she think that? You must have said something."

I didn't care for his tone one bit. Just like my father, he always felt the need to find a scapegoat. If something was wrong, someone had to be to blame. I hated that about both of them. "I didn't tell her you tried to murder her, if that's what you're implying."

He crossed his arms. "Then how would she get that idea?"

Rather than look into his accusatory eyes, I focused on the tiny galloping horse embroidered on his shirt, trying to digest how quickly our hospital truce had come to an end . . . along with the mirage that he was a decent, rational human being. "She's a child. How do they get any ideas they have? I told her you didn't do it. She knows you didn't do it, but she still *feels* like you did."

"You're not making sense. She was in your care. If anyone's to blame, it's you."

My fingernails dug into my palms as I looked at him. Standing before me was the only person in the world, with the exception of my father, who could take me from zero to fury in under a minute.

I noticed Craig watching him—a lion ready to pounce. I didn't want a scene to erupt with Isabella in the next room. I softened my voice. "It's no one's fault, David. Not yours. Not mine. I realize it's irrational, but girls sometimes feel things that don't make logical sense. You can't go at this problem like a math equation. It's more like—" I searched my mind for a worthy comparison—"abstract art."

I could tell by his incredulous expression that he wasn't anywhere close to getting it. I sighed. "Just apologize to her."

He looked at me like I'd lost my mind. "For what?"

"For trying to drown her."

"You're even crazier than your old man."

Craig threw his sponge into the sink, making water slosh over the counter. Before he could make a move for David, I put my hand up to stop him. A growl-like sound erupted from him as he stalked out the back door.

When it slammed shut, I felt the vibration run through me. "David, I'm trying to help you here." It was exasperating trying to explain to a man something I knew most women would understand instinctively. "It's like when you have a dream that someone you love hurts you. Even though you know they didn't really do it, your heart still feels the betrayal. Saying you're sorry isn't admitting guilt, it's . . ." I tried to find the words, but defining emotion was no easy task. "It's just the way she feels, okay? Just say you're sorry and she'll get over it."

David sneered at me. "I think the cancer's spread to your brain."

As I watched him tramp back to the living room, I contemplated how that man could be the one I'd spent nearly ten years pining over. I never thought I'd see the day I got over David Preston, but at that very moment, standing in the wake of his contempt, I was well on my way. Dreams long held are often the slowest to burn, and that was true in this case as well, but the fantasy had certainly begun to blacken and curl.

This realization was bittersweet. How much time had I wasted loving a man who wasn't worthy of my love? Had I let David go when I should have, might I have opened my heart to Craig when there was still time to do something about it? The suds from the counter glided slowly down the cabinet.

Rather than brood about my emotional retardation or allow myself to relive a past that no longer mattered, I forced myself back to the living room and leaned against the wall.

David and Lindsey held hands on the couch while Mama Peg rested in her recliner, feet up, eyes closed, wearing a hint of a smile. In her own world, Isabella played solitary Barbie on the rug. If Norman Rockwell had captured the scene before my eyes, viewers would assume this to be a happy, all-American family. Sometimes a picture was worth a thousand lies.

Isabella held a half-dressed Barbie in one hand and a gown-clad Barbie in the other as she mumbled a conversation that only she could hear. Her back remained to the group. I wasn't sure if I should force her to interact with David and Lindsey or if it would do more damage than good.

David let go of Lindsey's hand, leaned forward, and glared at me. "We don't need you to supervise."

Lindsey jerked her head toward him. "David!"

I let his hurled stone clank impotently against my heart's new armor. Although his words could no longer hurt me as they'd done in the past, they still had sufficient power to tick me off. "This is my house, right? I mean, I do live here and you are a guest?"

His gaze slithered down me. "Oh? I hadn't realized you purchased your father's residence."

I shook my head in awe of his pompousness. "Must you always show your—"

Mama Peg threw down the *TV Guide*. It skidded across the end table onto the floor. "You've got to be kidding me! After all you two just went through." She thrust her arm out, pointing in Isabella's direction. "After all that little girl almost lost and will lose. Are you really going to make her listen to her parents behave like Neanderthals?" Her gaze moved from me to David. "Really?"

I looked at Isabella. She'd stopped playing and was watching the exchange with eyes so sad. Hot shame filled me.

Mama Peg pulled up the lever on the side of her chair, lowering her legs in one quick motion. "I can't bear to watch you fools. I'm taking a nap." With great effort, she pushed herself up from the chair and grabbed the handle of her oxygen tank. "If I'm lucky, maybe I'll dream about a family that isn't a bunch of selfish ninnies."

I watched her walk away, her disapproval lingering in the air. No one made a sound until her bedroom door clicked shut.

Lindsey pushed off the couch and made her way to Isabella. "I used to love to play Barbies."

Of course she did, I thought. Little prima donna probably never climbed a tree in her whole life or touched a frog . . . unless you counted David.

David glowered at me. "Something funny?"

Still wearing my smirk, I shook my head.

Lindsey's sleek hair fell into her face as she knelt beside Isabella. She tucked it behind her ears, picked up a spare Barbie, and proceeded to make the doll do cartwheels. Isabella paused as she watched the gymnastics routine from the corner of her eye.

Someone touched my arm. I turned to find Craig in the doorway, motioning toward the kitchen. I followed him.

"What's up?" I asked.

He tucked his fingertips into the pockets of the jeans he'd changed into. "Why don't we get out of here for a little while and give them some privacy?"

I looked back to the doorway. "Isabella would freak if I tried to leave."

He scratched at his Adam's apple. "Maybe, but she'd get over it quick enough. I've got something I want to show you."

I smiled. "As long as it doesn't come in a little black box."

He didn't smile back. "I'm serious, Jenny. I have a surprise for you."

The thought of him proposing again sent a thrill of excitement up my spine. As flattering as his advances were, though, they were equally draining. I didn't think I could keep telling him no. With the ever-growing affection I felt for him, eventually I'd cave and further complicate an already-complicated situation. Besides, I was certain that Isabella would throw the world's biggest hissy fit if I left her with David. "Another time, okay? She gets so worried when I'm away from her."

"*She* gets that way?"

I opened my mouth to defend myself, but his puckered lips stole my retort.

His kiss sent a current more powerful than a bolt of lightning through me. Speechless, I touched my lips and looked at him.

"Did that change your mind?" he asked, looking pleased with himself.

When I shook my head, disappointment dulled his eyes. I hated that my answer always seemed to be no, but as much as he wanted my company, Isabella needed me more. "I'm sorry, Craig. She's just not ready." I gave his arm an affectionate squeeze and made my way back to the living room.

I laid a hand over my mouth to keep from gasping at what I saw there. Isabella now sat on Lindsey's lap while David lay on his side next to them. Isabella lifted a one-armed Ken doll from her case and held it just out of his reach. "Are you *really* sorry, Daddy?"

From where I stood, I couldn't see his expression, but whatever it was, it sent her into a giggling fit. She handed him the doll. The jealousy I felt was not far from what I felt watching David show affection to Lindsey. I knew it was wrong, but still I couldn't deny it.

I turned around and found myself nose to nose with Craig. His warm breath fell on my skin as he said, "I think they'll be okay without you."

CHAPTER THIRTY

GRAY AND GLOOMY, the afternoon sky couldn't have mirrored my mood any better. As Craig drove, I looked upward, thinking of Isabella and feeling more than a little sorry for myself. The rain clouds that had been cloaking the sun slid away before more could move in to take their place. Like a captive set free, sunlight burst through the windshield and into my eyes. I held a hand over my face as I pulled down the visor.

Craig shifted into the next gear, sending my shoulders thrusting back against the bench seat while my insides lurched forward. I laid a hand on my middle as if the gesture had the power to settle my stomach.

He gave me a worried glance. "You okay? You look a little green."

"Just a little." I turned toward the open window and drew in a deep breath. The air was so humid, it felt like I was inhaling kettle steam. Sticky tresses clung to my damp skin. I pulled my hair into a mock ponytail to get some wind on my neck.

"You need me to pull over?" he asked.

Not wanting to upset him, I shook my head. I knew when the flat land turned into rolling hills and the stink of manure filled the air that we were approaching Lemley's Dairy Farm. I winced and shut my window.

Craig did likewise, then turned on the AC. A Christmas tree air freshener swayed from the rearview mirror. Its original green color had long since faded to an ugly yellow.

I lifted it and brought it to my nose, hoping to counter the stench of dung. It smelled like old cardboard instead of pine. "Why do you keep this?"

He squinted as if seeing it for the first time. "Decoration?"

I raised an eyebrow.

"Actually, I didn't even know I had that thing. Probably came with the truck."

More amused than annoyed, I shook my head. "You might want to work on your powers of observation there, Sherlock." I stared out the window and watched grazing cows blur by. My feet vibrated against the floor, jostling my thin legs with the road's every bump and crater.

Craig tapped my shoulder with his fist. "My powers of observation might not set the world on fire, Miss Lucas, but there's something to be said for having the ability to filter out things that don't much matter."

My head felt heavy and I leaned it against the window. The trembling glass rattled my skull. Not relishing the thought of a migraine, I picked my head back up. "Maybe so, but you might find the ability to notice minute details comes in handy if you ever get married."

He took his eyes off the road for a split second to question me with a glance. "How so?"

I straightened a kink in my seat belt. "Your wife comes home from the salon after having her hair highlighted. Now she's standing in front of you, all expectation and smiles, asking if you notice anything different about her."

Craig made a face. "She wouldn't expect me to notice a few blonde streaks in her hair."

"Of course she would," I said. "Or if she had her eyebrows waxed, lost five pounds, or—"

"*Five* pounds? Oh, c'mon. That's like asking a woman to notice a new pack of drill bits in my toolbox."

"If she looked—" I breathed a puff of hot air onto the window and drew a heart with my finger—"she would probably notice." The fog on the glass dissipated, taking the heart with it.

Neither of us spoke for the next mile or so until Craig broke the silence. "*You* wouldn't expect me to notice those things, would you?"

I thought for a second. "I wouldn't *expect* you to, but what can I say? I'm a woman. I'd *like* you to."

He started throwing troubled glances at my hair.

"It's okay, Craig. It's not highlighted."

"Of course not." He grinned at me. "I would have noticed."

"No doubt in my mind." The air-conditioning began to make me feel like the abominable snow woman. I reached over and turned it down. "Is this why you had me dress warm?"

He stared straight ahead at the road. "Nope."

"Where are we going?"

"For the last time, you'll see when we get there."

"I need to know when I'll be getting back to my daughter. She needs—"

"She needs you to stop worrying. She'll be just fine. Lindsey told you that. I told you that. Even Isabella told you that. You'll be home before Ken kisses Barbie good night."

"Tell me where we're going."

"No."

"Tell me."

"Stop it."

"Please?"

"You need to learn to take no for an answer."

I huffed and crossed my arms.

He brushed my cheek with the back of his hand. "C'mon, Jenny. It won't be a surprise if I tell you."

"I hate surprises."

"Too bad, so sad."

"How about a hint?"

He grunted. "Okay, one hint. About a year after you left, someone discovered something very special in a neighboring town."

"What town?" I asked.

"I've said enough."

"Fossils?"

Craig scrunched his face at the road. "I'm not saying another word to you until we get there." And for almost an hour, he didn't.

Slowing the truck, he pulled onto the shoulder of the road and shifted into park. He reached under the seat, pulled out a striped tie, and held it before me. "We're almost there. I need you to put this on."

I looked at the tie and again at him. "What kind of place requires a woman to wear a tie?"

He held it up, leaned toward me, and laid it flat across my eyes. The silky fabric felt cool against my skin. His fingers brushed against my ear sending tingles down my neck, and excitement welled up inside me.

Once, when it my mother's birthday, my father had tied a blindfold over her eyes and led her from the house. Watching from the window, I squealed in delight as Mom's dress swished about her legs and my father grinned bigger than I'd ever seen him. I used to dream that one day David would do the same for me.

"Keep that on until I tell you, okay?" Craig said.

I could technically keep it on and still sneak a peek, right? "Okay."

"And no peeking."

I said nothing.

"Jenny, no peeking. Promise?"

I had hoped he'd interpret my silence as concession.

He didn't. "Jenny?"

I tucked in my lips and turned away.

His voice grew stern. "Genevieve Paige Lucas?"

Touched at his use of my full name, I turned toward him. "You know my middle name."

"Don't change the subject. Promise me."

At last I grunted in defeat. "Okay, already. I promise."

I felt the truck move again, and soon we made a right onto a surface smoother than the battered road we'd ridden in on.

"We're here," he said. "Remember, no peeking."

I felt for my seat buckle and unlatched it. His door slammed shut. I heard mine open and a wall of humidity met me.

Craig's hand grasped mine. "I've got you, baby. Come on out."

My heart fluttered at the endearment. I'd always wanted to be someone's baby. David had called me that once, but his halfhearted utterance rang flat and foreign. From Craig's sweet lips, however, it sounded as right as rain.

I climbed out of the truck and let Craig guide me by the elbow. It felt odd and a little disconcerting to be blindly led to a destination I couldn't even guess. I trusted Craig, of course, but still my stomach was a mosh pit of butterflies.

Each blind step I took was heavy with uncertainty. He led me through what must have been a parking lot. We paused and a door creaked open. I felt my way through it, fingertips grazing wood as I stepped inside.

The heat of the outdoors was superseded by cold dankness. The place smelled of earth and mildew. "How many?" a woman asked. Her voice was soft and shaky. I guessed her to be a slight woman in her sixties.

"Just us," Craig replied. He must have received a questioning look because he added, "I'm surprising her."

"Well, now, ain't she just the prettiest little thing you ever saw?" Her question sounded more like an accusation than a compliment.

"She sure is," Craig said. I could hear the smile in his voice.

"Is it her birthday?" she asked.

I was beginning to feel like a nonperson standing there, being spoken about instead of to, as though I weren't just blindfolded but deaf as well. "Not my birthday," I said. "He just likes to be dramatic."

She laughed. "Men are like that, darlin'. They like to accuse us women of being drama queens, but you just have to see a grown man sick once to know that's the pot calling the kettle black." She paused. "That'll be twenty even."

A rapping sound was followed by the ding of a cash register shooting open. It slammed shut again. "We'll wait about five minutes or so to see if anyone else comes; then Harry will take you below."

Below? I fingered the button of the cardigan that Craig insisted I wear, trying to figure out what sort of place we'd need to go down into. An underground casino? A tunnel? Maybe it was an old bunker from the cold war era turned into a museum. None of the possibilities seemed to warrant the wearing of a blindfold, but wherever we were going, it certainly beat sitting around the house watching Isabella bond with her new parents.

As we waited, I leaned into Craig. He laid his arm across my shoulder, enveloping me in his warmth and affection. I turned my face toward him and inhaled his smell.

After what seemed like far longer than five minutes, a gruff male voice axed through the silence. "We 'bout ready, Janice?"

I imagined he must be Harry. As soon as the words left his mouth, I heard the door open again and several sets of feet scuffle across the floor.

"Hello," a male and a female voice said simultaneously.

"Three?" Janice asked.

"What's wrong with her?" a boy's voice demanded. He sounded a little older than Isabella. I assumed I was the "her" he referred to.

"I'm surprising her," Craig answered.

"You can't see," the boy said in a mocking tone. He must have been very close to me because I could smell something like sour milk on his breath.

It left me uneasy to not be able to see his proximity, body language, or expression.

GINA HOLMES

"Do you even know where we are?" the boy asked.

The cash register dinged to life once more.

I shook my head, wondering if I could incite him into telling me. "I'll bet you don't know either."

Instead of filling me in, the brat said, "Nice try."

Craig laughed. "I like that kid already."

That made one of us.

"Let's get this show on the road," Harry said.

Craig gathered my cold hand into his warm one and helped me stand. Following the other footsteps and voices, he led me a hundred or so feet before we stopped.

"How long you gonna make the missus wear that thing?" Harry asked.

"Just until we get to the bottom," Craig answered.

"Well," Harry said, "make sure you've got her, then. Those stairs are mighty steep."

Craig tightened his grip. "Don't you worry. It would take an act of God to make me let her go." He placed my hand around a cold, metal rail and clasped my waist. "Jenny, just take it slow. Like he said, the stairs are steep."

As he nudged me downward, anxiety filled me. I wanted to know where I was and what waited below. I was certain it must be safe, but still apprehension filled me.

One slow step at a time, with Craig beside me, I descended into the unknown. The air grew colder and damper with each step, and a slow, steady drip echoed in my ears.

No matter how many times or ways I told myself there was nothing to fear, my heart still beat faster.

As I descended, Craig whispered in my ear. "I know that it must be frightening to think about dying, but the darkness won't last forever." His grip tightened around my waist. "The next step is the last and then it's flat ground."

"You're going to want to grab that young'un's hand." There was something foreboding in Harry's tone that made my stomach tighten.

I heard a loud click . . . then a scream.

"Turn the lights back on! Turn them on!" the boy yelled.

"It's okay," his mother cooed. "I've got you. I've got you."

Terror raced through me. Promise or no promise, I ripped my blindfold off. The darkest blackness I could imagine loomed before my eyes—cold, uncertain nothingness. The boy continued to shriek. Try as I might, I couldn't catch my breath. If Craig's hand hadn't been grasping mine, I feel sure I would have died of fright. I was on the verge of screaming myself when Craig whispered in my ear again. "But then everything changes in the blink of an eye."

Another click preceded the sudden onslaught of spot-lights.

As my eyes adjusted, an underground paradise came into view. Inside a cavern, man-made lights illuminated God-made wonders.

From the cathedral-like ceiling, crystals bound together to form what looked like a castle made of diamonds. Beneath it, a smooth pool of glittering gold lay undisturbed save for the one drip gliding down a formation into it.

All around us, rich, colored lights reflected off crystal formations, making me feel as though I were standing in the center of a giant crown of jewels.

As I looked up at the magnificence that seemed to have no end, my mouth fell open. Everyone's mouth fell open, even Harry's—who surprised me by being a small, neat man with a kind face. Still plastered to his mother's side, the little boy who'd been screaming his head off seconds ago now looked completely at peace with his wide eyes and cherub cheeks.

I turned to Craig. "This is incredible."

With everyone fixed on the cavern, he gathered me in his arms and locked eyes with me. "Do you see, Jenny? One minute blackness and the unknown, but then just like that, everything changes."

I felt myself start to choke up as I considered the analogy Craig had presented me. I'd known logically that when death overtook me, the pain and fear would be so very brief in the grand scheme of eternity. I knew that those few scary moments accompanying my passing would be nothing compared to the eternal splendor awaiting me on the other side. I'd wake up in heaven—pearl gates, streets of gold, mansions, and all of that. Even though my mind understood, until that very moment I hadn't truly grasped it in my soul. When it hit me, it hit me hard and it was all I could do not to drop to my knees.

Craig pulled me tighter against him. "I love you, Jenny."

In that moment of nirvana, my heart forgot all the reasons why I wasn't allowed to love him . . . and it just did.

CHAPTER THIRTY-ONE

THE REST OF the summer passed uneventfully. Isabella spent more and more time with the Prestons, while Craig and I became steady companions. When September was ushered out by October, it took what remained of my health with it.

I had always found it difficult to fully enjoy the beauty of autumn. The trees ablaze with color were certainly magnificent to behold, but to me, these brilliant flashes of gold and crimson fluttering to the ground were little more than a pretty curtain falling on a soon-to-be empty stage. I had always hated the thought of winter's impending arrival, and that was true this year more than ever.

As I did most mornings, I sat with an afghan tucked

around my thin legs, waving good-bye to my daughter as she trekked off to school, hand in hand with her cowpa.

Weeks ago, when Lindsey offered to enroll her in Tullytown Elementary, it was all I could do not to bawl. Not just because my little girl was no longer a baby, or the fact that I wouldn't get to sign her up myself, but because I hadn't even had the sense about me to think of it.

Watching my dad walking hand in hand with her reminded me of the father I knew as a little girl—the daddy who packed my lunch, walked me to the bus stop, and pushed me on the swing so high that my mother would shriek with terror. For the first time, I found myself considering that he may have loved me as much as I loved Isabella. Somehow this seemed both likely and impossible.

I called after them, "Bells, you have your lunch?"

She turned and held a small brown bag high above her head. Every day I asked her, and every day she responded the same way. I think the question was just my lame excuse to see her beautiful face one more time . . . just in case. I rocked back and forth in my chair, watching the two of them make their way to the very corner where I had waited as a child.

As they disappeared around the bend, I turned my attention to the lawn. By the time they lowered my casket into the ground, this grass would be faded to the color of straw. Seeing the vibrancy of the green bleed from it a little more each day was like watching sand slip through an hourglass, and boy, was it slipping fast.

A gust of wind rang the chimes that my father had hung the week before. Mama Peg said they reminded her of church bells, but to my ears they sounded like claws on a chalkboard. I pulled my sweater tighter and brushed a strand of hair from my eyes. The moment the chimes quieted, I felt another breeze, this one much warmer than the last. Strangely the chimes remained silent. Instead, I heard a familiar voice whisper, *Fall begets winter; winter begets spring.*

I rocked faster, trying to ignore it. More and more frequently, I'd hear what sounded like someone sighing cryptic messages into the wind. Instead of these strange little tidings that I'd long since given up trying to decipher, I wished they'd say something useful like "You forgot to put water in the teakettle" or "Hey, your zipper's down."

Now and then, hands I could not see would stroke my face or arm, covering me in a fresh crop of gooseflesh. Sometimes I would even smell strange fragrances, like incense or spices, for which I could find no explanation.

I liked to imagine that the closer I got to death, the more the spiritual realm opened to me, releasing glimpses of the afterlife. That's what I wanted to believe, but a little research indicated that David was probably spot-on when he suggested that the cancer had spread to my brain.

I considered scheduling a CAT scan so I could know for sure but decided it really served no purpose. Tumor or no tumor, it changed nothing. My body was in far worse shape than my mind.

After fifteen minutes or so, my father sauntered back and

kissed my cheek, just as he did every morning. His lips felt cold against my fevered skin. "See you later, pumpkin."

"Where you off to in those snazzy britches?" I asked.

He looked down at his checkered pants, then back to me. "I thought I'd teach Miss Rachael how to swing a nine iron. Her drive—" he chuckled—"or should I say *putt*, needs a little help."

"You've been seeing a lot of her."

He shrugged. "She's not your mother, but we have fun." He looked like he was about to say something else but changed his mind. "Tell your grandma I won't be home for supper."

I suspected his new love life had less to do with his fondness for Rachael or golf than it did with having an excuse not to be around me. I didn't think he could stomach watching someone he loved waste away . . . again. Although his growing distance bothered me, I figured if my dying jump-started his living, at least something good was coming from it.

"This must be getting serious. That's three times this week."

His face turned shades of red. "Oh, c'mon, Jenny. I just like having someone to pal around with. I've only been seeing her a couple months. It's no more serious than you and Craig."

I almost choked on that one. He obviously didn't understand what Craig and I had become to each other.

"Can you get Isabella off the bus this afternoon?" he asked.

"Of course."

He squatted beside me and gathered my hands into his. That gesture, coupled with the exaggerated concern on his face, made him look like a soap opera actor. "Are you sure you're up for it?"

I pulled my hands away. "Good grief, Dad. I'm not dead yet."

He looked as if I had slapped him. "I wish you wouldn't talk that way."

"I'm just tired of everyone treating me like I'm a china doll. I'm not made of porcelain; I'm not going to break."

Something hit the sidewalk. I looked down at an acorn, then up at the squirrel scampering across the gutter.

"I'm sorry," I said, turning back to my father. "Go. I'm fine. You kids have fun."

He stood and looked down at me. "Jenny, make sure you eat today."

It took everything in me not to say something sarcastic, but I reminded myself that his motivation was love. "I'll try."

He studied me a moment, then nodded.

I watched his car back out of the driveway, then gathered up my blanket and went inside.

The kitchen smelled of Mama Peg and maple syrup. My grandmother sat at the table with a half-eaten stack of pancakes in front of her. Her breathing sounded labored; her skin was the color of ash. In other words, she looked like she usually did.

I picked up her dish. "Finished?"

She glanced up from her crossword. A bit of breakfast clung just above her lip like a mole. "Put that down. I'll take care of it."

I draped my blanket across the back of a chair. "I've already got it."

She stood and took the dish from my hand. "You don't need to be doing that."

"I'm fine." I reached for the plate again.

She pulled it back. "Jenny, you need your strength."

I felt my cheeks catch fire and something inside me snap. "Stop it!"

She flinched. "Honey—"

"*Honey*, nothing. News flash: You're not the picture of health either, in case you haven't noticed. You want me to start treating *you* like an invalid?"

I snatched the plate back out of her hand and marched over to the sink. After shoving the pancakes into the garbage disposal, I scoured the plate as if it had an inch of caked-on grease, trying to work off my frustration. It seemed like a day couldn't pass without someone trying to remind me that I was dying—as if I could forget.

I scrubbed and scrubbed until my anger had slipped down the drain with the last of the suds. I wrung out the sponge and stood there, trying to get up the nerve to turn around.

Preparing to face her, I looked out the window at the lake, drew in a breath, and braced myself for retribution—the cold shoulder, a lecture, or at the very least, a disapproving scowl. When I turned, Mama Peg was doing none of those things.

Her reaction was something far more punishing—she was crying.

I don't think I'd ever felt as bad as I did at that moment. I hurried over and hugged her. "I'm so sorry, Mama Peg."

She lowered her hands, revealing glistening eyes and a trickling nose. "It's okay, Jenny. We all have our moments, and you were right."

I kissed her forehead. "I shouldn't have talked to you that way."

She picked a napkin from the table and wiped her face with it. "No, you shouldn't have, but I probably would have reacted the same way if you treated me like we've been treating you. I wasn't crying because of that, anyway."

I waited for her to explain, but she just dabbed at her face. Afraid I'd send her into another crying fit if I pushed the issue, I decided not to ask. My grandmother had always been our family's pillar of strength, and seeing her break down shook my sense of well-being, which was quaking as it was.

After we progressed past tears into small talk, I felt safe enough to excuse myself for my morning nap.

"Okay, kiddo." She blew her nose. "I'm going to putz around a bit. Then I might rest too."

I started to walk away.

"Jenny?"

I turned around.

"You know," she said, "sometimes I tend to focus so much on the future that I forget about today."

"Me too," I said.

"You're dying, Jenny, that's true; but you're also still living."

As I lay in bed, a strange buzz zipped past me. I looked around and saw no movement except flecks of dust hovering on a sunbeam. I shut my eyes. Not a minute later, there it was again.

I pushed myself onto my elbows and looked around my bedroom. Isabella's stuffed koala sat on the dresser. I squinted at him and he stared back with coal eyes. Suddenly one of the eyes took flight. The buzzing sound grew louder as the eye barreled through the air toward me like a kamikaze pilot. Before I had time to make sense of it or react, it crashed into the side of my face and dropped to the bed. I rubbed at my cheek and looked down, thankful to find not a koala eye but a way more logical stinkbug. He lay upside down atop my cover, his threadlike legs squirming in the air.

I gently flicked him upright and he flashed across the room again. I laid my head back down and was almost asleep when I heard, *Zzt, zzt, zzzzzzzt*. I let out a frustrated groan and sat up. The noise continued. Looking up, I spotted a blur of black slamming around the inside cover of the overhead light.

"How in the world did you get in there?"

David used to make fun of me because I wouldn't let him kill flies. Instead, I insisted he catch them and release them outside. He would mumble to himself as he obliged. After watching my mother die, I just couldn't stand to see anything suffer . . . not even an insect. I pushed myself off the bed as the bug grew more and more frantic inside his light-fixture prison. "Calm down. I'm coming to let you out."

An armchair sat by the window. I tried to lift it, but it was too heavy, and I was too weak. Giving up, I dragged it to the center of the room, just under the light. Cautiously, I climbed up on the cushion, reached over my head, twisted the tiny screws holding the cover in place, and removed it. The moment he tasted freedom, the ungrateful bug rocketed into my face again.

As I batted him away, I felt the chair cushion slip under my foot. I threw my hands up just in time to protect my face from colliding with the floor. Though my shoulder took the brunt of the blow, it was my foot that exploded in pain. I grabbed it and groaned.

Mama Peg called up, "Jenny! You okay?"

It took me a minute before I could even answer. She called again, this time panicked. "Jenny, answer me!"

"I'm okay," I called back, afraid that if I didn't answer right away, she'd try to come up after me, huffing and puffing, dragging that tank of hers. "I'm getting up." I pushed myself off the floor, cringing at the soreness in my wrists.

Lately, I hurt everywhere, all the time, but this was worse than usual. Slowly I made my way onto my knees and stood. The moment I put my full weight on my feet, a fresh jolt of pain shot up my toes to my ankle and knocked me back to the ground. This fall wasn't nearly as bad as the first, but when I tried to get back up, the room twisted and whirled, blood rushed to my head . . . and everything faded.

I don't know how long I was unconscious, but when I opened my eyes, two gluey-white pools blinked back at me. Labored breaths that smelled of syrup puffed on my face. Disoriented, I pulled my head back and squinted. Mama Peg lay on the floor beside me, her oxygen tank flat on its side. Wiry hairs sprung out from her off-center bun like coils through an old mattress. "Jenny?"

I wasn't sure if I was still dreaming. "Why are we on the floor?"

"You fell," she said. "Twice, I think, by the sound of it."

My body lay at a strange angle with my leg bent behind me as though I were preparing to kick a ball. I straightened it out, cringing at the pain. My right foot was double the size of my left. It took me a second to remember why. "If I'm the one who fell, then why are you on the floor?"

"Misery loves company." She wheezed through strained breaths.

"You sound horrible."

She coughed. "Thanks."

I motioned to her tank. "You made it all the way up here dragging that?"

"The things we do for love," she said.

I tried to push myself up, but my head pulsated with pain. I laid it back down.

"I quit trying too," Mama Peg said with a frown. "Looks like we might be here awhile."

"When's the last time you were up here?" I asked.

"I stopped doing stairs about five years ago." She turned her head and, eyed the room. "I like what you've done with this place."

I followed her gaze. It did look cute. I tilted my head back and glanced at the striped blue valances I'd hung. "I found those curtains in the attic."

She studied them. "They look a lot better in here than they ever did in the den."

"Thanks," I said.

We lay there awhile just staring at each other until I finally said, "I'm afraid if I try to get up again, I'll pass out."

Her bushy eyebrows looked even more unruly than usual. "I might need a forklift to get me off this floor."

"We should probably call someone to help us," I said.

She twisted her mouth thoughtfully. "I hate to be a bother."

I laughed at that.

"Glad you can find humor," she said.

"It is pretty funny."

She smiled a toothless smile. She must have removed her dentures to take a nap. "I imagine it would be, to you."

"What's that supposed to mean?"

"You always did find humor in strange places," she said.

"Wonder who I get that from." If I had inherited anything from Mama Peg, it was her sense of humor, and she knew it.

I leaned on my elbow and propped my head on my palm. My head throbbed, but a little less than the first time I had tried to raise it. I figured if I lay like that for a minute or two, it might settle down. "Hey, why were you crying earlier?"

She focused on the ceiling instead of me.

I regretted the question. "It's okay; you don't have to answer."

"No," she said, "it's okay. It just struck me that you were really dying." She traced her finger over a spot on the oxygen tank where the green paint had flecked off. "And that I was dying too."

I felt as if I should say something insightful or comforting, but what was there to say? We really were both dying. It probably needed to strike her sooner or later.

Her naked gums looked more gray than pink. I couldn't help but focus on them as she spoke. "What time does Bella get off the bus?"

Alarm and adrenaline filled me. "Shoot. How long have we been lying here?"

"Honestly, I don't know. We both were out for a while."

I looked at the alarm clock on my dresser. The dread I felt at missing Isabella's bus was far worse than the pain in my temples. "Twenty minutes ago."

With what looked like great difficulty, Mama Peg pushed herself up to a sitting position. "Kid, I'm sorry, but I don't think I can stand by myself."

My cell phone rang downstairs and I knew I'd never make it in time. It was probably the school. They had a policy of not letting a child off the bus unless an authorized adult was there to walk them home. This meant she was probably sitting in the office right then, wondering where her mother was and feeling abandoned. That would be the best-case scenario. I couldn't bring myself to entertain the worst.

Slowly I stood and looked down at my grandmother. Not knowing what else to do, I offered a hand to her.

She batted it away. "You try to help my fat butt up and you'll be down here again with me. Go call Craig to pick up Bella. I can wait."

It took what felt like more energy than I had to hop my way down the steps. When I finally made it to my phone to call Craig, it just rang and rang. I left a message and sighed. My father didn't carry a cell phone, so that left only David. If it hadn't been my daughter at stake, I would never have considered contacting him.

He'd been on his best behavior lately, waiting patiently for me to die so he could claim his daughter. Still, he managed to sneak in a jab every now and then when Lindsey wasn't around to chide him for it. And this was just the sort of thing he would rub in my face . . . discreetly, of course.

As I dialed, a frantic pounding bellowed from the front door. I didn't need to open it to know who was there. The school must have called David when they couldn't reach me. By the time I dragged myself over, I was so exhausted that I almost collapsed into his arms.

CHAPTER THIRTY-TWO

THE DOCTOR TOLD me that my foot was broken and needed to be set and cast. I told her, "Yeah . . . no."

Crossing her arms, she lectured me on what could happen down the road if it didn't heal properly. Did I really want to have my foot rebroken in six months? I told her that I'd take my chances. Her disapproving scowl made me laugh. Though I was third-world thin and as pale as her lab coat, the joke was apparently lost on her.

No way was I going to spend my final weeks in a hard, itchy cast. Once I explained that I was about to knock on heaven's door, pity replaced irritation. She wrapped my foot in Ace bandages and sent me home with her blessing and a pair of crutches.

And so I sat on my front porch, occupying two rocking chairs—one for me and one for my foot. The night air felt unmistakably autumn—crisp, but not cold. Gone were the floral fragrances of summer. In their place, the scent of cinnamon and apples drifted through the cracked-open window as Mama Peg baked a pie with the first batch of apples ever harvested from Mom's tree. My sweet grandmother was constantly baking and cooking my favorite things in an attempt to get me to eat more. Even so, I never managed more than a few bites before my stomach revolted.

Dressed in the only pair of flannel pajamas I owned that didn't slip down my meatless hips the moment I stood, I leaned my head back against the wood spokes of the rocking chair and surveyed the night. Under the light of the moon, I watched Craig's shadow move across the yard toward me. When I looked up, my gaze met his, and my heart fluttered right on cue.

I combed through the ends of my hair with my fingers. Even without undergoing chemo, it was beginning to thin. "Hey, stranger, where've you been all day?"

He took a seat in the empty chair beside me. "Working."

"I thought you gave up working weekends?"

"I was working on something else." His Cheshire grin told me it was something involving me.

"Oh?"

"Do you need me to drop Isabella off at David's?"

The window behind me clicked shut. I turned to see Mama Peg walking back to the kitchen. "My dad already did."

Craig slipped his hand under mine and I rubbed at his familiar calluses.

"You think she'll make it through the night this time?" he asked.

I sighed, keeping at bay the anxiety that rose every time I thought of how Isabella would adjust when I was gone. "I hope so. We're running out of time."

He nodded solemnly, brought my hand to his lips, and kissed it. "Even if she freaks out again, maybe this time it'll be 2 a.m. instead of midnight, and the sobs will just be whimpers."

I laughed. "You're as sick as Mama Peg."

Sweet Pea emerged out of nowhere and rubbed his side against Craig's pant leg. When Craig reached out to pet him, the cat predictably swiped. Craig jerked his hand back just in time. Sweet Pea hissed and sauntered to the other side of the porch.

Craig watched the cat disappear into shadows, then turned to me. "I've got a surprise for you."

A smile played on my lips as I rubbed the hem of his sweater between my fingers. "Please tell me it doesn't involve steps."

"Maybe a few."

I peered at him through my lashes. "Or a blindfold."

He looked up at the roof as if considering it, then shook his head. "I guess we'd better not, with your broken foot."

When he turned his head toward the yard, I noticed a streak of white running down his cheek. I wiped the coarse substance off him and brought my fingertips to my nose to investigate. It smelled like cleanser. "Have you been cleaning?"

He looked like a man caught with his hand in the cookie jar. "Maybe."

I wiped the powder from my fingers onto his jeans, earning a raised eyebrow from him. "What's my surprise?"

He brushed off his pants and stood. "It's at the saddle barn."

"You're going to make a lame woman hobble all the way over there for her trinket?"

"It's not a trinket, thank you very much, and there's no way to bring the surprise to you. You have to go to it."

I tried to feign a frown, but my smile won out. "Well, if there's no other way . . . You mind grabbing those for me?" I gestured to the crutches leaning against the house.

Craig glanced over but made no move to retrieve them. "I have a better idea."

He bent over me, slid one hand under my thighs, the other around my back, and lifted me into his arms. A year ago, I would have felt embarrassment, wondering if I was too heavy to pick up. Now I worried about being too light. A hint of what must have been shock glinted in his eyes, but if he was bothered by my featherweight, he was kind enough not to say so.

His chivalry soon made me forget my insecurities. I clung to him, glad for the peace and warmth his embrace brought. My visits with him were among the few times when I could abandon my worries about Isabella, Dad, and Mama Peg. I never felt I had to worry about him. He seemed to be strong enough for the both of us.

When I kissed his cheek, his fledgling whiskers scratched me. "You need to shave," I said.

He carried me down the steps and started across the lawn before answering. "I thought you liked me with a little scruff."

"A little, yes, but you're beginning to look like Leif Eriksson."

"Maybe I should buy one of those Viking hats. Would you like that?"

I thought that I just might but decided not to say so. "I wouldn't bother," I said. "We have nothing worth plundering."

He kissed the top of my head. "I beg to differ."

I laid my head against his chest as I bumped along in his strong arms.

"Do you really not like the scruff?" he asked, sounding vulnerable.

"No, sweetheart, I was just teasing. There isn't a thing wrong with the way you look. You're my dream guy, inside and out." I kissed his neck to emphasize my point.

At last we came to the saddle barn. It was a modest building, bigger than a shed but smaller than a full barn. It used to have a rustic look when its cedar siding had been painted barnyard red. That was before my father made it his retirement project to renovate the exterior to look like a smaller version of the main house—same white paint and black shutters.

He even added some finishing touches like flower boxes, in which Mama Peg planted geraniums each spring, accented by English ivy cascading over the sides. The geraniums were dead now, but the ivy would outlive me.

The inside renovations came after I moved away. Mama Peg said my father built the apartment in hopes I'd come home. When I didn't, he decided to rent it out to pay for the home-improvement loan. It was my good fortune that Craig happened upon the For Rent sign before someone else did. I couldn't imagine what the last few months would have been like without him.

When we came to the front door, I expected Craig to set me down. Instead he managed to turn the knob without dropping me. I was duly impressed.

"I can hop up the steps," I said. "You don't need to—"

He gave me a stern look. "I'm carrying you and that's that."

I grinned at him. "You'd make a great Viking."

Like a groom with his bride, he carried me over the threshold. He managed to flip on the light switch at the bottom of the stairs with his hip, and up we went. It was exciting just to be in the saddle barn. This was my first look at its transformation.

Craig hadn't brought me here before now because he said the temptation of us being alone and secluded might be more than we could resist. I didn't argue. Even with me dying, keeping our hands to ourselves was getting increasingly difficult. Thankfully, when one of us was weak, the other was strong.

When we came to the top of the steps, he gently set me down. I saw nothing but darkness and a few shadows of furniture until he turned on a lamp, flooding the room in soft light.

Nothing could have prepared me for the scene before my eyes. "Wow," I said, looking around. "This is . . ."

I couldn't find the word I needed, wasn't even sure there was a word. Oh, wait; yes, there was. "Groovy."

He smiled proudly. "It's seventies retro."

"Yes, it certainly is."

"I put the orange shag in myself. You wouldn't believe how hard that was to find."

I closed my eyes, then reopened them. Nope, it was still there. "I can believe it," I said.

"What do you think?" His eyes were bright with anticipation. "I know it's out there, but it's supposed to be. It's weirdly cool, don't you think?"

I took in the avocado couch, the tie-dyed pillows, and the peace sign poster, trying to find something encouraging to say. Finally I nodded toward his old floor-model record player and went with "Wherever did you find that?"

He rushed over and turned it on. "Do you believe some dummy was actually throwing it out? It still works." He knelt, opened the cabinet beneath it, and pulled out a real-life 45. He slipped it from its sleeve and put it on the turntable.

When he set the needle down on black vinyl, the Bee Gees sang "How Deep Is Your Love."

"You thought of everything," I said.

He looked as excited as a little boy on Christmas. He hurried over to me. "I haven't shown you the best part yet."

I was more than a little fearful of what that might be. A life-size wax model of Elvis, perhaps?

He wrapped his arm around me and helped me hop to his bedroom. We stopped at the doorway. I peeked in, not at all surprised to find a mirrored ball dangling from his ceiling. It scattered glittering sparkles over the walls. "Wow" was all I could say.

He grinned ear to ear. "Isn't that the coolest thing you've ever seen?"

It took me a minute to decide if I loved or hated it. In the end I found the uniqueness of Craig and his apartment to be irresistible. "You know, it sure beats the beige cookie cutter everyone else our age lives in."

When my gaze slid off the disco ball down to his empty bed, I lost my breath. Atop a smooth cover rested three matching pillows. The left was monogrammed with his initials—*CA*, the right with *GA*, and a small square pillow resting in between the two of them simply read *Bella*.

Tears choked me and I couldn't take my eyes off them long enough to look at him. Nothing had ever touched me as much as those three pillows and what they meant. His fingertips slid down the length of my arm as he lowered to one knee.

I let out a jagged breath and looked into his stormy eyes.

"Jenny, I've already asked your father's permission, and he's already told me no."

I laughed through my tears.

Craig didn't even crack a smile. He just ran his thumb over my ring finger, looking as nervous as a pig at a barbecue. "But he's promised not to kill or evict me for doing this, so I'm going to give it another shot. I know this apartment isn't much, but it's all I have right now. I'd buy us a house if our time weren't so short. Bella's bedroom isn't much bigger than a closet, but it'll hold her bed and a dresser. . . ."

He reached under his sweater, pulled a small velvet box from his pocket, and opened it. A diamond set on a ring of gold gleamed against a black backdrop. "Jenny, do you love me?"

I laid my hands on his shoulders to steady myself as my eyes became Niagara Falls. "You know I do."

"Then spend your last days with me . . . here."

His love consumed me and I was no longer sure of what I should say or do.

"Say you'll marry me. We only have a little while."

Staring at that symbol of his love, I couldn't think straight. "I don't know, baby."

"It's getting harder for you to take care of yourself, let alone Bella. Mama Peg can't do it. Your father won't say it, but he's stopped playing golf and going out because he's afraid to leave you alone."

I wiped tears from my eyes, but more replaced them. "He can't do that."

Craig lifted my ring from its box. "Please let me take care of you. You and Bella move in here, and we'll play house until I have to let you go. I promoted Jimmy to manager, and he's going to run the business until—"

"You can't do that for me."

"Already have. I've earned a vacation, wouldn't you say?"

The thought of us living together—Mama Bear, Papa Bear, and Baby Bear—was amazing. The best way I could think of to spend my last days. And if we were married, I could finally give myself to him the way I longed to. I loved him with everything in me and I knew it was the same for him.

I leaned down and pressed my lips against his. The kiss we shared felt almost holy. It seemed to last forever, but when he finally pulled back, I realized it hadn't lasted nearly long enough.

I wanted to say yes. I wanted that more than I'd ever wanted anything for myself—but I was a mother first, woman second. My time was short, too short to waste.

Was it possible that what Isabella needed could be the same as what I wanted? Why couldn't I transition her to David from here? What was the difference really, but a few hundred feet?

Craig's eyes searched mine for the three-letter word he wanted to hear. I didn't give him that. I simply smiled and extended my left hand.

CHAPTER THIRTY-THREE

LYING IN BED, I touched the engagement ring I wore on a chain around my neck. Like everything else I owned, it was too big for my emaciated frame. When Craig slipped it onto my finger, it had fallen right back off. The symbolism wasn't lost on either of us, but still we managed to find humor in the moment. Or at least pretended to.

I pushed off my pillow and leaned on my elbows so that I could better see out the window. The night sky was a clear navy blue with twinkles of starlight sprinkled throughout it. With a smile, I wondered if Craig was looking at this same sky and thinking of me. Had there ever been two people more in love? It just didn't seem possible.

I slid the ring back and forth on its chain, liking the feel of the smooth gold band against my fingertips. We'd have to marry as quickly as possible, of course, but that didn't have to mean a drab city hall ceremony. If the weather cooperated, we could exchange vows in front of the lake—that would be pretty. I bit my lip, considering it.

What in the world would I wear? Being as thin as I was, my choices were limited to something white that could hide my boniness. I wouldn't get to don the strapless princess gown I'd always dreamed of, but if Craig's eyes glinted with the same admiration on our wedding day as they did every other time his gaze fell on me, not even a frumpy white frock could make me feel less than beautiful.

I lay down again, bent my arms behind my head, and gazed at the reflection of glimmering moonlight on the ceiling.

First thing in the morning, I'd call the church and make arrangements, then city hall or wherever it was you got a marriage license. My breath caught as I considered that within days I would be Genevieve Paige Allen . . . Jenny Allen . . . Mrs. Genevieve Allen . . . Mrs. Craig Thomas Allen . . .

When I ran out of possible derivatives of my new name, my elation began to ebb. As it did, a twinge of guilt nipped at me—I was sentencing the man I loved to the fate of widower. Was it as selfish as it felt? Doubts sprouted in my mind like weeds until I remembered the words that Craig had whispered to me one night as we sat together on the porch swing, listening to the crack of thunder and watching lightning explode in the sky like fireworks.

Holding my hand, he told me that I was his fate, that he could no more stop himself from falling in love with me than the Nile could decide not to flow into the Mediterranean. My guilt slid away on a moonbeam as I drifted off to sleep.

It seemed that as soon as unconsciousness took me, the phone jolted me awake. By the third ring, I'd thrown off my sleepy confusion and regained my senses enough to know what the call meant. Isabella—once again—wasn't able to make it through the night at her father's house.

These late-night calls had become so routine that I didn't have to ask to know it was David, not Lindsey, on the phone, explaining to my father that Isabella was crying to come home. He would soon drop her off, shaking his head, looking as frustrated as I felt.

Isabella would crawl into my bed, lay her head on my pillow, and whimper a promise to do better next time. My reply was always the same—"You need to really try. One day soon, I'm not going to be here for you to run home to." Her beautiful eyes would widen with a look that broke my heart. Powerlessness would overwhelm me as I snuggled her tightly and kissed her wet face.

A knock came on the bedroom door, followed by my father's voice calling my name.

I covered my legs with the blanket and sat up. "Come in."

He pushed the door open and stood in the doorway. His normally neat hair stuck up like a troll pencil topper.

"Let me guess," I said.

He leaned against the doorjamb. "You know, they might just be ready to concede to her living here permanently and—"

"Dad, don't. It's not the house she's wanting; it's me, and I won't be here."

His blank expression told me that he had no rebuttal.

"David's bringing her?" I asked.

"That's up to you."

"What do you mean?"

"They're asking you to go *there*," he said.

I looked at the clock. "It's one in the morning."

He glanced at the time and again at me.

"Maybe I can try to talk to her on the phone."

He shook his head. "I suggested the same thing."

"And?"

"She won't stop screaming long enough to pick up the receiver."

My insides churned at the thought of my little girl being that upset.

"Do you want him to bring her back," he asked, "or do you want me to take you over?"

I hated the idea of going to David's house at any time, much less the middle of the night, but not as much as I hated the thought of not being there when my daughter needed me. "I guess I'd better go. We've got to try something."

"I'll be in the car."

❋

My father waited in the Buick while I, and my crutches, made our way up to David's front door. Before I could knock, it flew open. David nodded at me, then looked over my shoulder at my father's parked car. "Thanks for coming."

"You sure you don't want me to just take her home?" I asked.

He pulled at the neck of his T-shirt. "We can't keep doing the same thing and expecting a different response. We don't have much time, Jenny. I hate to say that but—"

"It's okay," I said. "It's true."

From inside the house, Isabella shrieked. David threw a nervous look behind him, stepped back, and gestured for me to come in. "I'm hoping you can calm her down a little, maybe lie with her a few minutes. Just until she goes to sleep."

I looked back at my father, sitting in his idling car, and held up a finger. As I stepped inside, Isabella let out a blood-curdling "I want to go home! I want my mommy! I want my mommeeeeeeee!"

Hurrying down the hallway, I followed the sound of her cries to a door that stood half-open. "Shh, it's okay, sweetheart," Lindsey cooed. "She's on her way."

Isabella sat on the floor, trembling. Her eyes were red and swollen from tears cried too long and hard. When Lindsey reached to pick her up, she buried her face in the crook of her arm and whimpered, "I want my mommy."

The door creaked as I pushed it open the rest of the way.

When Lindsey saw me, she closed her eyes in obvious relief. Isabella, clutching her koala, ran for me. I braced myself against the crutches just in time. She flung herself against me, and I winced in pain. With her arms wrapped tightly around my legs, she looked up at me with a haunted expression and lifted her arms for me to pick her up.

"Hang on, Bells; let me sit down." I made my way to her bed and sat. Before I could lay down the crutches, she climbed onto my lap and buried her head in my arm.

"I'm sorry it's so late," Lindsey said. "We just didn't know what else to do."

I rubbed Isabella's back as I rocked her. "It's okay. David's right. We've got to try something."

When I looked down at Isabella, her eyes were closed and she was sucking her thumb—something she hadn't done since she was a baby. I continued to rock her until her back stopped heaving. Lindsey leaned against the radiator, holding her silk robe closed and studying us as though she were watching a documentary. I realized then that she was probably trying to learn from me how to mother my daughter. I doubted she understood that what worked for me wouldn't necessarily work for her. She and Isabella would have to forge their own path.

After a few minutes of silence, Lindsey whispered, "Do you think it's safe for you to go now?"

Isabella's panic-filled eyes shot open.

"I've got another idea," I said. "What if I lie with you for a while?"

The fear left her eyes as she slid her thumb from her mouth. She stared at me a moment, then nodded. I eyed the single bed with its headboard painted to look like a giant tiara. Even this narrow mattress was plenty big enough for the two of us.

Lindsey laid her hand on the doorknob and turned around. "Is there anything you two need—covers, an extra pillow—"

"Water," Isabella blurted.

I shook my head. "Bella knows very well that she can't have anything to drink after seven."

Lindsey frowned. "We always give her a glass of water at night."

"It makes her wet the bed," I said.

"She's never done that."

"That's only because she hasn't slept through the night here yet. Right around four, she would. It happens every time." I thought of the last half-dozen times my father had brought Isabella home in the middle of the night from here. No wonder she always made a beeline straight to the bathroom.

It occurred to me then how many of those little details Lindsey didn't know about Isabella. She hadn't known to ask, and I hadn't thought to tell her. I moved the pillow to the top of the bed and patted it. Isabella crawled off my lap and lay on it.

Suddenly I remembered my father still waiting for me outside. As Lindsey closed the door, I called to her. "Could you or David drive me home later? I hate to keep my dad waiting."

In the shadow of the hall light, she turned to face me. "It's the least we can do. I'll tell him he can go home." The door clicked shut behind her.

I lay on the pillow next to my daughter and pulled the down comforter around us. When she smiled sleepily and curled her body tight against me, my heart ached. Soon I wouldn't be around to do this for her.

Cocoa fell from her fingers. I heard the clink of his hard nose hitting the wood floor as she clutched me instead. Leaning into her, I kissed her forehead and did my best to mask my sadness. "You know, Bella, you're going to have to get used to sleeping here without me."

"I know."

"You're going to have to be a brave girl."

Her eyes pleaded with me. "I'm trying, Mommy."

I stroked her soft cheek. "Why were you so upset?"

Her thumb found her mouth again, making her words slur. "I wanted you, and Daddy just kept telling me to be a big girl and go to sleep."

Of course he did. "What did Lindsey say?"

"She came after I was crying real hard."

"Was she nice to you?"

"I guess."

"Did she tell you to be a big girl too?"

Isabella reached over with her free hand and rubbed my earlobe. "No, she told me I could call you on the phone."

"So why didn't you?"

She didn't answer for a minute. Her bottom lip pooched

out as though she were getting ready to shed more tears. She continued to rub my ear as she let out a deep breath that smelled like bubblegum toothpaste. "I had a bad dream," she finally said and buried her face in my neck.

I heard a soft whimper. "What is it, sweetness? What's wrong?"

When she looked at me, I saw that same broken look in her eyes I had seen at the beach during our talk. "I dreamed you were drowning. You kept yelling for me to help you." Tears welled up in her eyes. "You were sinking . . . and I couldn't find you. Daddy made me stop looking."

Her words pierced the deepest layer of my heart. Her dream was, in a strange way, both memory and premonition—except that it was she who was sinking, not I. "Shh." I kissed her tears. "I'm here. I'm right here." I laid my cheek against hers, wishing I'd used the setting sun analogy instead of the ocean metaphor. "Bella, baby, Mommy isn't going to drown."

She sniffled. "You will. You're not strong anymore. You can't swim all the way across."

I pulled back and looked into her eyes. "I don't have to swim across the ocean. Jesus is going to carry me."

She rubbed her wet face against my T-shirt. "Is He a good swimmer?"

I held her tight. "He doesn't have to be. He walks on water, remember?"

"You don't."

I laughed. "You used to think I did. Please don't worry.

He won't let me drown, I promise. He's going to carry me all the way across."

She looked askance at the wall for a moment as though considering it. Finally her eyes began to flutter and eventually close. I was at the cusp of falling asleep myself when she asked, "Mommy, why didn't Jesus carry *me* when I was drowning?"

I tried to open my eyes, but they were too heavy. "Because He wanted Craig to do it."

I had intended to stay only until Isabella fell asleep. Instead, I woke hours later, scrunched up against my daughter in a princess bed with the bright morning sun shining through Barbie suncatchers into my eyes.

I shielded my face with my hand and looked up to see Lindsey's bright, perfectly made-up face in the doorway. "Good morning, ladies!" She sounded disgustingly chipper. Of course she would be a morning person. She probably woke up whistling, with bluebirds and bunnies following her around. I groaned and flopped over, giving her my back.

"Okay," she whispered. "I'll let you go back to sleep, but as soon as you're awake, David and I need to talk to you." She paused as if waiting for me to answer. "We've got a plan that I think you're going to like." She sounded far more enthusiastic than anyone should at . . . whatever time of morning it was.

Staring at the pink wall, I rolled my eyes. Oh, good, another talk. Those always led to wonderful things with the Prestons. "Can't wait," I muttered.

CHAPTER THIRTY-FOUR

When I kissed Isabella's cheek, she moaned and turned over. I quietly gathered my crutches from the floor and made my way out of her bedroom into the hallway. The crutches rubbed against my already-sore underarms as I hobbled past paintings of European landscapes hanging on rich, gold walls, toward the grating sound of David's voice and Lindsey's laughter.

My stomach tightened as I neared the room they occupied. I couldn't think of anything I'd like less than having a sit-down with my ex-boyfriend and his adoring wife. But the sooner we had our little talk, the sooner I could get out of there and back to the comfort and familiarity of my own house. Touching the diamond ring hanging from my neck, I inhaled a fresh breath of nerves and stepped through the doorway.

Lindsey sat next to David at an oval table, holding a glazed mug in her slender fingers and laughing. David grinned, looking pleased with her reaction. When she laid her head on his shoulder, I cleared my throat.

They both turned toward me. David's smile disappeared while Lindsey's widened.

Her cheeks flushed as she stood. "Jenny, I didn't mean you had to wake up now."

"It's fine," I said. "I needed to get up anyway. I have a lot of stuff to do today." I ran my tongue over my teeth, wishing I'd stopped at the bathroom to at least rinse my mouth out.

Lindsey wore a men's dress shirt over her designer jeans. It was the same shirt David had been wearing the last time he'd dropped off Isabella. Despite the fact that I loved Craig now, not David, jealousy still nipped at me.

"Are you hungry?" she asked.

"No, I'm fine."

"Thirsty? We have coffee, orange juice—"

"I'll eat when I go home," I said, hoping my tone didn't sound as abrasive to her as it had to me. "Thanks anyway."

"Please—" she gestured to an empty chair—"have a seat."

As I did, I scanned the room full of wood trim and clean lines. A dozen red roses occupied a vase in the center of the table. They were so perfect-looking that I couldn't tell if they were real or fake. Behind David's chair sat a lowboy, on top of which rested three black-and-whites in matching silver frames. The first was David and Lindsey's wedding portrait. The second was of Isabella sitting on a park swing, wearing corduroy overalls I didn't recognize. The third was a candid shot of the three of them playing in a pile of raked leaves in front of their house.

I leaned my crutches against the table as I thought of the photo album I had put together for Isabella. I needed to remember to give it to her while I still could. As she created new memories, I hated the thought that she'd forget the ones we had already made. Hated the thought that she'd forget me.

Lindsey stared at David expectantly. When he turned his attention to his lap, I knew this idea of theirs was going to be a doozie. My good leg shook back and forth as I waited for one of them to say something. When neither did, I decided to expedite things. "Please tell me you have some thoughts on what we can do about Isabella."

David's gaze moved from his lap to Lindsey and back again.

"If you do, I'm all ears."

Lindsey waited, but when David wouldn't look up to make eye contact, she turned to me. "Do you remember the day you broke your foot?"

Before I could answer, she giggled nervously. "Of course you do. That was a stupid question."

Already I didn't like where this conversation was headed. A chill moved through me, and I rubbed absently at my arms.

"We felt bad because your dad's only one man with two

sick women and a little girl to care for. That's a lot to put on him. Too much, maybe."

My eyes narrowed. "I'm not a complete invalid. Neither is Mama Peg, for that matter. Besides, it's not just my father. Craig's there too."

She looked at me as though I'd said something cryptic. "Your boarder?"

"My fiancé."

Lindsey looked as though I'd just thrown a glass of ice water on her. "I didn't know that." She frowned at David. "Honey, did we know that?"

"It just happened," I said. "Yesterday."

David gave me a slow once-over. I was sure it was all he could do not to state the obvious. To ask what the point of it was since it couldn't last. To call Craig crazy for wanting to marry a dying woman, and me crazy for letting him. For once in my life, I couldn't have cared less what David Preston thought.

They both looked at my left hand, then each other. I decided not to tell them where I wore my ring. The details of my engagement were sacred and special. I felt no desire to share any of it with them.

"Interesting timing," David said flatly.

Lindsey pressed her fingers against her lips as she studied his profile. Their reactions told me that whatever their plan had been, I'd just thrown a wrench into it.

David rubbed the back of his neck.

"Just spit it out," I said. "What's the plan?"

He nodded at Lindsey. She gripped her coffee cup, tapping French-manicured nails against ceramic. "We thought—David and I thought—that we might have a win-win solution to Isabella's problem transitioning to us and your problem of needing to be taken care of. If you were to move in with us, Isabella would get used to living here. Get used to us. And you'll have a live-in nurse. What I can't do, we'll bring in hospice to take care of."

I was so stunned by the ridiculousness of her offer that it took me a moment to pick my chin up off the floor. "Are you kidding me? You want me to spend my last days watching you two play Ozzie and Harriet? If I wanted hospice, I could call them myself. I already have the rest of my life planned out, and it includes seeing as little of you two as humanly possible."

Lindsey's hand stilled. "Jenny, it wasn't just an idea we pulled out of the sky. We spoke to a counselor, and she said . . ."

As she explained why the child psychologist thought my moving in with them was the only way my daughter stood a chance at acclimating to her new home and parents, my gaze traveled from Lindsey's pink cheeks to the healthy sheen of her hair, to her hand resting atop David's, and finally to the gold band that fit just right on her left hand.

Cutting her off midsentence, I said, "You can spin it anyway you like, but I'm marrying Craig." I stood and gathered my crutches, afraid that if I sat there any longer entertaining their insane idea, it might just happen. I couldn't live with them. I wouldn't. "This week." I slid the crutches under my arms.

Lindsey held out her hand as if to stop me. "Take your time. We don't need an answer right now. It's a lot, I know. Just think about it. We have a guest room all ready for you." Her smile seemed at odds with the troubled look in her eyes. "Do you want to see it? It's really pretty."

I made a face to show my disgust. "Do you really think I care if my room's pretty?"

David planted his palms on the table. "Sit down, Jenny."

I glared at him. "I don't take orders from you."

When Lindsey touched his shoulder, he added a meeker, "Please. Sit down and hear us out."

I didn't want to sit back down. I knew that if I stayed any longer and listened to their reasoning, I might just agree to sacrifice my last chance at happiness. David reached out to touch my arm. I jerked away from him and grabbed my ring as though he'd intended to rip it from my neck.

"Jenny, I know we've exchanged some harsh words and that I've hurt you in the past, but our time is short here. Isabella needs us—you, Lindsey, and me—to come together to help her make this adjustment."

My stomach turned to acid. "I've been trying."

"I know," he said. "I know you have. We all have, but it's just not enough. When she starts screaming like that—" he turned toward the hallway as if she were doing it right then—"she's absolutely terrified. You're here to comfort her now, but for how long?"

I swallowed the boulder that had risen in my throat. "No," I said. "No matter what you say, I'm not doing it. I can't. Please don't ask me again."

David stared at me, unblinking. "What are we going to do when you're not here to settle her? What is *she* going to do? I see the future and it's not good, Jenny. Don't leave us here with a little girl who's afraid of us." He buried his face in his hands.

My soul screamed from within me that this was wrong. I was supposed to be with Craig. Hadn't David taken enough from me? I had wasted my entire youth loving him. He was inheriting my only child, for crying out loud. Now he swirled the last drops of my life in his snifter and wanted permission to swallow it down?

"I've got cancer. I'm *dying*. I've just been proposed to by a man I adore and have a chance to live out my last weeks with him, and you're asking me to give that up? Is that fair?"

David's face blotched with red. "You want to talk about fair? If you hadn't kept my daughter a secret all these years, she wouldn't be afraid of me. She should be as comfortable with me as she is with you. I wouldn't have to come to you, begging for a little mercy. You owe me this. You owe her!"

"Why are you yelling, Daddy?" Isabella stood in the doorway, rubbing sleep from her face and holding her koala by the ear.

I saw the weight of the world reflected in her tired eyes and knew we had managed to fail her again. "We were just talking, sweetness. Sorry if we woke you."

Her expression made it clear that she didn't believe me for a second. She hugged Cocoa to her chest. "Mommy, can we go home now?"

CHAPTER THIRTY-FIVE

As I CAME to the pine tree that marked the beginning of the woods, Isabella bounded to my side like metal to magnet. "You left me!"

"I thought you were picking apples with Cowpa," I said.

She gave me the evil eye. "Don't leave me again." When I couldn't take the hand she reached out to me because I needed both of mine to operate the crutches, she trudged beside me wearing a scowl.

By the time we reached the stream, I was utterly exhausted. When I collapsed onto my sitting rock, the boulder's coolness penetrated straight through my sweatpants to my bottom. Ignoring this additional discomfort, I laid my crutches on the bed of pine needles to my right. Besides the ever-present smells of damp leaves, pine, and earth here, the cool air also carried the distinct scent of impending snow.

I glanced up, past the fading leaves still clinging hopelessly to branches, to the clouds shrouding the sun in hazy gray. It wasn't cold enough yet to do much more than rain, but the temperature could easily drop overnight, thrusting us out of autumn, straight into winter. The thought that I might live to see the first snowfall after all brought me no joy. My mind was too preoccupied with fears and fantasies to care.

Isabella sat at my side, zipping and unzipping her purple fleece. We said nothing as I gathered the stones scattered at my feet and threw them, one by one, into the stream. Droplets rose and fell with each deposit. When my arm grew too weary to continue, I leaned on my hands and turned to my daughter. "I think we're going to move. What do you think of that?"

Her eyes lit up. She jumped in front of me, fluttering her hands like a hummingbird preparing to take flight. "Back to our apartment?"

I shook my head. "No, Bells, we're never moving back to the city. Tullytown is our home now."

Her hands stilled as the sparkle left her eyes.

I painted on my most convincing smile. "Don't look so sad. We're moving somewhere even better—into the saddle barn with Craig!"

Her eyebrows knit together. She didn't need to say a

word. Her expression made it quite clear that she wasn't impressed.

"You should see your room," I said. "It's so pretty."

She gave me a look that must have mirrored the one I'd given Lindsey when she had said the same to me. "I don't wanna move there. His house is too small."

"It's bigger than it looks," I said.

"Why can't Craig move into Cowpa's house?"

"Because he lives at the saddle barn."

"Well, I live with you and Mama Pig and Cowpa." She crossed her arms.

I sighed. "It's only just across the yard."

She turned and gave me her back.

I touched her shoulder, and she yanked it away. "What is it, sweetness?"

"I don't wanna move anymore."

"Guess what, Bella?"

She threw a weary glance over her shoulder.

"Mommy is marrying Craig."

She stared at me a moment with an expression I couldn't read, then turned away. "You can't marry Craig."

"Why not?"

"Because you're going to marry my daddy."

"Bells, your daddy's already married to Lindsey."

"I asked God to take her across the ocean 'stead of you. Then you can marry my daddy and we can all live together at Cowpa's house."

Wow, I thought, leaning back, *how long has she been fanning the fire of that pipe dream?* "You shouldn't pray that. Jesus is taking *me*, not her. When that happens, you're going to live with your daddy and Lindsey at their house. That hasn't changed."

She kicked at a rotted tree stump with her boot. Flecks of brown peppered the ground as she knocked a hunk of bark from it. She looked up at me. "Mommy, once I'm a growed-up, I can live wherever I want, right?"

I ran the back of my hand across her cool cheek. "Yes, baby, when you're a grown-up, you can live wherever you want."

"Then I want to move back to the city with you, and since I *am* a growed-up, you have to do it!"

"You're not a grown-up yet, young lady."

"Yes, I am." She unzipped her fleece, planted her hands on her hips, and stuck her torso out as if she were Wonder Woman. "See?" Two mounds protruded from her T-shirted chest. My daughter had mysteriously gone from being years away from needing a training bra to a full B-cup, just like that.

Trying hard not to make light of her newfound womanhood, I kept a serious expression as I pulled the collar of her shirt away from her neck and glanced down her front. Inside out and twisted over her shoulders was my black bra. I pulled the silky fabric back to see what she was using for breasts. She blushed and pulled away from me. When she did, one of the apples fell to the forest floor. Her eyes grew wide. "Look what you did! Now I'm not growed-up anymore!"

I grabbed the bruised fruit from the ground. Its pale color, along with the green leaves still clinging to the stem, marked it as one of my mother's.

Isabella's quivering bottom lip told me that tears were on their way. I would have to work fast to distract her. "If you were a grown-up, would you really want to move back to the city?"

The diversion worked because her lip stopped trembling. She nodded.

"Why the city?" I asked.

"You aren't dying there."

My heart sank. Still clutching Mom's apple, I laid my chin on top of her hair and held her as tight as my weak arms were able. "Oh, sweetness. I'm dying no matter where we live."

Isabella pulled back and held out her palm. "I want my ninny back."

I looked from the apple I still clutched to her. *Ninny* was her word for breasts all the way back to her nursing days. I didn't know she still remembered. I held the bruised apple up and thought of Mom. Isabella grabbed it from my hand and crunched a bite out of it. As juice trickled down her chin, I laughed. "You are such a unique child."

She giggled at herself, then took another bite.

"You know," I said, "your grandma, my mother, planted that apple tree right before she died."

Isabella swallowed. "She did?"

"Yep. And do you know why?"

Her eyes were riveted on me as she shook her head.

"I think it was a gift she knew she could give to her family even after she went to heaven."

A pine needle hung from Isabella's curl, just as it had the first time we had come here together. And just as it had then, love overwhelmed me. As I pulled it from her hair, I remembered my purpose in coming here that first time. I had returned home not to fall in love, nor to find happiness for myself, but to ensure a future for my little girl. To protect her . . . because nothing mattered more.

A lump formed in my throat as I realized what I needed to do. I reached behind my neck and unlatched the gold chain from it. Isabella ate her falsie as I slipped the ring onto my finger. The diamond was almost as beautiful as the love it represented, but there was no denying the fact that it just didn't fit—despite how badly I wanted it to.

I pulled it back off. "Your daddy asked if you could sleep over at his house again tonight."

Anxiety filled her eyes. "I don't wanna."

I thought of Craig's blond lashes that I so loved to kiss, his wonderful smell, and how comforting it would have been to be held by his strong arms as I drew my final breaths.

My gaze moved down Isabella's arm to the half-eaten apple she held. I thought of my mother, thin as a rail, digging a hole in the dirt with what remained of her strength so she could plant a tree that she would never eat from. I thought of my daughter trembling on the bedroom floor, screaming for me as Lindsey tried to comfort her, and I thought of Mama Peg saying life was about planting a tree whose shade you never intended to sit under.

I couldn't think of a worse way to spend my last days than

with David and Lindsey, but a skeleton of a woman cannot throw on her cape and save the world. I barely had the energy to get out of bed in the morning.

Isabella, however, I could rescue.

This was my final chance to be a hero, even if I was the only one who would ever know it. I could give her something even better than an apple tree; I could give her peace. I doubted that she would ever understand the sacrifice I was getting ready to make for her, or how much it would cost me.

"What if I come too?" I said.

When the fear left her eyes, I knew I was making the right decision.

The wind whistled through the treetops. I listened hard for a confirmation from heaven that I was on the right path. The breeze died without uttering a word. The only thing I could hear now was the pounding of my heart.

"Come on, Bella. It's time to go." I picked up a brown leaf from the ground, crumbled it into a million pieces, and scattered it over the water. Isabella and I watched the debris float downstream, carried away to who knew where, to eventually fertilize who knew what.

CHAPTER THIRTY-SIX

ISABELLA AND I stood on the porch with everything we had to our name piled at our feet. When David pulled into the driveway, spewing gravel from his tires, Craig mumbled an expletive that I hoped Isabella hadn't heard. Given the circumstances, I thought it better not to chide him for it. He was already hurting enough, and besides, David really was what Craig had called him.

When David beeped the horn twice in quick succession, my father's nostrils flared like wings on a fighter plane. With his balled-up hands swinging from his sides, he soared over to the car. Whatever he grumbled into the window left David wide-eyed, red-faced, and apologetic. He quickly got out of the car and made his way to the porch.

Craig, my father, and David worked together to load our belongings into the trunk, while Mama Peg, Isabella, and I watched in silence. Although I knew my grandmother was as sad as any of us, she managed to appear as unshakable as she had the day I'd come home with Isabella in tow.

Craig was another matter entirely. As he worked, he drew in deep breaths, one after another. I knew it was all he could do to keep it together, but thankfully, he managed to.

Mama Peg pulled me to her ample bosom and squeezed the breath out of me. With my ear plastered against her chest, the rattle and wheeze of her lungs sounded as if they were being amplified by a microphone. Finally she let me go. "Genevieve Paige Lucas, I love you," she said.

"I know, Mama Peg. I love you too. You take care of Dad, okay?"

"What choice do I have?" A hint of a smile played on her pale lips.

Waiting for the odds and ends of pillows, covers, and stuffed animals to make it into the car, I studied Isabella's profile as she watched her father interact with the other two men in her life. I considered how differently this scene might have gone had I not been accompanying her. She turned and gave me a surprising smile. She bounced on her heels, looking excited and eager . . . but not at all fearful.

After David closed the trunk, he started to get into the driver's seat until my father directed him back to the porch with a severe look. David looked at him, hung his head, then joined us again. We all stood there silent, staring at each other like teenagers at our first dance, waiting for someone to make the first move.

Mama Peg pulled the oxygen tubing from over her ears, adjusted it, then put the tiny prongs back in her nostrils. "Where's Lindsey?" she asked David.

David winked at Isabella, who giggled in return as though the gesture were hilarious. "At home putting the finishing touches on the girls' rooms. You should see how excited she is. She's been painting, cleaning, and organizing nonstop for days."

"It's called nesting," I said.

David gave me a look that told me he couldn't care less what it was called.

"You've got yourself a good wife," Mama Peg said. Her eyes left David and fell on me. "Doesn't he, Jenny?"

If anyone but her had put me on the spot like that, I would have let them have it with a scathing retort, but I knew what my grandmother was trying to do. She was, in her unique way, trying to remind me of my mission.

"She's better than you deserve," I said, trying to sound more tongue-in-cheek than I was. We all knew it was the truth— I suspect even David.

He gave a toothy smile. "I'm still thanking my lucky stars."

I cleared my throat, wanting to end this conversation. "I think we're ready to go."

Without warning, Craig slid his hand behind my neck, leaned me backward, planted his soft, cool lips against mine, and gave me a kiss that tasted of root beer. It was a kiss I wouldn't soon forget. When I opened my eyes, everyone was studying the ground. Everyone except David. He stared at Craig as though he'd just caught him red-handed trying to hot-wire his car. Wrong as it was, the jealousy in his eyes left me almost as satisfied as Craig's kiss.

As we made our way down the steps, a fat ball of orange fur emerged from the shadows of the porch. Sweet Pea's tail pointed skyward as he sauntered up to Isabella. He rubbed against her leg, purring like a motorbike and leaving a trail of fur along her pant leg. She reached out to pet him, but I grabbed her hand in the nick of time. Though she was the one person he'd let touch him without retaliating, I didn't want to take any chances. She looked at me. "We almost forgot Sweet Pea!"

I shook my head. "We can't take him, Bells."

"Why . . . not?" Mama Peg said through coughs.

I turned around. She smiled mischievously.

If I had been a nicer person, I'd have let David off the hook by giving Isabella a firm no. Unfortunately for David, I wasn't that person. If ever two creatures deserved each other, it was Sweet Pea and David Preston. If they weren't different species, I would have sworn they were twins separated at birth. "It's okay with me," I said, not feeling half as guilty as I should have, "but I think you better ask your father."

Isabella's mouth spread into an ear-to-ear grin before the smile suddenly faded—replaced with her best manipulative pout. She batted her lashes at David. "Oh, please, Daddy. Can Sweet Pea come? He would help me be less scared. Please. Please. Pretty, pretty please?"

Red spread over David's face and neck as he glared at me, then at the cat, and finally turned his attention back to his daughter. "I wish we could, angel, but we can't take your grandma's kitty. She's had him forever. I'm already taking her two best girls. We don't want her to be lonely."

"I still have Jack and Craig," Mama Peg quickly added. "I won't be lonely. Really, David, I insist. It will be my going-away present."

David turned and gave her a weary look, then let out an exasperated sigh. "Yeah, thanks." He still had a scar on his left hand where Sweet Pea had gotten him good our senior year of high school. "Fine, but I am not putting that thing in its carrier. You know very well that it hates me."

"Oh, for pity's sake," Mama Peg said. "He hates everyone except Bella."

Craig watched the exchange with his fingertips tucked into the pocket of his jeans, looking as though he were losing his best friend, which of course he was. "I'll do it. I'll bring him with me tomorrow when I visit."

David rolled his eyes. "Great."

Mama Peg winked at me. "I'll see you soon, kiddo." To the unbeliever, her words might have been interpreted as a little white lie meant to spare us each from the harshness of reality. After all, she seldom, if ever, ventured farther than the yard those days, and I would soon be bedridden. But I knew as well as she did that even if we never saw each other again in the confines of our ailing bodies, our reunion in heaven would not be far-off.

My crutches rubbed against my armpits as we made our way to David's car. When he opened the door for Isabella and me to get in, I turned around one last time. Craig, Mama Peg, and my father all waved as if they were standing at a train station platform, sending us off with a happy little bon voyage. Not knowing how else to react, I waved back. I knew the second the car rolled out of sight, they would all break down.

I, however, would not have that luxury.

From the back window, I watched Craig bring his fingers to his lips to blow me a kiss. I did the same, chanting a mantra in my head not to cry. Isabella turned and waved both hands at them, squealing with delight at everyone's attention fixed on her.

To my daughter, this was not the same sad farewell it was to me. After my death, per our legal settlement, she would see my family every weekend until she was grown. This move with her mommy was nothing but another adventure. For me, it would be my last.

Craig's shoulders slumped as he watched the car pull away, and I could almost feel his heart breaking. I reminded myself that he promised to visit me daily, even if it meant being nice to David.

My father, on the other hand, said he couldn't make the same promise. He'd forgiven David's father for the most part, but David was another story.

As we rounded the corner, I took a deep breath and turned around.

CHAPTER THIRTY-SEVEN

As DAVID SAT at his desk on the opposite side of the living room punching numbers into a calculator, I sat in a wheelchair by the bay window watching the wind blow through barren treetops. If he was aware of my presence in the house, you wouldn't know it. How Lindsey could stand living with him was beyond me.

He was scarcely aware of anyone or anything's presence except his beloved Lindsey, his stock portfolio, and the television set when the Virginia Tech Hokies played. Apparently I was the only one in the house it seemed to bother, so I kept my opinions to myself.

Sweet Pea meowed at his feet. David frowned at him

and gently kicked the cat away with the side of his shoe. Sweet Pea's orange fur shot up as he bared his teeth. David flinched and drew back his legs. When the cat sashayed away, not making good on his threat, David mumbled something about a gift that keeps on giving and dove back into his spreadsheet.

I heard a car pull into the driveway. The side of David's mouth curled up, and I knew he was relieved to have his wife home. He needed her almost as much as Isabella needed me. After a few minutes, Lindsey fluttered through the front door, carrying department store shopping bags in one hand and holding my daughter's hand with the other.

"Look, Mommy!" Isabella ran to me. She patted the hot pink earmuffs she wore and grinned.

"Wow," I said, trying to keep my drooping eyes open. I'd been awake for only half an hour. I shouldn't be as tired as I was.

"Mommy Lindsey bought them for me."

My heart tripped on the new endearment. Lindsey couldn't have looked more guilty as her gaze flew to me.

If I hadn't been dying, the thought of my baby calling anyone besides me Mommy, Mama, or any derivative close to them would have broken my heart. But this, I reminded myself, was the goal of my being there. This was good.

Lindsey started to stutter an explanation, but I cut her off. "It's okay," I said. "That's what we want." A moment of panic overtook me. "When can we plant the tree? We need to do it soon before it's too late."

Her smile looked sad. "You already did. Your father helped you, remember?"

"That's right," I said, relaxing. "That's right."

Isabella's gaze traveled between us, then settled on me again. "Mommy, can you come play Barbie with us?"

I reached my hand out to touch her, but my arm was so weak that it dropped back to my side. "Maybe after my nap, sweetness."

Isabella crossed her arms. "All you do is sleep!"

Lindsey laid her bags down and hurried over to me. "Honey, your mommy's sick, remember? Isn't it nice that she stayed awake just so she could see your new earmuffs before she took a nap?"

Isabella's scowl dissolved. "You stayed awake just to see my earmuffs?"

"Of course," I said. "And they were well worth it."

"Do you really like them?" she asked, patting them once again.

"They sure do look pretty on you," I said with a yawn.

"Come on, Bells, let's help your mommy to bed so she'll have the energy to read you your bedtime story tonight."

I mouthed a thank-you to Lindsey. She had become such a godsend. Without her and my hospice nurse, I don't know how I would have survived the last few weeks. Mama Peg wasn't strong enough to bathe me or help me to the bathroom, and I was thankful I didn't have to let my father or Craig see me in such unflattering situations. But Lindsey handled it gracefully, affording me a dignity I know I wouldn't have been able to keep had I stayed at my father's house or with Craig at the saddle barn.

Lindsey wheeled the chair I occupied to my room, helped me pivot into bed, and covered me up. Isabella leaned down and kissed my cheek. Lindsey surprised me by doing the same. I would never have thought it possible, but somewhere over the last weeks, I'd grown to love this woman, who I knew had also grown to love me. I looked at them, my heart overflowing.

I studied Lindsey, with her doe eyes and sweet spirit, and finally understood why David had chosen her. I would have too, I thought without a twinge of jealousy.

Lindsey laid a finger over her lips to signal Isabella to be quiet as they started for the door.

"Wait," I said.

They both turned.

"Lindsey, please make sure you wake me before she goes to bed."

"I always do," she said softly.

"I'd like for you to come too this time."

She gave me a questioning look.

"Tonight's bedtime story is going to be about the day I brought Bella home from the hospital. I thought you might want to hear it too. I tell her that story every year on her birthday. And since you'll be pinch-hitting . . ."

She laid a hand over her heart as her eyes filled with tears. I could tell by the shape of her lips that she was trying to thank me, but the words wouldn't come.

"I love you," I said, making deliberate eye contact with both of them.

"I love you too, Mommy," Isabella said.

Lindsey covered her mouth. Tears trickled over her hand as she closed the door.

CHAPTER THIRTY-EIGHT

THREE WEEKS LATER, pain ripped into my right side. I tried to lift my head, but it throbbed so severely, I had no choice but to lay it back down. I must have forgotten to take my pain pill before I fell asleep. Lindsey was usually good at reminding me, but maybe she'd been distracted by Isabella and had forgotten.

I opened my eyes, surprised to find my father's head resting on the mattress beside me. "Daddy," I whispered. "Can you help me?"

His eyes shot open and he sat upright, looking shaken and confused. "What is it, pumpkin? What's wrong?"

My throat felt like sandpaper, but that was the least of my

problems. Every nerve in my body felt as though it were on fire. "It hurts."

"It's okay, Mr. Lucas. I've got her medicine right here."

A woman with black curls and a round, chocolate face leaned close to me. She smelled like cotton candy. "Hey, sweet stuff. Long time no see."

"Hi, Darlene." I winced. "How long?"

"You were out about two days this time. It hurts bad, doesn't it?"

"These tears aren't from joy," I said.

Her dark eyes filled with sympathy as she brushed the damp hair from my face. "I've been giving you your medicine as shots, but now that you're awake, you may want something you can swallow."

I ran my dry tongue over my teeth and tasted the mint of toothpaste. I wondered if it had been my hospice nurse, Darlene, or Lindsey who had groomed me this time. "I don't remember any shots."

Darlene smiled. "I'll take that as a compliment. So what do you prefer, injection or pill?"

I groaned in pain. "Whatever works fastest."

She must have already been preparing to give me a shot because she pulled a syringe from her lab jacket pocket. "I'm only going to give you half of what I normally do because you have some visitors and I don't want to knock you out again. It should be enough to take the edge off at least. Okay?"

I tried to look around the room, but the pain was so bad it had affected my vision. Before I could ask who my visitors were, I felt something cool wipe against my arm and a sharp prick like a bee sting. The pain was nothing compared to that which ravaged the rest of my body.

Within minutes, the fire began to cool and the throbbing dulled. I was finally able to lift my head. When I looked down, I noticed an air mattress pulled next to my bed. It had a crumpled afghan piled in the center of it. I recognized the blanket as the one Mama Peg had made my father the same year my mother died. I turned to him. "How long have you been here?"

He rubbed at the scruff on his cheeks. "Awhile. We all thought . . ."

"Wow," I said. "My father sleeping at a Preston's house."

He shrugged, caught between a smile and tears. "I figured if you could stand to live with him, then I could tough out a few nights too. Besides, anyone that gave Bella half her genes can't be *all* bad."

I almost couldn't believe my ears.

He leaned in and whispered, "But I have to say, I'm still glad you didn't marry the fool."

"Is that mine?" I pointed to a cup of water sitting on the bedside table.

"Mine, yours, what difference does it make? If you're thirsty, drink it." He picked up the glass and then the pillow behind my head.

The water felt so wonderfully cool sliding down my parched throat. "Where's Bella?"

Mama Peg answered. "In the living room, kiddo."

I turned to the far corner of my bedroom and grinned when I saw my grandmother sitting in a chair with her oxygen tank resting at her feet. "Mama Peg . . . you're here."

Darlene laid a damp washcloth on my forehead. "Everyone's here, Jenny. I asked them to come."

A moment later, Lindsey appeared in the doorway with my daughter in tow. Isabella moved to my bedside with a cautiousness that I'd never experienced from her before.

"Hey, sweetness." When I reached out to touch her, she drew back. My heart felt the sting of rejection until I noticed that my hand was the same shade of mustard that my mother's had been right before she died.

I brought my hand to my nose and cringed. It smelled of rotting fruit. "It's okay, Bells. I may look and smell bad, but it's still me."

Isabella scrunched her eyes closed, puckered up, and bent down as though being forced to kiss a frog. I suppose it would have hurt my feelings had I not been through the same thing with my own mother. Under the circumstances, I took no offense.

Isabella's gaze fell on the window as she pulled away from me. "It's snowing, Mommy!"

"Are you going to go play in it?" I asked her.

"I already had a snowball fight with Craig and Mommy Lindsey."

"Craig's here?" My heart skipped a beat. "Where?"

My father exchanged a worried look with my nurse. Confusion overtook me when Craig brought my hand to his lips and kissed it. "I'm right here, baby."

Before I could ask where he had come from, the ceiling rolled back on both sides like a great scroll, giving me a clear view into another realm. A wall, made of what appeared to be a perfect sheet of opal, opened. From within, I heard music so beautiful and joyous that it brought tears to my eyes.

I didn't know if it was the morphine, the cancer, or God Himself behind this vision, nor did I care. It was magnificent.

Everyone I loved was gathered at my side as though attending my funeral. I wanted to ask them if they saw the vision too and tell them not to look so somber, but my gaze would not move from the scene above me. My eyes were fixed upward and my mouth lay parted in awe.

Out of this glimmering gate emerged a woman who looked like a more beautiful version of myself. She wore a gown of finely spun lavender silk and a radiant smile. My mother was no longer the sickly, pitiful creature of my last recollection, but far more lovely than she had ever been in her youth.

My heart filled with joy, then sadness, as I realized that it was almost time to join her.

"Are you ready?" she asked me.

Almost.

The music faded. My mother closed her eyes and lifted her face toward a blazing white light above her.

Unable to withstand the brilliance of it, I turned to the

handsome blond kneeling at my side. "Let's dance in the snow," I said.

His eyebrows shot up in surprise. "You can't even stand."

"Carry me."

"Baby, it's cold. You'll—"

"What, catch my death?"

"Jenny," my father said. I expected him to lecture me about needing my rest. Instead, he surprised me with "Have fun."

Craig looked at me, unsure.

My grandmother coughed. "Oh, for pity's sake, the woman's dying. Craig Allen, if you don't dance with my granddaughter, I'm going to flick your forehead good."

"Make hay while the sun's still shining," I said.

He smiled through tears.

Lindsey and my nurse swaddled me inside a thick comforter. Craig waited for them to finish before scooping me from the bed into his strong arms. Strangely, for the first time in weeks, I felt no pain, just an uncanny sense of euphoria. I laid my head on his chest as he carried me outside. Though I tried to inhale his wonderful scent one last time, it was not him that I smelled, but the sweet fragrance of incense.

Craig carried me into the cold outdoors. Inches of powder coated the ground and tree branches as fat white flakes continued to flutter down over us.

Soft and cold, they hit my face, then melted. I felt something glide across my neck. I reached up and felt my engagement ring still hanging by its chain. I touched it, searching Craig's face. "I thought I gave this back to you."

Such sadness brewed in his stormy hazel eyes. I prayed that it was just passing through and would not take up residence there. He deserved to be happy. I laid my hand on his cheek. "I love you."

With great effort, I unlatched the necklace from my neck, slid off the engagement ring, and held it out to him. "I don't want it to be buried with me. It isn't mine. . . ."

He leaned his forehead against mine. Foggy white puffed from his mouth in quick, hot breaths against my lips. "It is, baby."

When I felt tears trying to form, I let out a deep breath to ward them off. I slid the ring and chain into the breast pocket of his coat. "It belongs to a woman who will love you almost as much as I do."

"There's not going to be anyone else." He nuzzled his nose into my hair. "You're the love of my life."

"The love of your life *so far*. She's out there, but you won't be able to give yourself to her if you're engaged to a dead woman."

His eyes glistened as he hummed softly in my ear, twirling me this way and that. I smiled at him and he grinned back. His blond lashes turned white before my eyes.

Watching us from my bedroom window were the delighted faces of those I loved most in the world. Isabella was among them, held up by her new mother. Using my last bit of strength, I waggled my fingers at them and they waved back.

"It's time now, Jenny," I heard my mother say.

When I looked up, it was not her looming before me, but a Man who was far more than a man. The closer I drew to Him, the more familiar He seemed. He gathered me into His arms and uttered beautiful, unspeakable things to my soul. Warmth and joy, so perfect and complete, overwhelmed me.

As He held me, I realized that all along, it was He my heart had longed for—not David and not even Craig. I was getting ready to ask if He was the one who had whispered to me in the wind and in my dreams, but He answered before I could utter the question.

I Am.

Epilogue

A BLANKET OF peace fell over me as I tucked my mother's notebook into the desk drawer and peered through the window at lavender tulips reaching heavenward through a dusting of snow.

Today marked the official start of spring, but like a lingering guest, Old Man Winter refused to believe the party was really over. Nonetheless, channel six assured me it would be seventy degrees by noon. Listening to the chickadees caroling outside my office window as an orange orb rose in the blue sky, I felt confident in their prediction.

This promise of life renewed brought a smile to my lips . . . that and finally finishing my mother's journal.

Reading it had affected me more deeply than I ever could have dreamed. My normally happy-go-lucky disposition hibernated as I became engulfed in my mother's melancholy musings. My husband, Ben, worried that I was sinking into depression, but I assured him it was her tears, not my own, streaming down my cheeks as I turned the pages. He no more understood that than why I'd been so compelled to finally read the notebooks I had carried with me for so long.

I explained to him that there was something about becoming a mother myself that fed the sudden desire to understand her.

Twisting a ringlet of hair around my finger, I wondered if she knew that I had grown up to be a teacher and married a man who loved me the way she always hoped David would love her. Or if she knew I was about to deliver her first grandchild, and that if she truly was a girl as the ultrasound promised, I would name her Genevieve Peg Wilkinson.

I picked up my mother's opal ring, fingering the delicate prongs holding the stone in place. After today, it would be tucked safely away with the rest of my memories of her, hidden from the little hands that would soon be born.

A curl of steam tickled my lip as I leaned in to sip chamomile from my mug. Through paned glass, I watched a robin poke its tiny gray head from a birdhouse hanging from our powder-coated willow.

Yes, spring was definitely here despite winter's vain attempt to hang on. The snow would be melted within the hour, unlikely to return until December. I wondered if the dogwood I planted last year would bloom. I wondered a lot of things as I sat there. Would I have been able to do for my child what my mother had done for me? Would I face my own death with the grace with which she faced hers?

I set the cup down and lifted open the window. Crisp air greeted me just as the phone rang.

A familiar string of numbers flashed on the caller ID. I picked up. "Hey, Mom." A twinge of guilt pricked at me as it always did when I called Lindsey *Mom*, but I recognized the false accusation for what it was and dismissed it. After all, the woman had raised me to adulthood. She'd earned the title through and through.

"How's Dad?" I asked, forcing myself to at least sound interested. My mother had been right about him. David had never become the father either of us had hoped he would be. Indifferent and moody, he cared more about numbers adding up than he had pushing me on a swing. But Lindsey loved him completely, and what he lacked in the parenting department, she had more than made up for.

Between Uncle Craig and his wife, Cowpa, Uncle Ted, and my late great-grandmother Mama Peg, I had never wanted for love or attention.

"His back is bothering him again," she said.

I tried to concentrate on the rest of the conversation, but my mind drifted off to the Noah's ark wallpaper border I still needed to add to the nursery. After a period of perhaps seconds, possibly minutes, I heard my name and it jostled me back to the conversation.

"You're doing it again, Bella."

"I was listening."

"Isabella Rose."

"Don't say my name like that."

She laughed. "Then don't give me cause to. So did you finally finish her journal?"

"Yes," I said. "Just before you called."

"I imagine it was bittersweet." I detected a tinge of jealousy in her tone. I appreciated that she tried to hide it, but being a mother-to-be myself, I understood. Though Lindsey had raised me from the age of six and was the woman I loved most in the world, she had never been Mommy. That role was reserved for the woman who bore, cradled, and nursed me—Genevieve Paige Lucas. My mother.

When Lindsey and I finally said good-bye, I hung up and glanced out the window at the same lake I had tried to cross all those years ago. Beside it grew three apple trees, one planted by my grandmother, one by Mama Peg, and the other by my mother before she died. One day, there would be a fourth.

But not just yet. I rubbed my growing belly. I had a few streams to ford in my lifetime before I could even think about crossing an ocean.

About the Author

GINA HOLMES BEGAN her career in 1998, penning articles and short stories. In 2005 she founded the influential literary blog Novel Journey. She holds degrees in science and nursing and currently resides with her husband and children in southern Virginia. To learn more about her, visit www.ginaholmes.com or www.noveljourney.blogspot.com.

crossing Oceans

A Conversation with the Author

Your blog, www.noveljourney.blogspot.com, grew out of your own journey to become a published author. How many books had you written before Crossing Oceans? *How long has your "novel journey" taken?*

Thanks for mentioning Novel Journey. It has been a labor of love, not just for me but for the whole Novel Journey team. It's a great place for readers to discover new authors and for writers to connect and learn. And unlike most things in life, it's a completely free resource. It really is the Novel Journey team's desire to spread the word about the tremendous choices and talent available today in the realm of Christian fiction, so forgive us if we unashamedly plug it. We'd love the whole world to discover the great Christian novelists there are to choose from—Francine Rivers, Charles Martin, Lisa Samson, Claudia Mair Burney, Frank Peretti, and on and on.

But to answer the question you *actually* asked, I've written four books that haven't been published before this one, *Crossing Oceans*, was contracted.

I've been writing toward the goal of publication for something like ten years. I've had lots of rejections and near misses along the way, but I'm so grateful for all of it. *Crossing Oceans* is my best piece of writing to date and a story I'm so very proud to debut with.

How did the idea for Crossing Oceans *come to you?*

I'm not exactly sure where the idea came from, but when I write, I'm usually working out something in my personal life, past or present. Often it's not until the story is done that I figure out exactly what. I think with *Crossing Oceans*, it probably was my relationship with my parents. They divorced when I was a baby. For the first years of my life, I was with my mother, and then when I was in second grade, I went to live with my father. I know what it's like to be torn, like Isabella, between two families who don't always like each other but who all love the child they share. Then again, maybe I wasn't working out anything! Maybe I just fell asleep watching something about a dying mother and woke up thinking I had a brilliant idea.

How much of Jenny did you draw from yourself?

Friends could probably be more objective in answering this question than I am. The honest answer would be maybe a little, maybe a lot. Each of the characters is drawn from parts of me, the good guys and the bad. I've got enough attributes and flaws to go around! Mostly the characters are their own creations, though. They borrow a little from me, a little from others, and take on their own personas as well. It's a combination.

Probably the one who's most based on myself is Bella. She's the glue that brings the two families together. I've always been a mediator type of person. I think most middle children probably are. However, I was more like Eeyore as a child than Isabella's sunshiny self.

All of your as-yet-unpublished novels were written in a completely different genre—thriller/suspense. Crossing Oceans *is quite a departure. Do you prefer or find your voice more easily in one or the other?*

I grew up reading suspense, so naturally that's what I thought I should write. I did okay with it and got some recognition in a contest and came close to getting contracted, but ultimately none of those suspense novels ever sold. Then I started reading some really amazing novels outside the suspense genre, and it was like another world opened up to me. It was no longer a thriller I longed to write, but a story that would change lives the way the books I read had changed mine. When I started *Crossing Oceans*, I presented it along with a suspense novel I was working on to my agent, Chip MacGregor. I asked which one he thought suited me better. He told me both were good, but that *Crossing Oceans* seemed more like my true voice, or something to that effect. It turned out to be a turning point and absolutely the right advice. I'm now writing what comes naturally and absolutely loving it. Chip's a genius.

As you reviewed novels and talked to a lot of novelists who have had varying degrees of commercial success, was there ever a "dark night of the soul" where you decided this wasn't what you thought it was going to be, wasn't worth pursuing?

Not worth pursuing? No way! There are so many worthy stories to tell, and it's my burning desire to do that. Not to say that I didn't have fleeting moments of despair along the way, particularly when I came close to getting a contract only to see it fall through at the last minute. But those moments really were fleeting, and I knew God's timing would be perfect . . . and it was.

King Solomon wrote, "My child, let me give you some further advice: Be careful, for writing books is endless, and much study wears you out" (Ecclesiastes 12:12). What's your perspective on the flood of new books you see each season?

Honestly, I'd rather see two books released that are fantastic than a hundred that are just okay. There are great books that often don't get the attention they deserve because they're buried in an avalanche of new releases. Of course, tastes in literature are as different as in clothing, food, and anything else. One of my dearest friends has raved about books I thought were just okay and vice versa. So who's to say which two books are the great ones?

Do you ever find your Christian worldview a challenge to convey in your writing or as you communicate with other novelists in the industry?

It's not difficult to convey in my writing, I don't think. At least not today. Hey, I'm a sinner. I wish I wasn't and I try not to be, but I always seem to fall short. It's the same for my characters. The thing with me and them is we get back up, dust ourselves off, and try to do better next time. My faith, in all its imperfection, isn't lip service. It's who I am. What I believe. That comes out in my conversations, my choice of clothing, music, friends, and in my writing. It's very natural for me.

As far as other novelists go, I guess it's not a challenge. I'm a Christian and not everyone's going to agree with what I do, what I write, or what I believe, and that doesn't matter. My mother said when I turned forty, I would stop caring so much what people thought and really start being who I am. I'm almost there, and as usual, she was right. I would say that in my personal life, everyone who truly knows me is well aware that I'm a Christian. I don't hide it in my professional life either.

Finish this sentence: "I will know that I have totally arrived as a novelist when . . ."

I don't think any of us ever "totally arrive" at anything. I'm a good mom, but have I arrived as a mother? No, I'm still learning and growing and trying to do better. It's the same with being a novelist. If I win a Pulitzer, that would be great—okay, really, really, *really* great!—but that still won't mean I've arrived. I'd still need to be learning and trying my best to improve with each book. I think once people start telling themselves they've "arrived," they start getting lazy and proud. Ultimately they become less than what they could have been had they remained hungry to improve. Only when I'm entering heaven's gates will I finally allow myself to say, "Now, I've arrived!"

Discussion Questions

1. At the beginning of the book, everyone in Jenny's family is hurting. What are some of the things that have happened to bring them to this state? In what ways have they brought about their own suffering or made it worse than it had to be?

2. How does Jenny's return home change the family dynamics? She didn't really want to go home, but she felt she had no other options. Do you agree? What would you have done in her situation?

3. Was Jenny right to keep Isabella's existence a secret from David? How might things have been different if David had known about Isabella from the start?

4. After making a snide remark to her father, Jenny wonders, "Why was I waving a red cape before this bull instead of the white flag I'd intended?" Why is it so hard to break long-standing relational habits, even when we realize they are hurting us or someone we love? Have you faced a similar situation with a family member or a close friend? How did you handle it, or how do you wish you had handled it?

5. Jenny's father has held Dr. Preston responsible for his wife's death for years. Is his anger justified? Have you or someone in your family experienced something similar to this? How did you or they respond?

6. While standing in David's yard preparing to tell him about Isabella, Jenny puts her hand out to catch flowers fluttering to the ground. Not one lands on her open palm. Instead they land on David. What do you think the author might have been trying to symbolize here?

7. After Jenny tells her father she is dying, she reflects, "For the first time in my life I knew—really knew— that my father loved me." Why is Jenny unconvinced before this of her father's love? Is there someone you love who, like Jenny, might not be aware of your love? What might you do to change that perception?

8. Despite her father's desperation, Jenny makes the difficult decision not to seek treatment for her cancer. Do you think that was the right thing for her to do?

What factored into her decision? Have you ever known anyone who had to make a similar decision?

9. Do you think the loss of Jenny's mother made Jenny's diagnosis easier or more difficult for Jenny to handle? for her father to handle?

10. When David comes to pick up Isabella, he stops in the driveway and honks as he used to when he and Jenny were dating. Jenny tells us, "For the first time, I understood why the gesture used to infuriate my father." What are some things you see differently as a parent, or simply as an adult, than you did as a child?

11. Describe the way Jenny's feelings for David change. Do you think she was ever really in love with him?

12. If you were in Lindsey's position, how would you have reacted to Jenny's return? What would have been the most difficult thing for you to come to terms with?

13. Craig is a true friend to Jenny and wishes to be more. Do you think he was right to ask Jenny to marry him? Should she have said yes even sooner than she did, or was she right to put him off?

14. Jenny's mother's epitaph is a far cry from that of the woman who lost four children. How do you suppose these differing views manifested themselves in each woman's life? Have you ever considered what you'd want your epitaph to say?

15. Have you ever had to communicate something life-altering to a child Isabella's age? What did you find was the best way to do that?

16. Jenny ultimately decides to move in with David and Lindsey, against her own wishes, because she sees it as a chance to be a hero to her little girl. Was she right? Would you have made the same decision? What are some of the things to consider when weighing our own needs and desires against those of the people we love, especially those who are dependent on us?

17. Jenny is predisposed to dislike Lindsey because of her jealousy. When does Jenny's impression of Lindsey begin to change? What causes the change? What relationships do you have in which your initial impression of someone gradually changed for the better? Why did it change? Do you have any relationships in which you are letting jealousy or other negative feelings prevent you from seeing the person's true worth?

18. Jenny seems to have a peace about dying. Would you have the same peace? Why or why not?

19. Jenny has an advantage over most in that she has time to spiritually prepare for her impending death. How would you minister to someone in the same situation?

20. If you knew you had only a few months to live, what would you most want to accomplish?

Don't miss the next novel by

GINA HOLMES

Dry as Rain

Turn the page for an exciting preview.

Available in stores and online spring 2011.

TYNDALE
FICTION

www.tyndalefiction.com

CP0393

"KYRA . . . MAY I call you Kyra?" He didn't wait for an answer. "Do you understand why you're here?" After casting her a sideways glance, he walked to the window and yanked on the end of a yellowed shade.

Kyra took a deep breath. "I guess someone thinks I'm crazy."

He took a seat across from her, retrieved a small bottle from his shirt pocket, and unscrewed the tiny cap. "Around here, *crazy* is a four-letter word." He tilted his head back and squeezed several drops into each eye.

She waited for him to recap the bottle and slide it back into his pocket before answering. "I'm not . . . you know, cra—insane, I mean."

His tearing, gray eyes reminded her of two frozen ponds just beginning to thaw. "I hope you don't think me too forward, but I need to assess your current state of mind. Please tell me what happened to bring you here."

And just like that, she found herself once again broken and bleeding in the emotional holocaust of yesterday. The crash. Flashing lights from an ambulance. Uncontrollable sobs. "Please, I just want to go home."

Interlocking his hands, he leaned his elbows on his knees, causing his tie to fall forward. He grabbed the end of it and tossed it over his shoulder. "I'm sure our staff has explained that we need to hold you at least forty-eight hours to determine your competency."

The oddness of the way he now wore the tie unsettled her. "Have I been committed?"

He pressed his lips together in a pause that seemed deliberately dramatic. "Not yet."

Not *yet*? Kyra buried her face in her hands. They still smelled of the orange she'd been peeling when Benjamin had called. She grimaced and pulled away.

"Kyra. I need you to focus on me."

She alternated her tired gaze between him and her wringing hands. Her nails wore a coat of pink that couldn't more than a few days old. When in her grief had she had the wherewithal to do that? Who dealt with her husband's death by getting a manicure? Shaking her head, she snapped herself out of it. Now wasn't the time to zone out.

Sitting up, she tucked a lock of hair behind her ear and squarely met his gaze. "It's only been a few days, Doctor . . ."

"Hershing."

She nodded acknowledgment of his name. A perfectly sane response. ". . . since my husband died. Then my son leaves home to join this godforsaken war. Of course I was hysterical. How do grieving widows normally act?"

His neutral expression flashed with surprise. "You think your husband's dead." It wasn't a question but a statement.

He didn't know. She slumped back in her chair and let her hands fall to her side. No wonder he pegged her for nuts. "Yes, he passed away." She tried to remember precisely how long it had been. Two days? A week? The fog inside her head wouldn't clear long enough to recall.

Dr. Hershing waited for her to sort her thoughts. After a moment, he licked his thin lips. "Tell me about Benjamin. He's just gone off to boot camp, I hear."

Her heart ached at the mention of his name. Having her baby leave her to join the Marines hurt every bit, and in some ways more, than the news Eric had died. Though she would never admit that to anyone but herself.

She reached to her neck, tracing her fingers over the bare skin where her pearls often hung. The pearls Eric had bought her their last anniversary, practically throwing the fancy box at her as he ran off to meet an unhappy client.

"Don't try them on yet," he said as he flipped his cell phone closed. "I'll put them on you when I get home." By the time he returned, she was sound asleep. Or so she let him believe.

"I know you want to go home." The doctor's voice jarred her. "In order for that to occur, I have to be sure you're not a threat to yourself or others. That you're *well*."

Forget the past. Concentrate on now. That's what a well *person would do.*

"Before I can ascertain your current frame of mind, I have to know what's going on. I need to know why you ran your car off the road and why you kept repeating that you wanted to die."

She had nothing to hide. She'd lost it. So what? Once he knew why, he'd understand. She ran her tongue over her teeth, tasting the chalky toothpaste the nurse had given her to use that morning. "First Eric, then Benjamin. I thought I was prepared for him to join the Marines. He wanted it so badly. And I wanted it for him."

Her gaze darted to the watercolor hanging askew behind his desk. "Well, I thought I wanted it. I wanted to want it, I guess."

"Go on."

"But when I got that phone call—" she drew in a deep breath, but it did nothing to cool the fire burning in her chest—"I felt as though I'd been punched." She shook her head. "No, not punched—gutted."

His eyes widened at her word choice, and she realized that although it was exactly the right description of how she'd felt, it was the wrong one to free her.

"He was a great son," she added.

"Was?"

Exasperation spilled from her in the form of a sigh. This constant monitoring of every word and deed was already getting old. "*Is*. I mean is. Handsome. Popular. The rare combination of homecoming king and valedictorian."

"You have much to be proud of."

"Yes, I'm very proud of my son. We were, *are*, very close."

"The phone call you mentioned—tell me about it."

"It was the hardest thing I've ever heard."

His eyes encouraged her to continue.

How desperately she'd needed to hear from Benji, one more time. Instead, it was Private Yoshida who'd contacted her. She sat up straight as steel and repeated his words verbatim. How could she ever forget them?

"'This is Private Yoshida. I have arrived safely at Parris Island. Please do not send food or bulky items. Do not call me. I'll mail you a postcard with my new mailing address. Thank you for your support. Good-bye.' I begged him to tell me he would be okay, that he'd call again soon, that he knew I loved him. But he wouldn't deviate from the script."

He handed her a tissue. "That would be a tough call to get."

She dabbed at her eyes, then wiped her nose. "There's a war going on. He could die."

"Is that why you drove your car into a signpost?"

"Even if I had wanted to die, which I didn't, I wouldn't kill myself."

"Why is that?"

"It's a sin."

"According to?"

"We're God's temple. We're not to destroy it."

He nodded. "I see."

She doubted it. "I was distraught. My son went off to the Marines. My *only* son. My husband, the love of my life, is dead. Dead! I hadn't meant to hit that sign. Maybe I was driving too fast; I don't know. But I wasn't and am not suicidal."

What seemed like genuine compassion glinted in his eyes as he leaned forward and placed his thick hand on her shaking arm. "You've been through a lot, Kyra. I want to help."

She pulled away. "Then let me go home."

He sighed. "I know you want that. I believe that your accident was unintentional and you probably would not kill yourself."

She tilted her head back in relief. "Thank You, Jesus." She looked at him. "So I can go?"

He shook his head. "Regretfully, no."

"Why not?"

He searched her face for an uncomfortably long time. "Because we still have one problem."

She crossed her arms. "What's that?"

"Your late husband is downstairs demanding to see you."